Sharon Dempsey is a PhD candidate at Queen's University, exploring class and gender in crime fiction. She was a journalist and health writer before turning to writing crime fiction and has written for a variety of publications and newspapers, including the *Irish Times*. Sharon also facilitates creative writing classes for people affected by cancer and other health challenges.

Who Took Eden Mulligan?

SHARON DEMPSEY

avon.

Published by AVON
A division of HarperCollins*Publishers* Ltd
1 London Bridge Street
London SE1 9GF

www.harpercollins.co.uk

HarperCollins*Publishers*
1st Floor, Watermarque Building, Ringsend Road
Dublin 4, Ireland

1

First published in Great Britain by HarperCollins*Publishers* 2021

A catalogue copy of this book is
available from the British Library.

ISBN: 978-0-00-845660-3 [TPB]
ISBN: 978-0-00-842445-9 [PB]

This novel is entirely a work of fiction.
The names, characters and incidents portrayed in it are
the work of the author's imagination. Any resemblance to
actual persons, living or dead, events or localities is
entirely coincidental.

Typeset in Sabon LT Std by Palimpsest Book Production Limited,
Falkirk, Stirlingshire

Printed and Bound in the UK using
100% Renewable Electricity at CPI Group (UK) Ltd

MIX
Paper from
responsible sources
FSC
www.fsc.org   FSC™ C007454

This book is produced from independently certified FSC™ paper
to ensure responsible forest management.

For more information visit: www.harpercollins.co.uk/green

For my Dad, Teddy Copeland, who told me all the best stories and provided me with an endless supply of notebooks and pencils

*If you genuflect to the same old gods,
you can get away with murder.*

PROLOGUE

Keep going. Don't stop. Run, walk if you must, but whatever you do, don't look back.

Her feet pummel the rough, uneven ground. The police station isn't far. She remembers passing it days before when they were in the car. Moving day. They had been delighted with themselves for getting the rental at such a cheap price. Had planned to make the run-down cottage into something more comfortable. After all, they weren't students anymore and they'd have good jobs before long. Young professionals, that was how they described themselves to the landlord.

She is trying to distract herself. To keep her mind from seeing the unthinkable. Her foot hits a rock and she lurches forward, falling to the right, bashing her knee. She steadies herself, not allowing the pain to register as she keeps running. If she feels the sting, then she'll feel it all, the true horror of what was in that cottage. She can't let it in. She has to keep that door in her mind shut; push against it with all of her strength.

The police station can't be much farther but she doesn't

1

know if she'll make it, if she'll manage to keep it together until she reaches safety. She's stumbling now, swaying.

It's as though she's on a fairground ride that's going too fast. She wants off but knows it won't stop.

She's certain she's going to be sick. Bile burns the back of her throat and she tries to spit it out while she's still moving, but it goes no farther than her chin. She wipes at it with her hand and smells that coppery-blood smell again and her stomach heaves. So much blood . . . No, she can't think about it. She can't let it in.

She's nearly there. Her breathing is ragged. Her heart is pumping so fast she fears it will explode. She sees the road. Sees the sign with the PSNI logo and the words 'Keeping People Safe' beneath it.

The glass doors open automatically and once there, standing in the reception area with an open-mouthed policeman looking at her, she no longer knows how to say it. How to put it into words and make sense of what has happened. Instead, she has what must be an out of body experience, for she sees herself from above – a girl with dark, straggly hair, covered in drying and caked blood. Clots of the stuff sticking to skin that had been bathed and covered in rose and peony scented body cream only yesterday.

The police officer is speaking. He's calling for help. They rush at her, asking where she is injured. Who has done this to her? Questions followed by more questions. Hands tugging at her, patting her down, looking for wounds.

She hears herself speak – giving her name, the address of the cottage – and then she says it, forms the words she doesn't want to hear herself say.

'They're dead. They're all dead. It's my fault. I killed them.'

And then she falls.

CHAPTER 1

This one was different from the start.

Bloodied and panicked, the girl had run into the local police station. Stated her name: Iona Gardener, the address of the crime scene: Lower Dunlore cottage, Larchfield, before conveniently collapsing.

Chief Inspector Danny Stowe had been in the game long enough to be surprised by nothing. He'd heard it all: the dog walker stumbling across a shallow grave; a witness, breathless and hysterical, calling the incident in on their mobile; a neighbour alerted to the screams and the cries of a mother trying to protect her children from an abusive husband; a drug deal gone wrong and the victim left splattered all over the scene. Cases come in all shapes and sizes. But cases with ready confessions? Well, they don't turn up every day.

Assistant Chief Constable McCausland had come up trumps and chosen Danny as the lead detective on this one, in spite of his sullied record. The Lennon case – a trafficked seventeen-year-old girl beaten to death by her handler – had nearly ruined him. Danny had messed up big time by losing his cool and smacking the perpetrator's head off of a gable wall. It could have been a career ending move but he had managed to redeem himself by keeping his head down ever since, volunteering for all the shit jobs no one wanted and making sure his clean-up rate was better than most. Diligence and penance were his watch words these days.

Now the Dunlore case had landed on his desk and looked to be as messy as it was big. Stabbings always involved too much blood for his liking. This one was done in a frenzied fashion that suggested passion, rage and loss of control, but he couldn't go jumping to too many conclusions. The arrangement of the bodies in the bed looked like a contrived staging, while the savagery of the attack spoke of chaos. The contradicting scenarios and other inconsistencies suggested that nothing was as it seemed.

His desk phone hadn't stopped ringing since he got the case that morning; every journalist he'd ever had a drink with, desperate to get something on the mass killings. The Dunlore stabbings would be the story of the decade.

'Get in line,' he'd told Louisa Richmond, his favourite reporter of them all. 'You'll have to wait for the official press statement.' Danny wasn't about to go leaking anything.

The phone buzzed again. It was an internal line this time, so he picked it up to hear Ian on the front desk, tell him he had a visitor.

'Ian, I'm not expecting anyone and I'm up to my oxters with this new case. Whoever it is, get someone else to sort it.'

'She says you'll want to see her. Good-looking doll, goes by the name of Rose Lainey.'

Rose Lainey. Now that was a blast from the past worth

dropping everything for. He didn't think this day could throw up anything more surprising than hearing Rose was in town.

'I'll be right there.'

Danny hung up and made his way to the front desk, checking out his reflection as he passed the window looking into the incident room.

Rose was the last person he expected to turn up out of the blue. He hadn't seen her for a good few years and never in Belfast. As far as he knew she never made trips back home. God, it must have been five – no, six – years since he last saw her. That last reunion. Most of them had been older, greyer and a little thicker around the middle. But not Rose. She had looked the same, if slightly more polished and refined. Her dark hair, worn down to her shoulders, was wavy and lustrous, almost black. She was still trim and lean, and she still held herself in that contained way, as if she was always ready for flight or fight.

There had been a time when the two of them were inseparable. Two Northern Irish exiles thrown together in the same halls to read Criminology and Psychology. Both competitive and ambitious students, they'd shared lecture notes, done essays together, and pulled all-nighters to make sure they both bagged firsts. And they had. After graduating, Danny had returned to Northern Ireland and enrolled on an officer fast-track training programme with the PSNI, while Rose had headed south to London and found work with the Met, dealing with immigration, drugs and terrorism. Rose had taken the clinician route, studying for her masters and then a doctorate. She was Dr Lainey now, a forensic psychologist. She worked in the prison service the last time he checked . . . and he did check, every now and then. Not that he'd ever tell her that. It was nothing more than an old habit, he told himself; he just cared about how she was doing.

He had a live crime scene to negotiate, a mortuary lab to visit, the team needed briefing and the press were breathing down his neck. But it could all wait. A visit from his old mate Rose Lainey wasn't something to happen every day.

CHAPTER 2

Rose looked around, taking in the nondescript decor, the sleek chairs and the coffee machine in the hallway. This could have been her place of work if she'd stayed in Northern Ireland, and if they'd been willing to overlook her family background.

'Rose Lainey. I never thought I'd live to see the day!' Danny's words as he burst through the door made her gasp with surprise.

'Danny!'

'Legend has it that if the fine Rose Lainey sets foot on these here shores, her beauty shrivels up and flees.' He opened his arms wide to give her a warm hug, squeezing her as hard as he could without breaking bones.

'Stick around and you might just see that happen.' Rose smiled at all six feet four of him. Brawny and good looking, with a sharp wit and a great analytical brain, he was the kind of man her sister Kaitlin would call a quare ride. To Rose, he was the best friend she'd ever had.

'What brings you to my neck of the woods?'

'Family business. You know how it is. Can't stay away forever.'

'Well you gave it a bloody good try. If it wasn't for the old Liverpool uni reunions, I'd never see you.'

The two had kept in touch over the years but Rose had always declined Danny's invites to come visit. Even his swish wedding invitation had been politely declined.

'So, how's life been treating you, Rosie?'

She felt self-conscious under his appraising eye. This is Danny, she reminded herself – he'd seen her hungover and devoid of any hint of the subterfuge make-up could offer plenty of times.

'Oh, you know, it's fine. Still in London and working for the prison service, but I sort of feel like I'm treading water.' She didn't tell him that she'd spent the best part of the last four months questioning her professional choices. Working in prisons and dealing with the worst category of offenders was starting to eat away at her soul. No matter what she did, it never felt like enough. She envied Danny and his role on the front line, being able to get his hands dirty and feel like he was making a real, discernible difference every single day. She sensed that it was too late for her to make any significant impact on most of the criminals she worked with. Many were beyond redemption.

'Time for a change?'

'I think so. I'm putting a few feelers out.'

'How long are you in town for?'

She shrugged. 'I'm not sure. I've leave to take, so I haven't booked my return flight yet. Thought I might stick around for a couple of weeks. Depends on how it feels to be back here, you know?'

'It's really good to see you, Rosie. You're looking well.'

Danny was the only person she'd tolerate calling her Rosie.

'How's Amy? Maybe I'll get to finally meet her.'

He looked off to the side and hesitated before saying, 'She's good. Yeah, we'll have to arrange dinner or something.'

'Definitely, though I've a lot of family stuff going on while I'm here.'

He nodded. 'Okay, but you are not leaving Belfast without spending some time with me. I'll show you around, let you see how much the old stomping ground has changed.'

It had changed; she couldn't deny it. Maybe it was the weather, but people seemed nicer, brighter and happier. There was less graffiti and more traffic. The peace dividend had paid off, by all accounts. Belfast was crawling with tourists and for the first time in a long time it felt as if it had something to offer beyond peace walls and political violence.

'I promise we'll catch up properly. I wanted to say hello before I head off to see to the family stuff. You know what it's like, it'll be "Auntie Joan needs to see you and Uncle Joe wants to take you to see such and such". My time won't be my own.'

She saw something flit across his face, his eyes opening wide. 'Hey, I have an idea. Would you have time to have a look at something that's just come my way?'

'What, like a case?'

'Yeah, why not? I can guarantee it's interesting and I could do with some of your hocus pocus input. If I can square it with my ACC, would you be up for it?'

'Hocus pocus?' She laughed. 'I'll have you know that forensic psychologists do a bloody good job of clearing up crime scenes quicker than any detectives.'

'I don't doubt it, Rosie. Think about my offer though. I'll see how we're fixed here and, if it works out, well . . . Say yes, for old times' sake.'

'We'll see, Danny. No promises. I'm here to take some leave, remember?'

'Rose, I know you. Sitting on your arse all day drinking cups of tea will drive you up the walls. Come play with me instead. I promise you, this case will be worth sticking around for. You said yourself that you're not happy in the prison service. Just take a look.'

'Take a look at what, exactly?'

'Let's head down to my office and I can talk you through it. I'd be eager to see what you make of it. Give me half an hour of your time, that's all.'

Danny had always been hard to resist.

CHAPTER 3

Danny stood back and watched Rose as she looked around the basement office, taking it all in. He knew the narrow windows were too high up to provide a view of the scorcher of a day outside and his row of filing cabinets, banked across one wall, made the room feel like a glorified store cupboard.

'So, you're in the arse end of nowhere. You must've pissed off someone pretty bad,' she said.

'They like to call it the Historical Enquiries Unit. I've been told it's the poisoned chalice, but you know me, I like a challenge.'

Up close, he could see she looked a little older. There were tell-tale fine lines around her eyes and her cheekbones were softened. He didn't care to think how different he might look. He knew a few detectives that wore their careers on their faces, all sunken eyes and dark shadows, never mind the expanding paunch telling of too many dinners on the run, and a fondness for whiskey and the beer. Funny how a few bad cases can catch up with you.

He wondered how life was really treating Rose. She'd always been something of a dark horse and the texts and phone calls had been few and far between since they'd graduated.

'Before we go any further – and I'm not saying I'm doing this, I'm just curious – what's the case?' Rose asked. 'And why me? I'm not exactly on the Serious Crime Unit's list of go-to consultants. I'm sure you have a bank of professionals to call in for cases that require a psychologist's input.'

'Yeah, this one's a bit different though. I was in a lull between cases, that strange time when you wonder if your working life is going to be logging records and tidying up documents for the Crown Prosecution forever.'

Rose nodded. She knew that feeling. That fear of never making a difference. Of being resigned to chasing paper leads instead of proper ones, of talking in circles to satisfy parole boards.

He noticed her looking down at the Mulligan file on his desk and continued. 'So, when the ACC called me in and gave me the gist, I was pumped and ready to go. Do you know Dunlore, just outside Lisburn? It's in a small village called Larchfield.'

'Yeah, I know it. Pretty little place, looks a bit like Kent.'

'Well, they have a small station – just a little outpost really – and get this, in runs this blood-covered girl, straight off the street.'

Danny knew he was reeling her in. Nothing a psychologist likes more than a case with a bit of intrigue, a mystery crying out for unravelling. They were like coppers that way.

'I still don't see what you need me for, or why you're on an active case when you've been sent to historical enquiries,' she said, but he could hear the piqued interest in her voice.

'Just take a look and you'll understand. Come with me for a wee ride to the crime scene.' He glanced down at the Mulligan case documents sitting on his desk, the dusty red box file holding years of false starts and dead ends.

'A day like this shouldn't be spent down in this dreary hole. Your family won't mind if you take some time out, would they?'

She put her head to the side and gave him a look. 'Danny, I can't go swanning off with you, no matter what the weather's like. Plus, it looks to me as if you have your hands full here,' she said, gesturing towards the folders.

'The files can wait. We've more urgent business to attend. Please Rose. Just trust me.' He was serious for a minute, worried that she wouldn't come with him.

'Fine. I'll give you half an hour and if I don't think it merits my time, I'm out. Well, what are you waiting on? Let's go.'

CHAPTER 4

Rose snapped on her seatbelt, ready for Danny to take off. She'd a good idea he'd drive like he talked, which was way too fast. They headed onto the motorway, the fields flying past in a blur of green and golden sheaves of wheat. It was a glorious day. The weather had been uncommonly good for Northern Ireland lately, so much so that there was talk of hosepipe bans, dogs having to be rescued from overheating cars, and elderly people dropping dead from heat exhaustion.

'Right, tell me what you know,' she said.

Danny filled her in on the blood-covered girl and her confession. 'Uniforms went to the address and found three dead, and one badly injured but still alive.'

'Where's the girl now?'

'Hospital – she had superficial knife injuries – but she isn't talking.' He blasted the air con up as high as it would go while Rose switched between radio stations, searching until she found something they could both agree on. 'Raspberry Beret' came on. A bit of Prince would do.

'I still don't see where you or I fit in to all this. Last time

I checked, historical enquiries don't throw up too many fresh corpses.'

'You'll understand when we get there.' She could sense him smiling beside her.

'The house is a bit out of the way. If you didn't know where to look for it, you'd never accidentally come across it. SatNav is useless on these country roads.' He overtook a red Audi that was being driven as slow as a tractor.

'This isn't somewhere a burglar or a madman would chance upon,' he said, checking his speed.

When they arrived in Larchfield, a young officer in uniform pointed them towards the crime scene. As they turned into the lane they saw police cars banked along the side of the hedgerow, and a strip of blue and white police tape tied across the entrance. Danny flashed his ID through the open car window and smiled, and they were waved through. The lane itself was little more than an overgrown dirt track that looked like it hadn't seen much traffic over the last ten years. There was barely enough room for one car to make its way down it.

They bumped slowly down the sloping lane and at the end of the track Rose caught her first glimpse of the house. It stood nestled into the landscape and the midmorning sunlight bathed its sandstone façade, making it look almost luminous, like something straight out of a story book. The cottage, which was bigger than Rose expected and more like a house, looked like it belonged to another era. Scratch that, she thought, it looked like it belonged to a time that had never actually existed in real life, as if it was from a world of quaint families, picnics of ginger beer and fruit cake, nights spent round an open fire. The kind of world where everyone looked out for each other.

The house was built in an L shape, with a curved front entrance at the axis. Three upstairs windows were visible, and a small bay window was situated to the right of the front door but they were like blank eyes looking out, giving nothing away. Rose noted that the garden was totally secluded, hidden from the main road by trees, bushes and a dilapidated stone wall. It was eerily quiet except for the chirping of birds in the fruit-heavy trees.

The surrounding hedgerows, shrubs, and trees were interspersed with wildflowers and knee-high dandelions, and the foliage had nearly consumed the house. But, for all its beauty, the scene didn't look right. It was too calm, too quiet. Rose was used to thinking of crime scenes as being a bustle of action. Uniforms gossiping, police radios crackling, tech bureau people in their space suits collecting evidence and looking self-important, barking at the detectives to mind their size elevens. Instead, there was one uniform on guard, looking a bit queasy and unsure of himself where he stood near the entrance.

'Here goes,' Danny said, handing Rose a packet of protective gear.

She looked at him. 'Are you really going to let me trample all over a fresh crime scene?'

'You've had the training and I know you've enough sense not to disturb anything. Besides, the SOCOs have been all over it already.' He'd always had a renegade streak. She was certain it had landed him in trouble more often than he cared to admit, but she was also sure he was a first-rate detective despite it.

They suited up in their blue plastic suits, hoods up and gloves on, and made their way over to the cop on the door. What is it with new recruits these days? Rose thought. Do they all have to look like they're just through puberty? This one had the pimply face of a sixth former, and ears that sat like jug handles on either side of his neat little head. The sun was pounding down and the young officer looked like he was developing a red welt of sunburn across his greasy face.

'Hello there,' Rose said in her best congenial manner to hide the fact that she was breaking every rule in the handbook by entering another jurisdiction's crime scene without good reason or permission. 'Dr Lainey and DI Stowe.'

The officer nodded and stood aside to allow them to enter. 'The pathologist is still in there.'

'Who were the first officers on the scene?' Danny asked.

'I believe that would be officers Richie Hughes and Anthony Clement, Sir.'

'Tell them we need a word when we're finished here.'

'Yes, no problem.'

Rose pushed the front door open. Someone had painted it an optimistic yellow once, but time and weather had left it peeling and cracked, showing the dull, grey undercoat lurking underneath. She checked the old rusty latch. No sign of a forced entry, she noted.

'Sir, the bodies are still upstairs,' Jug Ears said from behind them.

Danny turned to Rose. 'One victim found alive in a downstairs room, barely breathing – we don't know yet if he'll make it. The others were all in the bedroom upstairs.'

They stepped inside to the gloom of the hallway and Rose had a feeling of stepping into the past. The coolness of the interior seemed at odds with the blistering heat outside and the flagstoned flooring and dark wood architrave were like something you only see in period dramas.

Time and wear and tear had left the woodwork scuffed and peeling, but you could see money and craftsmanship had gone into the place.

Yet for all the quaintness and old-fashioned details, Rose's stomach did that sickening twisting thing, as if she knew they'd entered a place where nothing good could ever exist. She was starting to think she was becoming sentimental, a bit soft, but she knew from experience you can get a feel for a place the minute you step foot in it. Some places feel dirty and sordid. Others have that ghostly feel, causing that barely perceptible tug on the hairs at the back of your neck, that involuntary shiver. This was one of those places. She knew well enough to keep that to herself though. Danny would have called her a 'fecking buck eejit' for spouting such nonsense, but the eerie hush and the sharp contrast from the beautiful, lush countryside scene, made her want to find out more and bolt at the same time.

Rose looked down at the dried, bloody footprints that stood out against the uneven flagstoned floor of the hallway. Numbered evidence markers sat at each footprint like a place setting at a gory feast. 'Watch your step.'

Danny looked at her and nodded. She knew that whatever they were about to see, it wouldn't be pleasant.

The stairs creaked, announcing the departing pathologist.

'Raymond Lyons,' he said, introducing himself.

'You're new to the job, I hear,' said Danny, giving him a smile. 'Detective Danny Stowe and Dr Rose Lainey, forensic psychologist.'

'Aye, new to this job, but I bring twenty years' experience with me.'

Rose caught Danny smirking at Lyons' brisk reply.

'Anything of importance we should know about the victims now?'

'Nothing beyond the obvious. Need to get them on the table to tell you exactly what has gone on.' The pathologist was hitting sixty, but had that healthy look of careful living. Probably went cycling every weekend and limited himself to one glass of red a week. Rose envied his type.

'At first glance, what do you think we're looking at?' Rose asked.

'I prefer to keep my counsel until I know exactly what I'm dealing with, but I can confirm that there are three bodies, each with multiple stab wounds. Time of death probably no more than ten hours ago. I'll be in touch.' With that, he left them to it.

'Come on, in here first. This is what I want you to see,' said Danny directing Rose towards the living room. Rose stepped into the room, noticing the larger evidence markers on the floor that indicated where the first victim had been found. The small, square, sash window was covered by climbing ivy, allowing little light to spill in despite the brightness of the day outside. As Rose took in the scene around her, hyper-alert and curious, she gasped, realising why Danny had brought her here. Over a fireplace that was little more than a blackened hole, a scrawl of blackened chalk spelled out WHO TOOK EDEN MULLIGAN?

'What the fuck?' Rose said.

'I know, interesting, right?' Danny smiled like he'd just been handed a present tied with a scarlet-coloured bow.

'You're on the historical review case, and then the call came in about this?'

'Yep.'

Rose thought of the red box file she had seen sitting on his desk in the basement office.

'Do you know much about the Mulligan case?' he asked.

'Well, I know of it. Hard not to considering it's been in the news on and off for years. It's one of those cases that gets flagged up every so often, usually when the politicians start talking about legacy and issues of the past. Must be sad for the family.'

She examined the rest of the room, noting that the whole place was cluttered with furniture. Trestle tables, a sideboard and a large pale green velvet sofa sat in the middle of the room, facing the open stone fireplace, where the remnants of what looked like burnt papers lay in the grate.

'You need to get that checked out,' Rose said, indicating towards the ashes. They could hear the shuffle of techs overhead in the upstairs rooms.

'Are you up for having a look at what's up there?' He pointed to the room above them.

Rose nodded and they made their way up the threadbare carpeted staircase.

'Just don't touch anything.'

'What do you take me for?' she asked.

'A pen pusher medic,' he deadpanned.

Rose was prepared for the smell but when it hit her she felt nauseous. It was thick and viscous, as if you could reach out and touch it. Meaty with an undercurrent of metal, it tickled at the back of the throat.

The door of the bedroom to the right was wide open, inviting them in.

'Ladies first,' Danny said.

Rose rolled her eyes. 'Man up, Stowe.'

The two techs walked out of the room carrying evidence

bags. 'All done for now, just don't do anything stupid,' the second one said. 'It's not pretty in there.'

He wasn't wrong.

The scene was an aftermath of an orgy of violence – limbs, bloodied and splayed, entangled together as if they were one mass. Two men, one woman. All young – early to mid-twenties. Initially, it was difficult to identify which limb belonged to whom.

The girl was easy enough – blonde hair matted with drying blood, gashes to the neck and upper chest. She was wearing what looked like an old-fashioned cotton night-dress, yellowing with age and wide open at the front.

A man lay with his bloodied arm slung across the woman's small breasts, defence wounds obvious on his hands. He'd fought back, but the puncture wound to the neck had probably been enough to halt him. He was in joggers but no T-shirt, his chest slashed into vicious ribbons of flesh.

The other man was lying on his front and half-hanging off the bed, his dark jeans soaked, as if he'd pissed himself. Again, no top on. The bizarre twist of his head showed a substantial neck injury. It looked like he'd had his throat cut, possibly while his head had been yanked backwards by the hair.

They all looked young and somehow enchantingly pretty, in a twisted, grotesque sort of way.

'Christ, someone has gone full-on psycho,' Rose said. For once, Danny was quiet. Rose had expected him to give a running commentary on the scene, pointing out the obvious, coming up with surprising insights. She was aware he was watching her. Realised he was waiting to see how she read the scene.

The house gave off a vibe straight out of Grimm's night-mares. A twisted fairy-tale meant to unsettle and strike fear. Rose still wasn't sure what Danny's cold case had to do with this bloodied scene, but she had a sense that whatever the link, she was about to become entangled in a case she wouldn't easily forget. As they walked around the room their plastic shoe covers made sickening, squelchy noises as they stuck to the blood-covered floorboards. Danny crouched down to look under the bed.

'Nada. Just dust,' he said straightening up. 'Have to check though – you never know when you could get lucky.'

He opened the old, Victorian-style, mahogany wardrobe. It had two doors, a central set of drawers and a mirror. As the door pulled open, the image of the bodies on the bed reflected in the mirror looked like a still frame from a horror movie – too bloodied and bizarre to be real.

'It isn't the primary scene,' she commented, watching as he rummaged through the few outfits that were hanging up.

'Nah, there's too much blood on the stairs and the down-stairs floorboards.'

'They've been placed here, staged for some reason. This is the girl's bedroom by the look of the clothes. Not many clothes in there though so maybe they were on holiday?'

'Mm,' he didn't commit to an opinion. Too early for that.

He felt along the inside of the wardrobe door, reaching into the back and then above. Nothing.

Rose moved over to the window and looked out at the pastoral scene below. Swags of bindweed hung over the top of the outside of the window, but it looked like someone had partially cleared it to see the view.

'They're still relatively fresh according to Lyons,' he commented.

'Yes. The smell's bad, but not rancid. I've smelt worse. The heat hasn't helped things.'

'Yeah, it will have certainly sped up the decomposition.'

A couple of flies were now playing kamikaze against the dirty windowpane.

Footsteps creaked on the stairs before one of the local officers arrived at the bedroom door. 'Anthony Clement, Sir. I was told you wanted a word?'

'You and Hughes were first on the scene?' Danny asked. The young officer looked like he was about to piss himself, frozen in the doorway and not daring to step across the threshold. His eyes looked everywhere except at the bed.

'Yes, Sir.'

Danny moved away from the bed. 'I assume you followed protocol? Didn't risk tampering with anything? Better to tell us now if you did.'

'No, Sir, but we had to respond to the live one.'

'Of course. But you've handed your boots over to the techs?'

'Yes.'

'So, what did you find when you arrived?' Rose asked.

'We found the breathing one first, downstairs in the living room. Blood everywhere. We could barely find a pulse. It's not likely he'll make it, going by the amount of blood loss. Never seen anything like it. Not round here.'

'He was conscious?'

'No, he was out of it. Ambulance arrived within twenty-five minutes. This place isn't easy to find without local knowledge.'

'Any ID on him?' Danny asked.

'No, not a thing. He was wearing jeans and a shirt. No phone or anything else on him. We tried to patch up the wounds as best we could and radioed for back-up. As soon as the paramedics were on their way, we came upstairs, found the other victims.'

Rose looked at Danny then back at Clement. 'Then what? Did you search the property?'

'Yes. No sign of a break-in. Back door was locked from the inside, one of those big old-fashioned keys still in the keyhole. We came in through the front door. It was wide open, as though someone had left in full flight.'

'Right, that'll be all for now, but we may have to check in with you and Hughes again. Get your reports logged in the system by the end of the day.'

'Sir, there's something else.'

'What?' Danny said, impatient.

'Outside, in the garden, we've found some dolls.'

'Dolls?' Rose asked. 'What kind of dolls?'

'Old ones, hanging from the tree.'

CHAPTER 5

They made their way outside and let Officer Clement lead them to the tree at the back of the house.

'There, Sir,' he said, pointing towards the dolls before briskly heading back to the front of the house.

Rose and Danny looked up to where the dolls hung perfectly still in the warm air. They had been suspended by fine nylon twine from individual branches of the same tree but each was different: a bisque face, cracked and dirty; a rubber one without an eye; another with blank holes where the glassy eyes should have been. Two of them had shorn heads showing the pin holes where the hair had been threaded into the dolls' skulls. The one closest to them had her nose bashed in and the gaping hole where it should be was stuffed with some sort of sponge. The mouth hung open showing small, pearly teeth. Eyebrows painted in single brush strokes gave the doll a surprised look, as if she had experienced a fright.

They appeared to be partly handcrafted and had been made out of an assortment of parts, some with arms attached backwards, giving them the appearance of deformity. The twisting of limbs, the assault of features and the missing eyes all conspired to make them look like they'd been in the ownership of a sadistic child.

Rose recognised the face of one of them as being from a Tiny Tears doll. Its one remaining blue eye stared blindly. She had one as a child herself. They were popular in the eighties.

'Weird as fuck,' said Danny.

'Do you think they were left for us to find?' asked Rose.

Danny walked underneath the vast branches, the shade providing a cool, dark belt, and started taking pictures with his phone. 'Possibly. Could have been here before the slasher arrived on the scene, but we've got to check them out.'

'Plenty to work with.'

'Ha, I knew you'd bite,' Danny said grinning.

'I'm not signing up for anything. This was a cursory look, nothing more. Besides, your ACC might have something to say about me sticking my nose in where it's not wanted.'

'A case like this one needs someone like you. Leave McCausland to me.'

Rose decided she needed to lay her cards on the table. 'As far as my boss is concerned, I'm here for a few days' holiday to attend to some family business. He'll be expecting me back. I've no intention of getting messed up in a murder case.'

'Yeah, but you could ask for a secondment. Say, six to eight weeks? That's all I'm asking for.'

'It's not that simple, Danny.'

'Rosie, it's only as hard as you want to make it. Tell me you love London, love working with parole boards and

26

you've some English fella keeping your bed warm, waiting for your return, and I'll back off. But if there is a tiny bit of you interested in doing some real, meaningful work at the front end, then come on board and do this with me.'

'Who says my work isn't meaningful? The world doesn't revolve around Danny Stowe, you know.'

He held up a hand. 'Sorry, that came out wrong. Rosie, you and I, we go way back. Do you not remember the nights we spent talking about how we were going to set the world alight? Now's our chance.'

She said nothing and he took it as his cue to continue.

'The truth is, Rosie, I was put on historical enquiries because I've messed up. A previous case went badly wrong, and I was responsible. You landed back in my life on my first day of a big case, with a crime scene straight out of hell, and a crazed girl thinking she has committed murder. This is my chance to right a few wrongs and prove I'm worth a second chance.' He put his hands behind his head. 'Christ, I've just realised what I'm doing – it's like finals all over again – I'm relying on you to make me do my best work.'

'Danny, you don't need me. You never have done. Look, I'm not saying I won't consider it – a change from London and the prison service *would* be nice – I just don't know if I want that change to be *here*.'

How could she explain to him that she had spent so long running away from Belfast that she feared coming back?

CHAPTER 6

Going back to Belfast had never been part of the plan.

The phone call had come in the dead of the night, just as she always knew it would. She'd scrabbled for the switch on the bedside lamp, and propped herself up in the bed, bleary-eyed, her heart thumping.

'Roisin, it's me,' her sister had said.

'When?'

'Tonight. At half-nine. It took me a while to track you down as I've four different numbers for you. How did you know?'

'I get a phone call from you at God knows what time so it has to mean she's dead. Either that, or she needs help. I prefer the first option.'

'Well, you got your wish.' She could hear the reproach in Kaitlin's voice.

'I'm sorry. You know it's complicated for me. I was never the favoured child.'

They fell silent for a second, the sounds from the London street below – a taxi door being slammed, a siren in the

28

distance – offering a kind of solace. This was Rose's life now. Here, she didn't have to be wary of the city around her or worry about her family.

'The funeral will be on Saturday. You'll come?' Kaitlin says it lightly, but the hope is clear.

'I don't know. I'll have to see what's happening at work.' She racked her brain for a believable excuse as to why she couldn't go but settled instead on the truth.

'Look, I don't want to go. You can't expect me to jump on a flight home after all this time and act like everything is normal.'

'Come on. That's not fair on us.'

She'd no doubt that Kait knew full well that any return to Belfast would be under duress. But Evelyn was gone, so where was the harm in seeing her family now? There must be a squad of nieces and nephews that she had yet to meet.

'For God's sake Rosh, it's our mother. Your superiors will understand and you're bound to be entitled to compassionate leave. We haven't seen you for years. You owe it to her to go to her funeral.'

'I don't owe her anything.'

'What about the rest of us? You left us too.'

'It wasn't that simple.'

She thought of their family home and felt the tightening in her chest that she had spent years learning to breathe through.

'I'll text you the details when we get everything sorted with the undertakers. O'Kane's are doing it. She warned us not to go with the other crowd on the road.'

Rose laughed. 'Sectarian till the very end.'

Fifteen years. Had it really been that long? She had left as soon as she could at eighteen and was thirty-three now. Sleep had deserted her, and she was left with the pale, early morning light and a head full of infuriating memories. Funny how a familiar voice could drag her back into that world so easily. A world she had worked hard to leave behind.

Back then she had learned to keep her head down, to stay in the shadows, and she had survived by counting down the days until she could escape. Lying on the top bunk in a room she shared with Kaitlin, she'd promised herself that when she got out, her life would be different. The posters on her walls of bands like Joy Division, Pete Doherty and Oasis helped her visualise a life beyond the grey, breeze block walls of Belfast.

Sometimes she worried it hadn't really been as bad as she remembered. Had she perhaps been too quick to judge? But there was no escaping the reality of it: late night runs down south, transporting people, weapons, laundered money and God knows what. The rushed dinners as her mother was called away to deal with some urgent business that they had learned early on never to question. Her family operated on a need to know basis and Rose knew not to challenge that.

She had been Roisin back then. Roisin Lavery. Skinny and tall with shoulder-length dark hair, styled with a side fringe she wore long to hide behind. She'd had skin so pale people remarked on it, suggesting that she needed to get out more instead of spending so many days inside reading and listening to music.

When the last exam came around in June, she felt a surge of excitement laced with fear. She'd packed her PE bag with a couple of pairs of jeans, a few T-shirts, toiletries and the bundle of twenty-pound notes she had been saving for years.

Working three nights a week washing glasses in Madden's pub hadn't paid much, but she had been planning this for a long time and saving every penny amounted to freedom. When the examiner said, 'Time's up, please put down your pens,' Rose's heart had soared.

Liverpool offered her a chance to start over. An opportunity to be her own person, without the stigma of her family name. Months earlier, she had hidden the letter declaring she had been offered a place on a degree course in criminality and psychology. It didn't take Freud to work out she was exorcising some demons – even she could see the irony. Ensuring she achieved the grades needed to meet the criteria had been all she'd focused on and studying was easy when she could almost taste the freedom it offered.

Within a month of leaving she had changed her name to Rose Lainey. Officially, she was still a Lavery, but when meeting new people, she used her adopted name. Reinvention was essential. If she could pretend to be someone else then, maybe, she had a hope of creating the life she craved. She wasn't going to let her family, or Belfast, define her for evermore, so she'd separated herself from her family with distance, morality and politics. Funny how, back then, she'd grouped them all as one.

The family had always been run as a tight ship with their mother at the helm. What Evelyn said went and they were all powerless to stop her. Only Rose stood up to her mother's politics, and the others would look at her like she was crazy. She might as well have said that the earth was flat, rather than question the republican rhetoric that her mother so proudly espoused. The younger ones knew no better, but Rose could think for herself and she wasn't going to stand by and say nothing. Leaving had been her only option. She couldn't imagine what would have happened if she'd stayed. Evelyn had a mean streak and she wasn't averse to hurting her own children. There'd been many a household battle that had ended in hair pulling and slaps that stung beyond the red welt left by a palm.

Yet Evelyn could also be wildly loving and entertaining when the mood took her. When they'd lost their father, in the worst circumstances possible, Evelyn had made sure each of the children knew she was there for them, that she was going nowhere and that they had each other. None of it, for Rose, was enough when weighed up against the other stuff, the things she never wanted to dwell on.

She'd worked hard all these years to eradicate her past. Her way of speaking took a bit longer to go than the name, but now she spoke with an indistinct English accent that people could never quite place. She'd managed to create a life built around her work. If she didn't get too close to anyone, they didn't care enough to dig and discover who Rose Lainey really was. Though who's to say that the girl she left behind defined her any more than the woman she had become?

When Kaitlin had called with the news of their mother's death, Rose had waited, expecting an avalanche of emotion, something to shift inside and show her that she was changed by Evelyn's passing. That shift didn't come. She wondered if that was partly down to the fact that she had spent so much of her adult life shored up against emotion, controlled and considered in her approach to everything to such an extent that she no longer knew how to feel.

Despite her initial reluctance, she'd arrived the previous day and found that, despite the obvious changes, driving the roads of Belfast felt natural, like her muscle memory had been woken from a long sleep. The hire car, picked up at the airport, was functional and nippy but she wasn't going to be impressing anyone pulling up at her family home in a Fiat 500. They'd probably piss themselves laughing at her. She remembered that snarky humour that only family can get away with. She was sure her siblings' banter wouldn't have changed. At least, she hoped not.

The cars parked outside the wake house gave it away, along with the huddle of smokers in the tiny front garden. Rose could have found the house in her sleep anyway. Her mother had never left the family home. Twenty-three Hyde Street. It was in the Markets area of Belfast, a nationalist enclave situated right beside the bustling city centre. Hyde Street was in a row of red brick terrace houses that had been renovated by the council to make them fit for purpose. In any other city, the close positioning to the city centre would have made the area genteel, expensive and sought after, but not here. For a long time, these homes had been the dregs offered to working class Catholic families without a say in the government at Stormont.

Rose parked at the end of the street and walked back up. She paused at the gate, conscious of the eyes watching her. Someone whispered within ear shot and she heard her old name, Roisin. She'd be a curiosity to them all. The one who ran away and never returned.

She entered the narrow hallway and turned into the living room at the front of the house.

'Rosh! You made it.' She felt herself be pulled into an embrace without knowing whose arms were wrapped round her. She looked up and for a second, she couldn't place the greyish-green eyes. Then, as if the kaleidoscope had shifted, it all fell into place – Kaitlin.

'Kait, I'd hardly know you!'

'That's what happens when you move away and forget to come home.' Her voice was warm but the hint of admonishment in her words was clear.

'Come on in, they're all waiting to see you. Or would you like a few minutes alone with Mummy?' She jerked her head in the direction of the coffin where it had been placed along the far wall, beneath the window. The curtains were closed against the late evening light. A gloomy low glimmer from two church candles cast a sombre feel over the room.

Rose could see the coffin was open and shook her head. She had no desire to see her mother's corpse. She was here for the living, not the dead. Kaitlin nodded in understanding.

'Okay then, come in and see the others.'

When she followed Kaitlin into the kitchen the room fell quiet. She felt as if they had all turned towards her, watching.

A man on a wooden chair rose to his feet and walked over to offer her his hand. She shook it and realised it was her brother Pearse. He was different from how she'd remembered him, balding and heavier. The softness of youth was long gone. She wondered what he thought of her in return.

'Hello, Roisin.'

The murmur of conversation started again and she realised she had been holding her breath.

'Hi Pearse. Good to see you.' She searched his face for the brother she remembered.

Someone offered her a cup of tea and she took it, glad to have something to do with her hands. Conversation buzzed around her and she picked up threads – *the funeral director had done a good job, the mass was all organised, the order of service pamphlets would arrive any minute*

34

now and yes, they had chosen a lovely photograph of Evelyn for it. The priest was going to say a decade of the rosary over the coffin and would anyone like to join them in the front room?

The room thinned out as some went to say the prayers. Rose stayed where she was with Pearse at her side.

'You're not the religious type then?' he asked.

'No,' she said, looking up at him. 'You?'

'Only when I have to be.'

'I forgot, that's the way it is here. Religion: a necessary evil that keeps everyone in their own lane.'

'That's one way of looking at it. How have you been, Rosh? Life treating you well?'

'I can't complain. And you?'

'Aye. I'm doing all right for myself. Married, did you know? Two kids.'

'I heard. Sorry I didn't go to the wedding.'

'Or the christenings, or the first communions . . . You've missed a lot, Roisin.' He said it with a touch of bitterness, as if she had deliberately slighted him by missing out on his family's milestones.

Kaitlin rescued her. 'Roisin, Aunt Marie wants to see you before she goes.'

She let Kaitlin take her by the hand and lead her into the living room. 'Thanks,' she mouthed as the responses to the prayers rumbled in the background.

CHAPTER 7

Rose and Danny were both quiet on the drive back to the station. She was processing, working out what needed to be done, considering tasks in her head even though this wasn't yet her case to consult on. She was tempted to stay. All it would take was one phone call to her boss, Bernard. He had been telling her for months that she needed a break and she was sure he wouldn't hesitate to recommend her for a short-term placement with the PSNI, if they wanted her.

'So, what have we got?' Danny said, breaking her stream of thought.

'A bloodbath. At first glance, you'd think the three of them had been in bed together, but as it didn't look like the primary scene, we're going to have to work out who placed them there, and why.' She paused, thinking about what they should do first. 'Iona Gardener. She's where we start. You need to find out where they've taken her and talk to her.'

'It would help to have you with me.'

'Danny, come on. Get real. I can't exactly turn up and interrogate someone when I'm not officially working on this case.'

'No, I know that. I'm just saying you'd be a great help. This is a complex murder investigation. We have a confession that I'm pretty sure is false and a whole heap of questions that need someone with your experience to unravel.'

Rose looked out of the car window. Northern Ireland sure looked a whole lot prettier in the sunshine. In her memory, it was a dull, grey place, with pavement markings of red, white and blue, or green, white and orange, depending on which side of the community you found yourself in.

'Christ, I only called in for a catch-up. I didn't expect to spend my day knee deep in a crime scene,' she told him. 'The Killing Moon', an old Echo and the Bunnymen song, came on the radio. She glanced over at Danny and caught his eye before smiling. They'd both got drunk and played that song many times.

'Sure, you know me. Never a dull moment. This song takes me back. Do you remember dancing to it at the union bar?'

'No, I think that must have been some other girl. I don't dance.'

'Oh, but you do. If I remember correctly, it requires a brave few vodkas, but Rosie Lainey has been known to pull a few moves. I even think I've pictures somewhere to prove it.'

He turned up the radio and sang along. She couldn't help but smile. He hadn't changed. She wondered why she had let him drift away. Danny Stowe was probably the best friend she had ever had.

* * *

37

When they were back at the station, Danny grabbed some lunch for them both from the canteen.

'We'll get peace if we eat it down here,' he said, placing the tray containing two packets of cellophane-wrapped chicken salad sandwiches and two Diet Cokes.

'It's not like the old days when the boys in balaclavas phoned you up to tell you what they'd done, only too happy to take the credit. This one's got a bit of intrigue about it, wouldn't you say?' He looked at Rose and she held his stare. He was working hard to draw her in. No small talk, no 'what have you been doing with your life?' One of the perks of being a psychologist meant that you could read people well. Danny wanted her – no, *needed* her – but she hadn't yet worked out why. She had no doubt that he was good at his job. Whatever had happened to see him assigned to cold cases on the Historic Enquiries Unit had been a blip. She was sure of it. He would prove himself worthy once again and move on.

'This one's going to be messy and drawn out. I can feel it in my water,' Danny said, checking his emails.

Rose sat on the end of his desk, almost knocking over a pot of pens. 'You can keep your divining water to yourself. Okay, tell me, what do *you* think you are dealing with?'

Danny rubbed his hands together as if he was readying himself for a big job.

'A house like something out of the land that time forgot, in the back arse of nowhere. Three dead bodies – now identified as Olivia Templeton, Henry Morton and Theo Beckett – all mutilated. We've one survivor in intensive care – Dylan Wray – and then the girl, Iona Gardener, who walked in off the street to announce the murders. She's also currently in hospital. I'd say we've a lot going on.'

'Plus, don't forget the "*Who Took Eden Mulligan?*" scrawl over the fireplace. What's that about?'

'I was hoping you were going to tell me,' Danny said.

'I haven't even agreed to open the case notes yet, so don't be expecting me to have any illuminating insights.'

'Yeah, but you are interested, aren't you? You've done a lot of work around false confessions.'

'Been keeping tabs on me, have you?' She raised an eyebrow.

He had the good grace to look slightly sheepish. It was true she had specialised in working with witnesses and ensuring credible testimony, which included uncovering coerced-internalised false confessions. It was an area of research she had been interested in since her uni days when she had done her dissertation on suggestibility and negative priming.

'Hey, I look you up from time to time. Make sure you're still living. Can you blame me when you don't do Facebook or care to pick up the phone? Friendship's a two-way street, you know.'

She looked down. 'Okay, *if* for old times' sake, I talk to my boss and ask for six weeks' leave to work with you, how would we go about it?'

'I thought Iona's confession would be hard for you to resist.' He smirked, looking pleased with himself. 'I'll have a word with McCausland. The false confession thing needs a professional like you on board. Like I said, this is a big investigation. We can't afford to get this wrong.'

Rose wasn't going to admit it, but she was glad to have been asked to consult on the case. Her work in London was starting to drag and she had resorted to reviewing case studies, writing up reports and doing all the dull shit she swore she'd never do. She never handled inactivity well. This Dunlore case looked interesting even before she had delved into it properly. Rose could see the attraction of proper police work.

Maybe it was time to come back. Evelyn was dead so Rose had little reason to stay away anymore. In some ways, it would always be home, even if it had meant fear, lies and danger. She'd run to get away from all that, hoping that her degree course in Liverpool would offer her a different kind of life. Now she realised that she'd achieved everything she'd hoped for, but at a cost. Her life in London was uncomplicated, just as she wanted it to be, yet sterile. No messy family dynamics.

That had suited her fine but now she wondered: was she missing out?

When she thought of Liverpool and her friendship with Danny it was always with fondness. He had taught her how to relax, to live a little. He'd dragged her to clubs in dodgy areas and made her forget her reluctance to dance to stupid rave music, knock back shots of foul green liquid, and laugh at herself.

Initially she had kept her distance from Danny as she didn't want to cling to the only other Irish student in her lectures. She'd gone out of her way to escape Northern Ireland after all and she figured life would be simpler if she left all connections with home behind. Try as she had though, Danny had been hard to avoid.

Once, he took her to a party of people he had met at the library. Standing in the queue to check out books he had naturally – for him – got into a conversation and discovered they were hosting a party that night. When they'd arrived, after ten, it was in full throttle. REM was playing and some fella was pogoing with such force that it was only a matter of time before he whacked into someone and started a fight. The atmosphere had had an edge to it that suggested someone had supplied pills and Rose could smell cigarette smoke laced with weed. She never partook in any of that herself. She never wanted to take anything that rendered her loose-mouthed and out of control.

Danny had leaned in close to her and said, 'Hey, do you think we're the only sane people here?'

'Looks that way. Don't recognise half of them. You said the house is rented by a pile of medics; they are always a bit whacko. Must be the long hours and all the blood and guts.'

Danny smiled at her. 'There's a few from our course over there.' He'd jerked his head in the direction of the kitchen as he spoke. Rose caught sight of a couple of girls she knew from her seminar. Neither of them appeared to be bothered by the rowdiness of the crowd. By comparison, Rose felt gauche and innocent, like a poor relation fresh from Northern Ireland. The others, with their accents and posh schools, had a sense of confidence and entitlement that Rose envied.

At times like this, she felt out of her depth. When she had lain in bed, back home in Belfast, imagining this new life, she'd pictured herself struggling in the lectures, having to work hard to keep up, when in reality the work was fine. It was the social side of things that she found challenging. She didn't have the right clothes, the right haircut, the right bag. When she opened her mouth, she was immediately seen as different. Other. Danny had made the transition easier for her. He attracted people, and by being his friend Rose had found that she didn't need to make too much effort to be included.

Now she realised that she was tired of feeling like the outsider. Maybe it was time to give Belfast another chance and get to know it all over again.

CHAPTER 8

As it happened, Bernard had been more reluctant to allow Rose the leave than she thought he would be. He sounded concerned that she was prepared to stay in Northern Ireland to do police work without any prior notice.

'Belfast? Are you sure?' She could hear the incredulousness in his tone. The unspoken 'why' left hanging.

'Bernard, it's not like the stuff you've seen on TV over the years. They're actually civilised now, you know.'

The truth was, Rose hadn't a clue what it was like now. Sure, the peace process had brought about a stability that she'd never imagined could be possible. Growing up in a ghettoised nationalist area, all she had known was violence and intimidation. Riots and Land Rover Saracens. Army searches, handbags checked before going into shops in town, a sense of something about to kick off all the time. But Belfast had moved on, even if the rest of the UK hadn't realised. The Troubles had been the soundtrack of her childhood – police messages played out on secret transistor radios, plastic bullets, bin lids rattling out a coded warning down rain-washed entryways, shoot to kill policies, knee-cappings and the rally cry as petrol bombs were launched towards police barricades. Home sweet home. A far cry from Bernard's middle-class Shropshire background. She couldn't explain it to Bernard any more than she could explain it to herself.

It had taken some time, but Bernard had eventually agreed and Danny had squared it with his superiors. Before she knew it, references, proof of qualifications and other administrative details were all being emailed across from her HR department in London. Apparently, Danny had argued that the need to have a psychologist on board was vital, owing to the fragile mental state of Iona Gardener.

When Danny called Rose to share the news, he told her McCausland had given in when he had been told that she was the best in the business. She had been assigned a desk in the basement of doom and was to report to McCausland first thing in the morning.

'I need to nip out for a little while tomorrow,' she said.

She heard Danny do a mock sigh down the phone. 'Jesus, first day on the job and you're already slacking off?'

'It's a family funeral. I did tell you I had come over for family business.'

'Anyone close?'

'No, not really, but I said I'd attend. I shouldn't need to be away for more than a couple of hours.' She had never explained her family to Danny and she wasn't going to start now.

'All right, no bother. I'll cover for you.'

'See you tomorrow then.' She hung up and decided if she was staying the full six weeks, she'd need to sort out some clothes. Thankfully, she had brought her laptop with her and the apartment she'd rented for her visit would be fine for accommodation. It was central and not too expensive. Her flat in London would be stuffy by the time she returned, and she dreaded to think what she'd find growing in her fridge, but she was kind of glad of the change. Left to her own devices, she probably would have stayed working for the parole board until she'd died of boredom. Danny's timing was perfect. This case was the shake-up she needed.

The funeral was held in St Malachy's chapel in Alfred Street. Rose slipped in at the back and watched as her family gathered themselves into the front pews. It was a beautiful, ornate church. The vaulted ceiling reminded her of icing on a wedding cake and had a Gothic feel to it, though she recalled learning at school that it was designed in the style of the Tudor period.

She turned her head and looked at the mourners. Some looked familiar, faces from the past, aged and altered but still recognisable. She jolted as she saw the one face she had hoped not to see. Sean Torrent. He had loomed large in her childhood. A thickset man who wore an air of repressed violence, as if he was at odds with the world and everyone he encountered in it, he was a figure who demanded fear and respect in equal measure. She hated how her mother had revered him, had answered his every call and dirtied her hands clearing up his messes. Sean Torrent was an IRA commander. Funny how when she was young, Rose had never known to put that title to his name. It had taken time and distance to enable Rose to see him for what he was: a murdering bastard who had a strange hold over her mother. There had been knocks on the door in the middle of the night and whispered voices in the hallway. Usually Evelyn would be whisked away – to do what, Rose was never sure. Her imagination filled in the gaps.

The funeral mass was predictable, its familiar rhythm coming back to her, soothing and hypnotic. Funny how some things stay with you, she thought. It was as if the responses had been branded into her DNA and came out of her mouth without conscious thought. Parts of the mass had changed since she had been a regular attendee as a girl, but she felt the intimacy of it carry her along. Her brother Pearse stood and walked to the altar to do the first reading from St Mark's gospel. His voice lulled her into nostalgia, and her mind drifted back to the days when they were kids. He had always been messing about with Colm, the two of them fighting over which television channel to watch. There was only a year between them, so they had seemed like a pair to her, always getting in her way or making her late because she had to mind them when her mother had taken herself off God knows where. Now, she realised, she didn't really know either of her brothers. She had left before they were teenagers. In her mind they were still just annoying kids.

Colm was at the altar now and was reading. 'The response to the Psalm is: to live in the house of the Lord . . . all the days of my life.' The congregation echoed the words back to him. She had yet to talk to Colm. He had held back at the wake and had avoided her. Being the youngest of the family, Rose had the sense that their mother's death would hit him hardest. She could remember him crying when being left by their mother as a small child. He always needed reassurance that she'd be back soon.

There was one evening he had fallen off the bunk bed – he had been playing about with Pearse and ended up tumbling from the top bunk, hurting his shoulder. He had sobbed in Rose's arms as she tried to console him, crying for his mummy to come and make it all better. Rose could still recall the feel of his damp cheek buried into the crux of her neck as his little arms and legs wrapped around her like a monkey. He had been a cute kid. All pudgy limbs and fair curly hair.

Afterwards, the mourners gathered in a local hotel function room. Platters of sandwiches arrived, and Rose helped herself to some tea. She could sense uncles and aunts talking about her and caught the odd stare, as if she was a gate crasher, here for the free food and drink. She stood at the edge of the room, refusing to get involved. What was the point in chatting or pretending that she shared their grief? It had been a mistake to come. She could see that now. She had promised Kaitlin she would stay for an hour but already she was glancing at her watch and wondering if she could slip off quietly. She was scanning the room, looking for the easiest route out, when Kaitlin appeared at her side.

'We're heading back to Ma's house this evening. Just us, the immediate family. You will come, won't you?' There it was again, that pleading cloaked in assumption. Like she owed them something.

'Kaitlin, I don't know. I might be working.'

'Working on what? I thought you worked in London?'

'I do, but I've been asked to confer on a case here for a few weeks. I thought I'd stick around for a bit.'

Kaitlin nodded in approval. 'All the more reason to come

47

tonight. We want to see you. Spend some time with you. The wake wasn't the place for that.'

Rose considered what that might mean. Recriminations, accusations. She didn't have the strength for it. 'Listen, Kaitlin, I left. It wasn't as if you didn't know I was okay. I made sure you all knew I was alive and well.' She had written to them explaining that she was studying in England. 'Life moves on. I don't expect any of you to understand but I needed to go,' Rose said.

'Roisin, we just want to see you. That's all. You're here now, so why not make the effort to give us a bit of your time? Don't you owe us that much?' They stood watching two young children play with plastic straws, pretending they were swords, swiping at each other and giggling.

Rose turned to Kaitlin. 'I'll see if I can get away. No promises, though. I have to get back to work now. What time will you be back at the house?'

'Seven.'

'Right. I'll try.'

CHAPTER 9

Rose was grateful for the distraction of work. The gathering of Evelyn's clan had been unnerving. Too many people who knew too much about her. She was used to being in her own contained world. No one to question her past or to share in her shame. It was better that way. Coming home threatened to crack that protective shell right open.

Danny had set up a desk for her opposite his and she busied herself reading the information about the murders that had been logged into the system.

'So, we have a confession. The holy grail of crime solving, but we're pretty sure it's worth shite all.'

Rose watched him as he strode across the room, stopping at the high-up window to peer out at the rectangle of clear blue sky, before he returned to his chair. He had spent the morning in the incident room, making sure that his team had been assigned tasks and were following through. Rose had opted to stay in the background.

'We're more than pretty sure.'

'What, so you don't think there's any possibility that Iona did it?' Danny asked.

'No. Not by herself, anyway, since the victims were moved. If she is of average height and build for a girl of her age, then there isn't a chance in hell she acted alone. She couldn't have carried the bodies up those stairs.'

'As much as I hate kicking a gift horse in the mouth, I know you're right. But she has to have been involved in some shape or form.'

Rose stood and stretched but quickly sat again, suddenly conscious that she had been showing a glimmer of her taut midriff. 'What could her motive have been?'

'I've no idea.'

'Well, what we do know at this stage is that if she did do it, she didn't do it alone. I'm still not convinced she was at all responsible. But then my next question is: why claim she was if she wasn't?'

Danny leaned back on the chair. 'Maybe she thinks she did it, like you said. Or *wanted* to do it. She has to have played some part, even if she didn't orchestrate it.'

'Who was she working with, though?'

'What about Dylan Wray, the one in intensive care? We could be looking at a murder-suicide pact that Iona was part of.'

'It's possible but not likely. Most murder-suicides involve family members. Any update from Dylan's doctors?'

Danny checked his phone in case there had been any recent texts he hadn't heard pinging in. 'Not since this morning. He lost a lot of blood and he's still unconscious. Doctor said it was fifty-fifty as to whether or not he'd make it.'

'Then I think it's time we paid Iona a visit,' Rose said.

* * *

Within minutes, they were on their way to the Royal Victoria Hospital, located on the Falls Road. The visitors' car park was full, so Danny reversed into a no parking section and slapped a card in the window saying the vehicle was on official police business. They were heading to ward 7C, where Iona Gardener was being treated for superficial knife wounds and shock.

They were met at the entrance to the hospital by a huddle of smokers, all taking a quick drag before entering the building. The irony of smoking outside a hospital seemed to be lost on them.

The maze of wards and side bays were easy to navigate, and they quickly found where they needed to be. Danny approached a nurse at a desk and asked where they could find Iona. She quickly scanned the computer and glanced up at them with a face that looked like it had seen too many night shifts. Her pallor was somewhere between yellow and grey and her hair was cut utilitarian style in a short, neat bob.

'I'm not sure she is able to have visitors at the minute. You might need to come back tomorrow,' she said, her voice carrying the lilt of a Derry accent. Rose did the needful with her medical ID and the nurse nodded and told them to go to the room at the bottom of the corridor. A police officer was standing at the door of the private room where Iona Gardener was being treated.

'Maggie, holding the fort on your own?' Danny asked in greeting.

'Matt McCabe will be back in a minute. He's just nipped to the loo.'

'Has she said anything?' Rose asked, nodding towards the door.

'Not a word to us. Doctor's in there with her now. The parents are here too, somewhere.'

Rose knocked on the door and stuck her head into the room. 'Excuse me, forensic psychologist Dr Rose Lainey and Detective Inspector Danny Stowe, here. We would like to have a word with the patient.'

The doctor looked up from what she was doing. She adjusted her glasses and turned to the nurse, instructing her to return to do the stats on an hourly basis, before walking across the room and speaking to Rose and Danny in hushed tones. 'Can we speak outside please?'

They backed out of the room into the corridor.

'Ms Gardener has minor injuries, some knife wounds and bruising – nothing life threatening – but as you can see, she isn't really fit to speak to the police. I don't think you'd get anything worthwhile out of her while she's like this. Maybe if you come back tomorrow, we can reassess.'

'Is the tox screen back yet? Any drugs or alcohol in her bloods?' Rose asked.

'All clean. We have her on pain medication now, and something to help relax her. She was very distressed when she came in. Here are her parents coming now. They were making calls.' Rose looked behind and saw a dark-haired woman with a pinched-looking face walking beside a tall, grey-haired man. They both looked drained and shell-shocked, as if they couldn't quite fathom what they were doing in a hospital when they should be at work or having lunch.

'Mr and Mrs Gardener, this is Dr Lainey and I'm DI Stowe. Can we have a word?' They looked into the room to check on their daughter, but she was still motionless.

'Michael Gardener,' the man said, before turning to the woman. 'And Christine, my wife.'

'Do you know what has happened yet? Who did this?' Christine asked, her face stern and pale, devoid of make-up.

'That's what we are trying to decipher, Mrs Gardener,' Danny said. 'We understand that Iona walked into the police station at Dunlore and reported the incident. We currently have three bodies and another victim in intensive care. Iona told the officers at the station that she was the one responsible for what happened at the cottage.'

'That's ridiculous!' Michael Gardener's complexion flushed pink, his ears reddening in agitation. 'My daughter has been badly injured, and God knows what she has witnessed or experienced, or can you not see that, Inspector?'

'Mr Gardener, we have to speak to Iona to try and ascertain what happened. I'm sure you can appreciate that this is a very serious situation. Do you know if Iona has any enemies? Any reason to feel threatened?'

The woman's head whipped up. 'No, of course not. She's a happy, settled girl. Never given us a day of bother. She gets on with everyone.'

'We have to ask. Let me introduce myself properly: I am Rose Lainey, a forensic psychologist working with the PSNI on this case. I'm here to help Iona as much as I'm here to help the police. We all want to get to the bottom of this and it is in Iona's interests to cooperate with us,' Rose offered.

The father gave a terse shake of his head. 'Christ, who could have done this?'

'That's what we are trying to find out, Mr Gardener, but we need Iona's help to do that. Does Iona or either of you have any connection to Eden Mulligan?'

He shook his head. 'The woman who went missing years ago?'

Rose nodded. Even after all these years, Eden Mulligan was still burnt into the public consciousness.

'Why do you ask?' Michael Gardener said.

'We're not at liberty to disclose that yet,' Danny answered. He turned to the doctor. 'We need to conduct a preliminary interview.'

'Well, keep it short and if she gets too agitated, you'll have to go,' she said.

Michael Gardener looked into the room, watching his daughter as she lay on the bed, and Rose could see the mother was about to cry. Her shoulders were hunched forward, and her head was buried into her chest, as if she wanted to curl up and hide away.

'We have to go back in to our daughter. This is not the time or place for interviewing her. Anyone can see she has been traumatised,' he said.

Danny stepped forward, blocking the door as they attempted to move past. 'I'm afraid that it won't be possible for us to speak to her at a later time. We are dealing with a multiple murder inquiry and we don't have the luxury of time to wait around. Miss Gardener may be able to help us.'

'Has she spoken to you about what happened?' Rose asked, her tone softer than Danny's.

Michael Gardener shook his head. 'No, she hasn't said a word.'

'The best thing we can do for Iona is to clear up the notion that she is responsible. If she didn't do it, we need to find who did. I'm sure you both want that too,' Rose said.

Michael Gardener looked to his wife and she nodded.

'Trust us to do our jobs,' Rose said.

They looked at each other and Michael spoke. 'Okay, but we stay with her. She's been through a terrible ordeal.'

When they entered the room, Iona was lying deathly still, with an IV hooked up to her hand. Her eyes, a clear blue, were opened, staring, but it was as though she was unaware that anyone was with her. Rose moved towards the bed. Iona's left hand was bandaged, and they could see the crisscross of light scratches farther up her arm. She wore a regulation hospital gown of blue cotton and a white sheet was pulled over her, up to her chest.

'Miss Gardener, we're from the PSNI. We're here to ask you about what happened,' Danny said quietly.

The girl turned her head as if to acknowledge them for the first time, but then closed her eyes as if to block them out.

Rose took her chance. 'Iona, I'm a psychologist. We're here to find out what happened at the Dunlore cottage. I know you want to help us. We just need to ask a few questions. Is that okay?'

She nodded.

'Well, ten minutes. No more,' the doctor said. 'I'll be back soon, Iona. If you need anything just push the buzzer.' She placed the buzzer in Iona's hand, the way you would with a child.

Rose sat on the chair beside the bed and Danny stood close beside her. 'Iona, can you tell us what you remember?'

The icy blue eyes opened, but appeared glazed over as she said quietly, 'They're dead because of me.'

Then, before any of them could respond, the girl was out of the bed and ripping out the IV needle stuck in her left hand. In one fluid movement she was at the window, pushing it with her hands, trying to open it, but it was on a safety latch, and only opened a few inches. Danny was there before Rose, grabbing the regulation hospital gown, trying to drag the girl back, before she could get the window open wider. The mother screamed, 'Iona! Stop! What are you doing?'

Rose hit an emergency button.

'Iona, you're going to hurt yourself!' Danny shouted as he held on to her by her shoulders, the gown ripping away to expose pale skin. The father grabbed at her, holding her arm, trying to pull her back from the window. She seemed to have strength and force beyond her fragile physique.

She didn't listen to their pleas, nor appear to care about their concern, as she launched herself against the reinforced glass, smashing her head against it as if she wanted to knock her brains out.

CHAPTER 10

Back at the station, Danny watched as Rose opened a file to start making notes on Iona. They had little to go on, but he was certain that, given time, she would get beneath Iona's skin. While the girl's confession was infuriatingly intriguing, they had to adhere to protocol and they had to be cautious in how to proceed. They needed to establish her competency to be able to gain full access, or they risked a repeat performance of what had happened at the hospital. She had eventually been calmed by an injection of a sedative, but not before causing herself a minor head injury.

'So, Iona's in psychiatric evaluation after her meltdown, and we can't get near her for questioning.' Danny sighed as he mulled it all over. 'Do you think the hospital incident could have been a convenient act to buy her more time?'

'Nah. I don't think anyone could put that on as a show. At least, it appeared real enough to me. She seemed terrified. Scared out of her wits enough to jump out of that window. Makes me think, what's she frightened of?' Rose said.

'Or *who*? What went on in that house and what did she see?'

'Yes, exactly – and why was she spared, if she isn't the murderer?'

Danny felt a surge of energy. He loved this initial stage of an investigation, when the details began to filter into focus. There was so much ground to cover – people to interview, evidence to examine – but at the beginning of every case was the endless stream of questions.

Rose's return was making Danny feel nostalgic. He found himself humming songs from years back – Nirvana, Radiohead and Nick Cave and The Bad Seeds – bands they had listened to in Liverpool. He'd find himself smiling at some daft memory and then check his phone to make sure he hadn't missed her call. For the first time in months he wasn't dwelling on Amy or the fucked-up Lennon case. He had tortured himself for weeks after he'd smashed that pimp's head into that wall, thinking that maybe he was losing his control and ability to function. It was his job to catch the bad guys, make sure every scrap of paperwork was exactly as it should be to prevent barristers weaselling the scumbag's way out of being banged up. His marriage troubles had affected his work. He couldn't blame Amy for his reaction to finding that girl brutally murdered with the imprint of a DM boot smashed into her face, but he certainly hadn't been his best self when it happened. Now, Rose and the Dunlore case were providing him with the perfect distraction.

And she was as lovely as ever.

Now that she was here, he couldn't help reminiscing about the early days of their friendship. The first time he'd been invited into her bedroom, in her shared student house, he'd been struck by how tidy she was. The single bed was perfectly made up, the pillow plumped and the duvet pulled so tightly that he was afraid to sit on it and crease it. A row of novels sat on her bookshelf: Orwell, Graham Greene, Iris Murdoch. All worthy and so Rose. She had no posters or photographs to adorn the walls. No trinkets or reminders from home. Everything was monastically simple. His own room had a few posters and a Liverpool football programme displayed along with photographs of his mates back home. One of the photos had been taken on the last day of school, the friends' arms around each other's shoulders as the sun beat down on them. All smiling and thinking they were the dog's bollocks.

He'd noticed that whenever the subject of home came up Rose became spiky and irritable. Once, when he'd asked if she'd be getting the ferry home for Christmas, she nearly bit his head off. Eventually he learned not to ask and assumed money was part of the problem. She obviously didn't come from a family with enough money to cover frequent trips back like he had. If she didn't want to hark on about back home the way some people did, then that was okay with him. They both loved Liverpool and were making sure they got the most out of their university experience.

There was an insecurity about her, a sense of uncertainty, as if she didn't know her own worth. He saw it any time they were out with others. She became a spectator, sitting on the sidelines and letting the conversation brush over her, rarely offering an opinion or interjecting. Once, they were in the union bar and were discussing New Labour, a subject on which he knew Rose had plenty to say. He watched, amazed, as she let Gillian waffle on about why Tony Blair was a godsend to the party and how Gordon Brown wasn't worthy of being party leader, never butting in to put her right. She seemed to doubt herself when in the company of the others, never shining the way she did when she was alone with him.

The conference room was situated on the first floor, right beside the main open-plan office. The wall of windows provided a view of the car park, and though the bright blue of the sky made up for it, the heat of the sun beating in had cooked up a scent of old trainers with an undercurrent of fried food. Notice boards littered with the ghost pin holes of past investigations hung on the pale green wall at the back, while a wide projection screen dominated the wall to the front.

The chairs and small desks were ordered into a lecture hall formation, making Danny feel like the teacher standing at the top of the class. He surveyed the room, and saw the usual faces looking back at him: Tania Lumen, Malachy Magee, Jack Fitzgerald, Jamie King, and a few others he didn't know well. While every case was important, seeing the team assembled and waiting, he realised how make or break this case would be for him. The case that would either secure his future in the PSNI or prove everyone's doubts to be right.

He knew that word about the Lennon case had seeped through the office like damp through paper. Whether they agreed that the scumbag had deserved getting his head smashed in or not, none of them would condone it. The days of police brutality were behind them. They were a different kind of force and he'd risked all of their reputations by acting like a prize dick. The PSNI Discipline Branch had thrown the code book of ethics at him, and the board had threatened suspension, but he had managed to avoid the police ombudsman being brought in and McCausland had argued his case. The basement of doom and cold cases was the compromise.

He knew he shouldn't complain, but he felt he had served his time and now he was ready to set about proving his worth once again. A case this big and complex needed the best and those in the room, like him, were aware that they were lucky to have been selected. This case was going to get plenty of attention both from within the force and from the public. The media were already hounding them for quotes.

He was pleased to see that the room was already set up with a map of Dunlore estate, a floorplan of the cottage and photographs of each of the victims displayed on a board. The team sat expectantly, waiting for Danny to address them. He could feel tension in the air and knew it was either a reaction to the new live case or they were preparing to give him a hard time.

He took a deep breath and began. 'Right, you have all had the briefing notes earlier. We are dealing with a major investigation. Whatever you're working on get it tied up or handed over to someone else. This case will demand your full attention.

'As of yet, we do not know if the killer, or killers, planned and orchestrated this attack or if it was a crime of opportunity. In a planned attack, we expect to see a level of control, limiting the evidence left behind, and we can't say yet if that was the case here. The scene is messy, with a lot of blood, but until forensics come back, we don't know what else has been left behind by the killer or killers.

'The cottage is out of the way but don't let that prevent

you from looking for witnesses. Someone may have seen something suspicious. We don't know for sure if the killer entered the property after the victims, if he was already there, or was permitted entry by one of the group.'

Danny was aware that he was stating more about what they didn't know than what they did. Despite the carnage in the cottage they had little information to go on. He paused to make sure everyone was paying attention. He needed to have the team on side, to trust him as their case leader. He was sure talk around the station had been that he was losing his touch.

'The offender's actions after the event, in leaving the scene or perhaps in returning to their home, may lead to suspicion falling on them with others seeing out of character behaviour or blood-covered clothing. On the other hand, if the killing was planned or if the killer at least contemplated the use of violence by carrying a weapon, they may have come prepared to cover their tracks.'

He paused and looked at the map.

'This area surrounding the cottage has limited electronic data traces. Any potential CCTV and other types of digital imagery – such as electronic data relating to telephone calls or financial transactions – in the nearby areas must be traced. Mal, can I ask you to oversee this aspect of the inquiry?'

Magee nodded. 'On it.'

'One more thing that we need to address is the dolls found hanging from a tree in the grounds of the property.' He clicked on the remote control and a picture of the hanging dolls flashed up on the screen.

The image looked eerie and sinister, the dolls hanging by thin wires from the branches. It was clear the arrangement had been designed to unnerve whoever came across them. Danny felt sure there had to be meaning behind them.

'What do these dolls say about the killer? What reason were they placed there? Keep the dolls in mind as you go about the investigation. I don't think it's a coincidence that they were found. Forensics are examining them at present – we hope to get something back from them in a day or so – and we should be able to find out from the owners of the estate how long they might have been there.

'Right, moving on.' He looked towards Tania Lumen. 'Tania, I'm making you lead coordinator. I want everything correlated and up to date on the system. Whatever aspect of the case you are working on, Tania needs to know. Everything must be logged in the system and we all need to keep the communication channels open.'

'Yep, no problem.' Tania looked pleased to have been singled out.

'I need good judgement on this case. If you can't get hold of me you will answer to Detective Sergeant Malachy Magee. Think of him as my second in command.'

Someone howled like a wolf.

'Deputy dawg Magee,' Jack Fitzgerald piped up and the room sniggered.

Magee stood and took a bow.

'All right, knock it off. There's too much to be done to be pissing around,' Danny admonished. They had a lot of work ahead of them. Long days and possibly weekends too.

'Right, one more thing,' Danny said, catching Rose's eye. 'Dr Lainey is working with us on a consultancy basis, dealing primarily with Iona Gardener and the confession angle. She is also conferring on the possibly connected historic cold case, that of the disappearance of thirty-three-year-old Eden Mulligan. It is of interest to us since the words "*Who Took Eden Mulligan?*" were found scrawled on the living room wall in the Dunlore cottage.'

He clicked on his laptop and a photograph of the slogan flashed up on the board.

'Dr Lainey is going to speak to you now. If anything relating to the Mulligan case crops up during your investigations, make sure you bring it to our attention. Dr Lainey, over to you.'

Rose walked to the front of the room and Danny noticed the team sat up a little straighter in response to her. Her dark hair was tied back, she wore little make-up and she was still strikingly beautiful. Danny could see there was a quiet confidence to her now that she never had when they were young. He could sense his team appraising her. Outsiders never got an easy ride, but he was sure Rose could hold her own.

'Thanks, DI Stowe. A historic cold case is not usually concerned with present day crime scenes, but as you can see from the graffiti on the living room wall, our two lines of inquiry are crossing. Right now, we have nothing else that connects Lower Dunlore cottage to Eden Mulligan's disappearance.'

Rose nodded to Danny and he clicked on his laptop to bring up a photograph of Eden.

'To refresh your memories, Eden Mulligan went missing from her Belfast house in July 1986. The exact date she went missing isn't actually known but it is thought that it was sometime between 17 and 22 July. The five children she left behind tried asking the police for help to look for her, but were told she would turn up when she was ready. The children's father is believed to have been working in

London at the time of her disappearance. He returned to see them on a regular basis, but – significantly – never came back once Eden went missing.

'When neighbours became suspicious that the children were on their own, social services were informed. The RUC at the time did not investigate the disappearance, claiming that there were more pressing crimes for them to deal with, and it was suggested by the police that the young mother had gone of her own accord. The children, the youngest being six and the oldest thirteen, were adamant that she would not have left them unattended. The neighbours supported this.'

Danny straightened himself up. 'Any questions?'

'Sir, you don't suppose the graffiti was just a random coincidence? Like, there's no direct connection between the victims and the cold case, is there? We can't go wasting resources looking for a mother who ran away over thirty years ago.'

Rose sighed. 'What's your name?'

'Aaron Dixon, Ma'am.'

'Well, Aaron, it was that attitude that meant five children grew up without a mother and without any answers as to what happened to her. We have a live crime scene with a red flag screaming "investigate the Mulligan case", so we will follow up all angles.'

Danny voiced his support. 'Dr Lainey is right. We can't afford not to link the investigations. No one is saying that you're to go haring off, ordering digs to find Eden Mulligan, but you are being asked to keep an open mind, to have an awareness of the 1986 case, and to bring anything of significance to our attention.'

Rose stepped forward and placed her hands on the table.

'Exactly, keep Eden Mulligan in mind. The victims found murdered in the Dunlore cottage – Theo Beckett, Olivia Templeton and Henry Morton – are of no relation to the Mulligans. Nor is Dylan Wray, who is still hanging on in the ICU, or Iona Gardener, who is in the psychiatric ward in the secure unit at the Shannon Clinic. So, *why* was the Mulligan slogan written for us to see? If the victims have no known connection to the Mulligan case, then we need to ask: did the killer?

'My role as a forensic psychologist can offer insights into the mental state of the perpetrator. As police officers, you are used to using your expertise to examine evidence and question key witnesses. Most people think forensic psychologists are brought in to provide profiling, but that's not the main focus of our work.' She paused. 'We are dealing with a vulnerable witness – Iona Gardener.'

Danny pointed to the picture of Iona on the board as Rose continued.

'Understanding her motivation to confessing and helping her to unburden herself of what she has experienced in the Dunlore cottage will help us to solve this case. Forget all notions you may have picked up from television about what a forensic psychologist does. I'm not about to get into the killer's mind and solve the case on intuition alone. Any insights I can offer you will be based on logic, behavioural evidence of key witnesses and my extensive research and experience.'

Danny moved forward. 'Right, team, get cracking and don't miss a single thing.'

CHAPTER 11

The house on Hyde Street was small – a terrace house reconfigured and extended to accommodate the family of six. It had changed since Rose's time there. The kitchen and the living room at the back of the house had been knocked into one large space. A row of modern, grey, kitchen cupboards ran along the length of the back wall, and a small window above the sink looked out into the yard. Rose could remember hanging out the washing there and the drudgery of looking after her siblings when she should have been carefree and experiencing the best years of her life as a teenager, without the responsibilities that had been thrust upon her.

The sight of her siblings gathered around the table, so familiar yet altered, hit Rose like a punch from nowhere. She gasped and averted her gaze. What did she expect? They'd have hardly stayed the same, but even so, it was unnerving for her, trying to readjust the mental image she had of them. The air in the room felt charged. Her arrival had been expected and heads swivelled in her direction as if in unison, an army of eyes examining her, waiting for a proclamation or some sort of acknowledgement. A cold sweat gathered at the back of Rose's neck. She felt sick, like she'd suddenly been swept up in a tidal wave, her feet on unsteady ground. She took a chair at the table and accepted a cup of tea from one of her sisters-in-law. She had yet to work out which brother the blonde girl was married to. She cast her gaze around, looking for something familiar to anchor her. Everything was so different but then her eyes found the clock on the mantel; it had belonged to her granny and it sat where it always had. The room had changed but the slice of backyard could still be seen from the window, the sun low in the sky but still brilliantly bright and dazzling. It didn't feel right. The Belfast from her memory was a dark, dismal place of dreary, grey, rain-laden skies.

. She was aware that everyone seemed to be treating her with caution, as if she was somehow fragile and incendiary. The chat was circling around the weather, the payment of the undertakers and the success of the funeral arrangements. It was as if she was on the outside looking in. None of them had asked about her life or had enquired as to how she was. It was as if her absence had been decided to be of no great importance to them. She could see how relaxed they were in each other's company – the shorthand, the banter. Kaitlin's eyes were red from crying, but she laughed now as she talked to one of the children. Pearse and Colm both looked tired. Up close, it was easier for her to see the boys they had been within their grown-up features. Stronger jawlines, stubble and thinning hair had masked how she recalled them. Colm retained some of his fair hair while Pearse was almost totally bald. Premature balding was a Lavery family trait.

The last few days had been tiring for them. The rituals of visitors calling to offer their sympathy, the wake, the mass and the burial, followed by the gathering in the hotel function room would've been draining. She could see it in all of them and was reminded that she was the outsider.

Their mother's death was not something Rose could claim to feel emotional about. She had buried whatever feelings she had for Evelyn many years ago, and the numbness that had descended since Kaitlin had called in the night, was welcomed. Better to feel nothing than everything. Looking at her siblings now, she could see her mother's funeral had been something they had experienced and endured as one entity. Each there for the other. There was a sense of belonging between them that she never had. The price she'd paid for her escape was high. That strong family connection was something she rarely saw in London. Everyone seemed to come from somewhere else. The absence of family in her life was never questioned there. But here, in Belfast, family was as vital as air. Everyone was connected in a web of relationships to be relied on and tolerated in equal measure.

Rose's mother once told her that how a family buried its loved ones said a lot about their relationship in life. She had been referring to the death of a young man from their area, Francie McAvoy, who had overdosed on epilepsy pills stolen from his brother's legitimate supply. Rose had been fourteen and upset that the family had been so vocal about their grief. They had talked to the local newspaper, the *Irish News*, about the tragedy, had asked mourners to wear Manchester United tops to the funeral, in honour of Francie, who had supported them. They spoke about the funeral as a way to celebrate the life that had been snuffed out. Rose had thought it undignified and Evelyn had scolded her for judging them. 'Consider that poor mother. All she can do for her son is to give him a big send-off. She's throwing herself into the arrangements, wanting to honour him the only way she knows how.'

Rose didn't buy it. She thought of the paramilitary-style funerals she had seen on television and one that had been waked from a house in their area. A group of men and women wearing military-style regalia – black berets, army green jumpers and black trousers, with balaclavas and sunglasses – stood in formation, saluting the coffin as it was carried out of the house. All of it had sickened Rose. They were like overgrown children playing dress up as Action Man. She knew better than to criticise it in front of her mother again, though. Evelyn probably considered it an honour to have such a funeral.

Sitting here among her family now, the memories were tripping over themselves to be acknowledged. Funny how when she was away, she could only recall the bad times. It seemed as if she had deliberately focused on the aspects of her family that she detested. The happier memories felt closer to the surface now, threatening to spill out and upset her carefully held façade.

She excused herself to find the toilet. The small bathroom had been refitted and looked completely different. There was no sense of the room where she had locked herself in and cried when it all became too much. It was the only place where you could hope to find privacy in the house. She had shared a bedroom with Kaitlin so when she longed to be alone she would stand in the shower, letting the tears fall. When she came back down the stairs, she found two dark heads bent over an iPhone on the bottom steps. 'You must be Laura and Donal,' she said. They looked at her with identical brown eyes that were as familiar as her own.

'Yes, and you're our Auntie Roisin.' The boy said it with a note of challenge in his voice, as if he dared her to correct him.

'Well, it's Rose now, but yes.'

'Why'd you change your name?'

She shrugged. 'A few different reasons. I got fed up of spelling Roisin to the English.'

'Aye they never get our names right. There's a girl in school called "Grainne" and someone pronounced it "Grannie" once when she was on holiday across the water.' They laughed.

'You're Kaitlin's kid, right?'

'Yeah and she's my cousin.'

'My daddy is your brother, Pearse.'

'Oh, yeah. You look like him.' The girl rolled her eyes.

'Better looking of course,' Rose added, and they laughed again.

'Roisin, good to see you.' Pearse greeted her as she returned to the living room. He stood blocking her way with a bottle of Budweiser in his hand. His tone said he was anything but glad to see her. Rose guessed he had been drinking all day. Funerals in her family tended to end up being drinking sessions. The morose story telling of days gone by and memories embroidered to make the deceased look better in death, could easily turn surly.

'Pearse, give her a break. She's here, isn't she?' Kaitlin said.

'What does she want, a medal? Doesn't come near any of us for years and then thinks she can swan in looking down her nose at the rest of us. We're beneath you now, is that it, *Roisin*?' He spat the words at her.

'It's okay Kaitlin. I'll go. I didn't want to come anyway. I don't expect you to understand, and to be honest Pearse, I don't care either.'

Kaitlin grabbed at her arm. 'No, please Roisin, stay. *Please*, for me.' There was an urgency in her voice that made Rose hesitate. While she wanted to leave this house, and get on the next flight to London, she'd committed to staying, at least for a few weeks, and there was something in Kaitlin's eyes that tore at her heart. This was her sister. In some ways, she felt she owed Kaitlin everything. She had left her behind to deal with all of the shit on her own. To save herself, she had thrown Kaitlin under. The death of their father had been devastating, which heightened their mother's republicanism. After all they had been through together, she felt that Kaitlin deserved to have her support now. Kaitlin relaxed her grip on Rose's arm and led her into the living room.

'Don't let Pearse get under your skin. Ignore him. He's pissed. He's been drinking all evening.'

Rose sighed. 'He's right, though. I've no place here. It was stupid of me to come. I knew that I wouldn't be welcome.'

'You are welcome. *I'm* glad to see you. Surely that counts for something?'

Rose's eyes filled with tears. For so long, she had shut down the part of herself that allowed her to be vulnerable. It was a necessary form of protection. If you can't feel anything then at least you know that the bad stuff can't hurt.

Kaitlin placed her hand on Rose's. 'Hey, do you remember when we used to sleep in the same bed just so we could be close?'

Rose smiled. 'And make up stories to entertain each other. God, what was that awful ghost story we used to add to every time?'

'The Hairy Hand of Grot McKee!'

'Yes, that's it.' They laughed. 'We used to have to get Daddy to check under the bed to make sure the hand wasn't lurking.'

At one time they had been a happy family, before they knew to fear what was around the corner. When they were young, Rose never realised how the outside world would encroach upon them, taking away all sense of security.

Kaitlin sighed. 'You have to stay a while. We've too much to catch up on.'

CHAPTER 12

The next morning Rose woke early and got ready to return to the station to do her first proper full day on the case. Running back to London had been tempting. It would have been easy to pack up this part of her life for good; to consider her mother's death to be the final footnote in her Belfast history. But maybe Danny and Kaitlin were worth hanging on for.

Once she had showered, she dragged a brush through her hair and tied it into a low ponytail, sprayed on some deodorant and went in search of something to wear. She'd no time to be messing about with make-up and breakfast would be a coffee at the station.

Down in Danny's office, she looked around at the pale yellow walls, paint peeling in dried-out patches, and at the far corner of the room there was a bloom of damp spreading upwards across the ceiling. There was a musty smell, something earthy and fungus-like, that reminded her of wet dogs and old slippers. The wall of filing cabinets, some drawers

74

over-spilling, stood taunting her, as if to suggest this task would be too great for any one person to take on. She shrugged off her jacket, undeterred, and took a seat at her desk. A red box file marked 'confidential', with 'Mulligan' printed at the top, sat unopened. One case out of hundreds, but for some reason this one mattered more to the powers-that-be. For some reason they had yet to discover, it mattered to the killer at the Dunlore cottage too.

The Historical Enquiries Team, initially set up to examine unsolved murders committed during the Troubles, had been wound down in 2005, owing to budgetary constraints. Now, political pressure from Stormont meant that they had been given limited funding to set up a small unit to look at specific cases. Rose knew enough about Northern Ireland to recognise that the unit had been a trade-off – a political win for one side against the other. She didn't care. The exact reasons that brought her to this posting were irrelevant. She intended to do her job diligently and efficiently.

Rose placed her hand on the box file almost reverently, knowing that the minute she opened it and began reading the contents, it would consume her every thought. It would hound her until she had reached some sort of resolution. One of the many reasons why she had ended up in the field that she had.

Rose was seven when her father was shot for the first time. Two men on a motorcycle had waited on him coming out of his place of work. The lone bullet skidded over his shoulder, causing nothing more than deep grazing. The next one, three years later, didn't miss. It went straight through his temple, exiting at the other side. They pumped a few more in, just for good measure.

It was five years later that Rose discovered the bullets

that killed her father would've been better placed in her mother.

The republican creed was Evelyn Lavery's religion. She was evangelical in her politics and in the movement she found a reason to live. She believed her feminist agenda was served by the movement and she happily subjugated her family's needs to that of her comrades.

The last time Rose saw her mother had been on the morning of her Maths A level; Evelyn had been bustling around the house before rushing out the door. An image of her in a red trench coat, her hair pulled into a ponytail, was seared into Rose's consciousness. It was probably bedtime before Evelyn would have realised Rose was gone and wouldn't be coming back.

The murder of her father, along with her mother's murky past, certainly played a part in her career choice. But there was also just something about being able to employ logic-based intuition coupled with research, learning and understanding of the human condition that really appealed to her. Lately, so much of her job had been looking at the macro elements of criminality, seeing how society dealt with wrongdoing and how to improve upon the rehabilitation of prisoners. Working with Danny and the PSNI was a return to something more dramatic – an up-close study of how to unpick the criminal mind. Part of her job in the early days of her career was to use profiling as a device to formulate a scenario that brought the killer and victims together. She was schooled in the complex psychological apparatus of deviants. The contents of the folders that came across her desk brought her into contact with individuals she wouldn't want to meet in any other context.

She lifted the Mulligan box file and placed it on her desk.

All cases carried secrets buried under the weight of time; truths eroded and retold with careful editing. The Mulligan case would be no different in that respect. She moved her hand to pull back the lid, when a sharp knock at the door made her jump.

'Dr Lainey, I see you found your way down to your new home.' Assistant Chief Constable Ian McCausland entered the room without waiting for Rose to say come in. He carried himself with the presence of a man who knew he had power and liked it, and was built like a Saracen tank, broad and squat.

Rose stood. 'Assistant Chief Constable, good morning.'

'Dr Lainey, please sit down, no need for formalities. I wanted to welcome you to your new post, and to have a little chat about what the job involves. Make sure you understand the role and how we expect you to handle yourself within the remit of our investigation. DI Stowe was most insistent when he requested your input.'

'Yes, he is aware of my background and experience in handling cases of this nature.'

'And what nature would that be?'

'Cases whereby a confession is offered voluntarily but is almost certainly false. Some people like to confess, feel a need to unburden themselves, even when innocent of the crime.'

He grimaced as if last night's dinner had repeated on him, making it clear that what she had stated offended him.

Rose continued. 'There are many reasons why someone might confess to something they didn't do. They can be protecting someone else or simply seeking attention and notoriety. Others believe they truly are guilty and want to be punished.'

'Well, whatever you uncover, keep in mind that we have a multiple murder case on our hands. It's only been six months since the Lennon case. You may not be aware of it, but DI Stowe is still dealing with the fallout. Finding himself exiled to cold cases was part of his penance. The Dunlore cottage murders is his chance to redeem himself.'

Danny had alluded to the case and Rose sensed that he was trying to make up for his mistakes. She knew that in Belfast, payment for past sins was always demanded.

She sat back in her chair. It squeaked in protest, as if the mechanisms had been rusted by the dampness hanging in the room.

'I understand that we are to consider the Mulligan case as part of the investigation,' she said.

'Yes, we have been asked to reopen the file, to see if we can provide some sort of comfort to the family. But there's a good chance that the graffiti on the wall at Dunlore is irrelevant to the murders. One of those strange occurrences that can be thrown up during an investigation – it has to be looked at, but will most likely prove to be a mere annoyance.

'As you probably know, my officers are under greater pressure than ever before to be seen to be righting any wrongs from the past with clear-eyed scrutiny.' It sounded like a rehearsed sound bite.

Rose noticed the roll of flesh bulging from his thick neck, pressing against his too-tight, starched white collar. He had straw-like hair that had probably been blond when he was young, but age had weathered it to a dull gold. He walked across the room, taking in the scruffy decor, the window too high up to show anything but a glimpse of metal railings, and too narrow to let in any natural daylight to make a worthwhile difference. She knew McCausland would have to answer to the policing board and was expected to be active in pursuing any leads in historic cold cases.

'As an outsider, you need to understand we are working within a politically hostile environment. Sure, things have changed, but the force is still treated with contempt by many within the communities of this province. Those in the nationalist community will always have a sense of distrust, and now the Unionist community feel we have sold out. We can't win.' He turned around to look at Rose with his hands held up, as if in surrender.

'Are you up to the job, Dr Lainey?'

'I'm well aware of the challenges, Sir. I'm from Belfast originally.'

'Yes, but you've not worked here before and this place isn't easy to crack. Don't be fooled into thinking you have the measure of us just yet.'

'No, Sir. I appreciate the complexities at play.'

'Good. I hope you do.' He looked directly at Rose, seeming to assess her worth, his eyes boring into her.

'It helps that you are an outsider in some ways, but never forget that we have lived through hard times. There are always reasons for every judgement call.' He paused to let his words sink in. 'That being said, we want the past to be looked at in a completely different way. Previously, we have been accused of examining certain cases with less intent than others. That needs to be addressed. They think we have shown leniency and have misinterpreted the law to suit our own agenda. Well, not on my watch, Dr Lainey. Any case you look at, I expect to have full disclosure, a clean ripping off the sticking plaster. If we don't like what we find, then too bad. Unfortunately, crippling budget cuts and diminishing police numbers mean that I can't offer you much manpower. You need to work smart. Call in resources only as and when they are essential.'

He rested his back against the filing cabinets. 'What I want DI Stowe to do is, in effect, take the political out of the cases in here.' He slapped the metal cabinet and it shook against his bulk. 'Treat them like any other cold case. Her Majesty's Inspectorate of Constabulary's destruction of the Historical Enquiries Team unit was short-sighted. It seems that the politicians have started to realise that, but rather than make a public announcement, and actually give us a proper budget to work with, they are trying to go around the back door. You two do a good job – who knows? Maybe they'll see the worth of funding a proper unit again.'

He smiled like he was offering her the promise of a reward, something to keep her on track. But she had read the subtext. If it didn't work out, then the blame would lie at her feet.

He looked down at the red Mulligan box file.

'This case has been flagged up as being of political significance before the Dunlore murders occurred. It's hoped that by examining the evidence, we can assuage some of the current hostilities, and, as you well know, it is now implicated in the current investigation by deed of the reference to Mulligan found on the cottage wall.'

'So, the Mulligan review is a whitewash you want to use to help keep the Ministers in Stormont in their jobs?' she asked, trying to keep the annoyance out of her voice.

Rose understood the political trade-offs. It wasn't that long ago in Northern Ireland that tit-for-tat meant shootings, one side of the community against the other, now it was horse-trading, the offer of resolution for one old injustice in exchange for another. Political trade-offs played out to help those in power keep it at all cost.

'Not at all, Dr Lainey.' He looked like he had a bad taste in his mouth when he said her name.

'You'd do well to check that attitude. Historical enquiries are of great significance in creating a sense of fair-dealing. People need to feel heard and respected. Police work is about more than clear-up rates.'

Rose considered ACC McCausland's words. He was making all the right noises about fairness and justice, but she knew that it would take more than words. Actions cost and if he wasn't prepared to put the funds in place to give Danny and her the backing required, there was only so much they could do.

She could see McCausland was hoping for a tidy review of the Mulligan case. A mere paper shuffling exercise that would be neatly tidied up within a few weeks, not something drawn out, bloody and messy, like the crime scene she'd witnessed in the fairy-tale cottage.

CHAPTER 13

Danny felt the buzz and hustle of a case in the early stages. That time when anything is possible, and all leads are up for grabs. He'd enjoyed the look on Rose's face when she saw the message on the cottage's living room wall. No cop worth their salt would be able to resist the lure of a fresh case and he knew Rose would have made a brilliant cop. He could sense a restlessness in her. Her work wasn't sustaining her and maybe it was time she came back to Belfast for good. All that prison research and dealing with Home Office policy must be mind-numbing. She needed what he could offer her – work with real meaning and fulfilment. But at the same time, he had enough insight to know that he wanted her back for his own reasons too. Historical enquiries were all well and good, but he needed the adrenaline rush of the chase. Cold cases were all paperwork and dusty files. He'd lose his edge if he stayed in that arse end of nowhere bunker too long.

Malachy Magee had been assigned to the case with him. He could hardly complain. DS Magee was good; a steady hand and a reliable cop. But Danny felt a spark when working with Rose. Even at uni, she pushed him to do better. She made him try harder, just to keep up with her.

Magee was back out at Dunlore cottage, but they had agreed to meet at four o'clock, to assign tasks to the wider team. The air in the office was stagnant. He had a wild thirst for a cold pint of Heineken but made do with a paper cup of water from the water cooler. He glanced out of the sorry excuse for a window to the remains of a beautiful day, and he was instantly reminded that it was marching season. The Twelfth of July parades would be in full flow by the end of the week. Wee hellions would be out in force on the eleventh night, drinking Buckfast and Frosty Jacks by the bottle, and shouting profanities about the Pope. Forty-feet-high bonfires would be erected, burning effigies of every nationalist politician who ever got on their tits. All in the name of loyalist culture.

He refilled the paper cup and went back to his desk to consider what was known about the murders, and to identify what was still to be assigned and uncovered. At the beginning of an investigation the objectives were wide ranging and all encompassing. The narrowing of focus would come later. The first priority was to gather all relevant material, though knowing what was significant and what was dross at this stage was virtually impossible. They needed victim statements – not easy with one in ICU and the other in the Shannon Clinic Secure Unit to undergo intensive psychiatric evaluation – and then the exhibits and images, intelligence reports, and a list of offenders who could be potentially active in the area, all needed to be gathered. The details of this ground work needed be logged into the system to allow for gap analysis later on. It was too soon for hypotheses. Christ, they had so much work to do before they reached that stage.

His phone rang.

'Magee, what's up?'

'Just letting you know SOCO have signed off the cottage now and Lyons says it will be a couple of days before we get the autopsy report. He doesn't like the fact that the three bodies were lying so closely together. He's worried about messing up samples and obscuring ante-mortem trauma, whatever the fuck that is.'

'Right, get back here then. Lots to do.'

'Too right. Overtime will rocket on this one. See you in half an hour or so.'

It was time to check on Iona Gardener and Dylan Wray. It took a few attempts to get through to someone with any knowledge of Dylan Wray in ICU. Eventually, Danny got Dylan's assigned nurse, Paula, on the phone and she told him Dylan was still critical – he wasn't conscious, so an interview was out of the question. A call to Constable Maggie Bolton told him that Iona Gardener had been transferred to ward J at the Shannon Unit. She was currently heavily sedated and under the care of Dr Helen Gracie. Again, no use to him. He felt a tight knot of frustration pull at his guts. They both needed to wake up and tell him what they knew.

CHAPTER 14

Home had meant darkness. A place of threat and worry, a drawn out war of retaliation. Eerie entryways and narrow alleys of bins and gurgling drains, where terrorists dealt out knee-cappings. Belfast had been a grey place with flashes of anger and violence so brutal it took your breath away. Rose could remember listening to the local news, waiting to see which side of the community had been slain, knowing that revenge would come the following week. A cycle of us and them, fear and distrust cloaking every conversation. News of hi-jackings and buses being burnt out, families ordered out of their homes, taxi drivers being made to deliver bombs to police stations, teenage boys moving weapons, and punishment beatings dealt out within a warped alternative justice system.

Life seemed to change – full of possibilities for the first time – when she met Scott, her first boyfriend. To Rose, aged sixteen, he seemed almost from a different planet. He lived in leafy East Belfast and attended Methodist College, where the posh Protestants went to school. His world was rugby, house parties, ski holidays, and family dinners at the golf club. Rose made sure he knew little of where she came from beyond the fact that she attended a Catholic grammar school. They weren't from the same community, but he didn't seem to mind. Rose marvelled at his lack of caution. His openness and his innocence. His world didn't have riots at the top of the street. Undercover police cars clocking your every movement. Fear and mistrust.

Scott was the eye opener. His life of safety and comfort inspired Rose to seek something better for herself. She was smart enough to know that she couldn't carve out such a life in Belfast. She'd have to escape to make it different. She'd have to reinvent herself and never look back.

When Evelyn got wind of her plans, all hell broke loose.

'No daughter of mine will be seen running around with a Prod. Do you forget where you come from, what sacrifices we've made to fight the Brits?' Always with the Brits.

The notion of Scott ever seeing how she lived in the terrace house in the Markets filled her with dread. Not that it was shame of where she came from; no, it was more a sense of embarrassment that her family were so trapped in their thinking. That her mother, in particular, was bigoted and spiteful.

Rose knew that by moving to England, her mother would be infuriated and that her heart would harden further. Maybe she did do it to spite her. Looking back, Rose could see every decision she had made had been chosen in defiance of Evelyn.

It was the Mulligan mystery, coupled with Iona's false confession, that sucked Rose in and demanded that she listen, hear the voices whispering secrets and asking questions. She could've been one of the Mulligan five, the abandoned children. Or her mother could've been the one orchestrating the disappearance. When Danny said he knew the Mulligan angle would reel Rose in, he'd no idea. As far as he was concerned, the challenge of a cold case caught up in the midst of a fresh murder hunt was temptation enough. But it went deeper than that. She'd lived in the same area that the Mulligan family had lived. She understood the insidious whisperings of suspicion.

Rose glanced at her watch. Late afternoon and she still hadn't formulated a concrete plan of action. She knew that a current murder case had a set of procedures clearly laid out for officers to follow: forensics, feet on the ground talking to people, gathering vital information and physical evidence. A cold case was different. Any potential witnesses could be long dead, or their memories fogged by time. There was always a possibility of using technology that had been absent during the original investigation, but with no concrete evidence to examine with this case, this option was out.

There was also the fact that sometimes the original detectives assigned to the case were overworked or neglectful. If McCausland was to be believed, the original case simply didn't merit action. Missing mothers weren't high priority at that time. Belfast had other concerns.

Rose had made herself familiar with The Stormont House Agreement, which outlined a mechanism for dealing with the past, part of which was the establishment of the Historical Enquiries Unit. Their mandate was to progress investigations into outstanding Troubles-related deaths. Part of the problem lay in the fact that Eden Mulligan's body had never been recovered. They had no definite proof that she had been killed. No body, no witnesses, no evidence. No real case.

Unsolved murders are never officially closed. Sometimes you hit a dead end and all investigative power and effort dries up. The next big case comes along and all interest and manpower is directed towards it. Well, she would have to go back to the beginning, gather sufficient information about Eden Mulligan, create a character profile and assess the family relationships. All of Eden's relationships would need to come under scrutiny, along with her daily routines. To complicate matters, it would be necessary to manage any expectations the family might have. Rose couldn't promise them anything, but she would need their input and cooperation. She would begin by getting up to speed with the contents of the files and doing a proper review of the actions taken at the time of the initial investigation.

Rose was about to create a sequencing timeline on her computer when Danny appeared at the door. She looked at his hands, wrapped around a copper-coloured plant pot with an ugly, twisted green thing within.

'What is that?' she asked, screwing up her face.

'A cactus. Call it an office warming present. Anything to liven this place up a bit. We're only one step up from working in an underground concrete bunker. You do realise that, don't you? I need to be seen upstairs, keep an eye on the team, so you'll have this place all to yourself at times.' He handed the plant over to her.

'It's a bit scary looking. Are you sure it's not dead?'

'No, it's not dead. I bought it this morning from a man in St George's market, who assured me it's a fine specimen of its type. I figured even *you* can't kill something used to barren, inhospitable landscapes.'

'Cheers. That's a great endorsement of my nurturing skills.' She laughed, looking at the wonky, spiked plant.

'I had to do something to make this cupboard a bit more homely for you. I've seen homeless people spending their night in better spaces than this. It can't be good for the psyche. Tell Sweaty Balls McCausland to find us something better, or you'll go off on the sick, owing to mental anguish.'

'Wind your neck in. I'm fine. Once I start reading this lot I'm lost to the world. I really don't care what the office is like. In fact, if you must know, I like the quiet down here. No listening to office gossip and snarky comments, or Malachy Magee belching into his fist after his second sausage roll. Down here it's just me, Iona Gardener and Eden Mulligan. Nothing else matters.'

CHAPTER 15

After Danny left to meet with Magee, Rose resumed her sequencing document. She wanted to have a sense of what Belfast was like around the time Eden Mulligan had vanished. What were the big stories people were talking about? From memory, life really was all bombings and shootings. She turned to her computer and typed in 'Northern Ireland 1986' and then clicked on the Conflict Archive site to find information and source material.

It was all pretty bleak. A society living from one attack to the next, checked by a police service represented largely by only one side of the community it served. The dry statistics detailing bombings and shootings began to feel meaningless after the third page. It wasn't Rose's usual habit to go trawling the internet for blogs concerned with real-life crime stories, but in this instance, she thought it might be worth having a look to see what information there was beyond official reviews of the case, or monotonous news reports.

The first few links she opened were rehashings of the newspaper articles that had been written at the time. The website of the Families for Justice campaign had a few links and it was one of these that led her to a blog site set up to extrapolate what had happened to Eden Mulligan.

The Disappearance of Eden Mulligan: What We Know to be True

By Joel Ellis

Eden Mulligan was born in Portadown to a 'mixed faith' family – her mother was Catholic and her father was Protestant. The family lived without intimidation in a Catholic enclave. When Eden was seventeen she met Geordie Mulligan and moved to Belfast when they married two years later. The young married couple chose to live in the Markets area of Belfast, which was close to the city centre.

At one time, the area had fifteen markets, the oldest being St George's Market, which still operates today. The Markets is one of Belfast's oldest communities. Despite being virtually part of the city centre, it still remains a residential area. In the early nineteenth century, houses were built in the Lower and Upper markets, to provide housing for labourers and working people in the area near the River Lagan. The wealthier merchants and commercial classes lived in the Georgian terraces of the Upper Markets.

This is by the by. The Markets area that Eden made her home in was at that time a close-knit community of mainly Catholic families. By 1986, the year Eden disappeared, she was a young mother of thirty-three with five children to care for. Her husband, Geordie, was often living in London or Liverpool, working on building sites.

The first investigation into Eden's disappearance did not happen until six months after she was reported missing. Unlike other cases of a similar nature, neither the IRA nor the UVF ever accepted responsibility for Eden's disappearance. This led to speculation that Eden could have left her family of her own volition and that she could be still alive, as a body was never discovered.

The Mulligan children found themselves separated. Cormac, thirteen years old, and Eileen, aged eleven, were sent to a children's home in Downpatrick. Paddy and Lizzie, eight-year-old twins, were adopted by a married couple who had no children of their own. Six-year-old Eamonn was passed around a succession of foster homes before landing in a convent home for troubled children.

In 2007, the Police Ombudsman acknowledged that a formal investigation of Eden's disappearance was never carried out. Instead, the RUC had conducted a minor review of the case and had lost valuable opportunities to investigate properly. The Ombudsman concluded that there had been no evidence that Eden Mulligan had acted as a police informer, an assertion that the press had made in the years following her disappearance.

Rose clicked onto a different site that made reference to the Unknowns, two secret cells within the IRA tasked with abducting, killing and secretly burying the bodies of so-called informers. The victims were often transported to the Republic of Ireland, where they would be tortured and killed. Their bodies were then buried in remote parts, never to be found.

Rose finished reading and clicked on the link to the pages of accompanying photographs taken during the seventies and eighties – grainy black and white stills of British soldiers patrolling the streets. One showed a squaddie down on one knee, looking through the view finder of a rifle, while a mother and her small son walked by, apparently unconcerned.

Rose was aware that MI5, the Security Service, was also involved in Northern Ireland during this time, carrying out surveillance and running its own network of agents and informers within republican and loyalist paramilitary organisations. She wondered what they would have known about Eden Mulligan's case. Would it have been on their radar at all?

She continued reading the screen, clicking from one site to another and scribbling down the odd note. If Eden had simply vanished of her own free will, the chances were that she would have turned up on the system before now. Staying off the grid is hard to do without specialist assistance.

And though no body had been recovered, that didn't mean that she hadn't been murdered.

Scrolling through other links, Rose came across an interesting extract from a book called *The Innocents Left Behind*:

There have been many casualties of the war on both sides, but sometimes the ones who are forgotten are the most vulnerable of our society. This was the case of Eden Mulligan's family. Five motherless children left to fend for themselves. Eden disappeared one July evening, never to be seen again. Her children, now

*grown up, some with children of their own, have never
given up hope that one day they will know the truth.
Know who took their mother, what they did to her
and their reasons why.*

Rose had a sense that whatever had happened to Eden, it
hadn't been without intrigue and wrongdoing. It was time
to seek out her children.

CHAPTER 16

It was late afternoon by the time Danny and Rose headed to meet Eden Mulligan's oldest son, Cormac. Danny knocked on the door of Cormac Mulligan's flat and waited while he heard a shuffle of footsteps. The door opened and revealed a man who had an air of having been beaten down by life. He looked older than his forty-five years. His skin had a washed-out pallor, which told of too much drink and too many fags, and his hair had receded so far back that it made him look exposed and constantly surprised.

Danny flashed his ID. 'Cormac, we talked on the phone? This is Dr Rose Lainey. She's working with me.'

'Aye, so what are you doing here? I told you I'd nothing to say to you.' His voice was hoarse, as if he'd been smoking for as long as he could talk. He smelt of smoke too. Acrid and bitter.

'I've some questions about your mother's case that I felt it would be better to discuss in person. Can we come in?'

He didn't budge from the door and ignored the request. 'I've been through this all before. It didn't get me anywhere then, so why should I expect this time to be different?' His tone wasn't belligerent, just uninterested.

Danny shrugged. 'I can tell you, I'm different. I'm not following an agenda. My job is to look at the case afresh, see if we can identify new lines of inquiry. Dr Lainey here will be able to provide insights that we haven't had before.'

'They sent an English copper last time. Told us he would be able to assess the case without prejudice. Fuck, should have told Alanis Morissette to put that in her song. They didn't even mean it as a joke.' He sounded desolate, as if all the hope and fight had been kicked out of him long ago.

Danny nodded. 'I know you've been messed about before. The Historical Enquiries Team promised more than it could deliver and they shouldn't have done that. My job is to open the case, look at the documentation, talk to a few people, and see where it takes me. If we find a fresh lead, we follow it up. Where's the harm in that?'

He laughed, sardonic and sad. 'The harm lies in how it screws me and my family up. Every. Frigging. Time.' He stood back and allowed them to enter the hallway, but didn't invite them any farther into the flat.

Rose offered her hand, but he ignored it.

'I'm sorry, Cormac. I know it can't be easy, but surely it is better to try to get some sort of justice than to simply assume we are about to trample all over your life. Maybe this time it will be different,' she said.

Cormac took a packet of Benson and Hedges from his tracksuit pocket and lit a cigarette with an orange disposable lighter before taking a long, slow draw on it. 'You know they are waiting for us to all die out. Once my generation is cold in the ground there will be no one to keep the memories alive. No one to pass on the information that we've had to dig up for ourselves. When we die, any chance of justice dies with us.'

'Then take a chance. Work with us,' Danny urged.

Cormac looked at them, his eyes cold.

'Fuck away off and crawl back under whatever rock you came from.'

Rose grimaced. 'Look, you don't need me to tell you that the disappearance of a loved one is one of the most traumatic and distressing things to live with. It's the uncertainty of it that eats away at you. It must have been hard growing up without your parents.' Her voice was soft and her tone measured.

'You've no bloody idea.'

'The relationship between a mother and a child is the deepest and most important one we have.'

Cormac shook his head, as if dismissing her words.

'You must have struggled. Every birthday, every Christmas, every new school year without your mother there to make it all right.'

His shoulders dropped ever so slightly.

Danny moved forward. 'Let us help, Cormac. Explain to us what happened. You don't know what we could uncover this time round.'

Cormac took another deep drag on his cigarette and blew out a stream of smoke, not caring to tilt his head away from Danny. 'We don't talk to cops. Not anymore.'

CHAPTER 17

Rose watched as Joel Ellis – the author of the article she'd found on Eden's disappearance – crossed the road like he was avoiding sniper fire. He dived in and out of the traffic, raising his hand by way of a thank-you, as he ran to reach the café and get out of the midday sun. It was another baking hot day. She climbed out of her car and followed into French Village. The aroma of good coffee seemed overpowering in the heat. She longed for something cool and refreshing.

'Any more of this and they'll be cancelling their package holidays. Sure, they always say there's no place like Ireland, with the perfunctory "if you get the weather". Of course you get the bloody weather. Rain is weather too, isn't it? Buck eejits the lot of them.' Rose listened as he made conversation with the blue-haired waitress with pale skin. The combination of the beginnings of a gingery beard and round, thin-rimmed glasses spelt out hipster. She could imagine Danny calling him a wank-stain, or something equally derisive.

She let him settle himself into a chair and watched as he reached for the menu before she approached him.

'Joel Ellis?'

'Who's asking?' he said warily.

'Dr Rose Lainey. Can I join you?'

'Free world.'

Rose took the chair opposite him and lifted a menu from the table.

'What do you recommend?'

'Pasta and prawns, or their sandwiches are pretty good. Are you buying?'

The waitress approached and took his order. 'I'll have the pasta with prawns and a glass of still water.'

Rose ordered a sandwich and gave the menu back to the waitress.

'Botanic Avenue is the place to be on a day like this,' he said.

They watched as two lads by the window sat appraising the body of an attractive blonde girl, in an off the shoulder top, as she walked by.

'Would you look at them. The wee girls are running around in all sorts of skimpy sundresses without a care in the world and wee shites like them are drooling with their tongues hanging out. Fellas trying to look cool while catching a crafty glimpse of a bare leg. Jesus, you'd think they'd never seen a half-dressed woman before,' Joel said, shaking his head, half laughing.

Rose had the impression that Joel seemed to find most people annoying. She knew he was a law graduate, now working for Families for Justice, providing advocacy for families affected by the Troubles.

'You never returned my calls,' Rose said.

He opened his phone and scrolled through the messages, opening the one from Rose telling him she was interested in the Mulligan case. 'Ahh, I'm busy, you know how it is. Thought I'd follow it up when I was back at the office. I have to tell you though, any interest in the Mulligan story is worth shite all. That case needs someone with a time machine. The lies, the lost witness statements, and the deliberate tampering with evidence has meant that any time we tried to get to grips with it, we reached a dead end.'

Their food arrived and Joel began eating as he continued.

'The press like to throw petrol on the dying embers of the Mulligan case every now and then. For them, it's an interesting narrative, providing a different take on the Troubles. When they were bored by the tit-for-tat shootings and car bombs, Eden Mulligan's disappearance – and what happened to her children after – proved to be a more salacious and sorrowful story in a time when violence was normalised and routine.' He took a long drink of water.

Rose finished chewing her bite of beef and caramelised onion sandwich before speaking. 'So, you felt that the case was messed up to begin with. That there wasn't a thorough investigation carried out?'

'You could say that.' He looked at her, as if deciding whether she could be trusted.

'I still stay in touch with one of Eden's children – Eamonn Mulligan. I check in every now and then to see how he is doing. It's the least I can do after all he'd been promised.'

'Promised?'

'Let's just say, I was bright eyed and naive, straight out of Queen's with a law degree, thinking I could take on all the wrongs of the world and make them right. Well, I fucked that up spectacularly and Eamonn Mulligan nearly paid for it with his life.' He set his fork down.

'Eamonn trusted me and I let him down.'

CHAPTER 18

The first rule of any new murder case is to phone the wife and tell her you won't be home in time for dinner. DI Desmond Henderson told Danny that on his first day on the job. He was fresh out of Garnerville, having just finished his student officer training programme, and all raring to go to get the bad guys.

'Keep the wee wife in the picture, but don't bring the job home, lad,' Henderson had told him. Not that he had to worry about that now that Amy had gone. There was no wife waiting at home. She had watched him, glassy-eyed and silent, as he'd packed, throwing anything he could place his hands on, into his gym bag. He could work all the hours the case demanded without worrying about her. He'd no one to answer to but the job itself.

It was a small mercy on a depressingly gorgeous day. The weather had been brutally good and it only compounded his feeling of being wound up. What use was a sunny day to him when he had corpses to worry about, and no one to share a glass of cooled wine with on the patio come seven o'clock?

He wondered where Amy was. Would she be at home, in the new build they'd bought in East Belfast, languishing on the sofa thinking about him, or would she be round at her mother's, being cared for like she was a fragile doll, too delicate to be left to her own devices? He knew he should be more sympathetic, but he'd reached his quota for good feeling towards her. Anorexia had destroyed her and their marriage.

It hadn't always been bad. There were times when she had been, well, full of life and plans. Those were the times he missed, when they could pretend that she was all right, and that one day they would have a proper life, away from clinics and therapists.

She'd hate this weather, he thought, as he adjusted the vertical blind to keep the sun from baking the office. Amy much preferred to drape herself in jumpers and cardigans, layers of protection from the outside word. The sun's brightness would be too illuminating, too revealing, for her liking. He still thought of everything through the prism of her mind. If he put the television on, he automatically searched for what she would want to watch. When he bought a book, he considered if she would want to read it after him. He'd have to learn to think for himself again. To take her out of the equation of his life, just as she had done to him.

The case would provide him with the distraction he needed. He hadn't had one as complex and compelling before. The perfect remedy for a broken heart.

Right, buck up out of it, he told himself. It was time he got a grip of himself and try to move on. He had been single before, he could surely work out how to live as a free agent with no ties, no one to hassle him if he left the wet towels on the bathroom floor, or, God forbid, the toilet seat up.

The smell in the office was of processed food, something fried and salty. Danny promised himself that he would start eating better. Now that Amy was gone, he had allowed himself to fall into a pattern of eating toast for dinner. Cheese on toast. Beans on toast. Toast on toast. Not that he couldn't cook. If anything, he was the one who had done most of the cooking when they were together. He just didn't have the motivation to cook for one. He had yet to tell Rose, or anyone for that matter, that his marriage was over. It was easier to pretend that all was well.

He had to admit, having Rose back in his life was proving to be a nice distraction from his marital woes. She was as beautiful now as when he'd first met her. That dark hair and those green eyes reminding him of a misty seascape. Back then, he had fallen for her straight away, but he'd learned early on to keep his feelings to himself. She was impenetrable. It was clear that she had no interest in him beyond friendship and he was content to settle for that.

Their first encounter had been in the halls kitchen. He'd walked in and found a girl standing with her back to him. All he could see was the dark hair and the skinny waist, legs clad in tight jeans and a pair of Doc Martens that looked too heavy for her thin legs. When she turned to look at him, he had felt an almost involuntary reaction. Then she spoke, and he could hardly believe the Belfast accent, reminding him of everything he knew and felt comfortable with.

He was grateful he had had the sense to not push it with her. There'd been moments when they'd both be lying on a sofa, pissed and talking a load of oul shite, and he'd think, this is it – now's your chance. But just as he would be steeling himself to make a move, she'd break the spell, making sure it wasn't to be. Their friendship remained intact as a result and for that he was grateful.

The office was busy. He was glad to see people were putting the hours this case demanded in and it was time for him to also focus his mind and get on with the investigation.

'Boss, this came for you.' DS Tania Lumen threw a brown envelope onto his desk. 'And the box of strange dolls has arrived back from forensics. Where do you want them?' Tania asked Danny.

'Give them to me. I'll take them down to see what Rose makes of them.'

'Knock, knock,' he said, as he arrived at the door to the Rose's office. 'I've a wee present for you – the weirdo dolls are back.'

'Let's have a look,' she said, getting up from her chair. 'Here, let me clear this away.' She removed her files of papers to make room for the dolls.

Danny opened the evidence box marked with the serial code, and took the dolls out one by one, still in their plastic evidence bags.

They stood back and looked at them spread out on the table.

'They're grotesque, aren't they? Any thoughts on their significance?' he asked.

Rose stared down at them, examining each one. 'I've done a bit of research into dolls found hanging from trees in other places. There's an island in Mexico – Isla de Las Muñecas, or Island of the Dolls – where there are hundreds of dolls and their body parts hanging from trees, much like the ones we found. Apparently, a young girl drowned there and the man who found her came across a doll soon after, which he believed belonged to her. To honour her memory, he hung the doll from a tree, and it began a tradition of sorts. Others began hanging old dolls in solidarity. Some said they were to ward off evil spirits.

'Then there are corn dolls, which are used in an ancient pagan ritual, but are also associated with the Christian faith. I found a newspaper story that said some had been found in hedgerows and trees all over Comber a while back. They're made out of straw and are a similar idea to the St Brigid's cross. They are used around harvest time and Halloween, and made out of the last crops harvested to encourage new growth the following season. Some people think they're creepy and connected to witchcraft.

'The dolls we found at the cottage were wreathed in spider webs, suggesting they were stored somewhere pretty run down and neglected. We've some missing limbs, and others with the wrong limb attached making them look weird as fuck.'

Danny nodded. 'Forensics said most of them were home to insects, suggesting they had been lying somewhere for a long time. They'd traces of insect activity on their mouths or eye sockets and crawling through their nylon hair. And they're older dolls, not the kind of dolls you would buy nowadays. Any thoughts on what they signify?'

'Childhood and play are the obvious associations. Interacting with dolls is thought to help develop empathy, and understanding, but a doll isn't a replica of a baby because the world it suggests is imaginary. It's a metaphor rather than a symbol of babyhood and demands imagination to engage with it. A doll represents the hidden, inner life rather than the more obvious representation of the life the child sees around them. I think these dolls are a talisman. A form of protection and hope.'

Danny opened the forensic report up and began to read.

'The tree the dolls were suspended from has been identified as a white willow. Normally planted as an ornamental feature, the mature white willow can grow to twenty-five metres and often has an irregular, leaning top crown. The grey-brown bark usually develops deep fissures with age and produces slender though strong and flexible twigs. The name "white willow" is derived from the white appearance of the undersides of the leaves.

'The dolls were attached to nylon twine and suspended from the branches. It appears that each doll has been made up of parts of various other dolls, so that no one doll is complete in its original form. Tracing the origin of the dolls will be difficult as they are not distinctive and can be commonly found.'

There was no denying that the crime scene had an eerie quality, from the time warped house to the bloodbath, even before they factored in the freaky dolls with their mismatched body parts and their glazed eyes.

The dolls were meant to be seen. Whoever had orchestrated the scene had done so for maximum effect.

On the surface, the murders looked frenzied, yet there was something of the macabre in the placement of the bodies on the bed.

Could it have been a random, even sexually motivated crime? An arousal of hate? The feverish nature of the wounds suggested a loss of control, yet the dolls and the placing of the bodies felt too orchestrated.

The dolls had been handcrafted in so far as they had been altered, like a naughty school boy tormenting his sister's favourite toy. An arm removed here, an eye extracted, a leg attached from another doll. Each slightly different. No features had been added to the faces, but they had been dressed in simply made outfits to differentiate the gender. The fingerprints were smudged and worth nothing. It didn't take Sherlock Holmes to work out that they represented the victims in the cottage. Five hanging dolls and five victims. Three dead, one on life support and Iona Gardener, the one who got away.

CHAPTER 19

The following morning, Rose arrived early to find Danny already at his desk in the open-plan office.

'What's on the agenda today?' she asked him.

'I'm getting individual updates from the team and then getting stuck in.'

'What about me? I can't get access to Iona Gardener yet. There's a protocol in place for dealing with patients like her. I can't go trampling all over another doctor's territory.'

'McCausland has had a word with the hospital where she's being held. The doctor in charge has asked for a twenty-four-hour assessment period. After that, they will be willing to work with us.'

'And until then?'

'Are you able to continue with the Mulligan case for me? Get a feel for the background and maybe talk to a few people? We'll need to make contact with the other siblings since Cormac wasn't interested.'

'Already on it. I'll follow up with Joel Ellis from Families for Justice. If I can't get near Iona, it makes sense to see if the Mulligan case has any bearing. The graffiti was there for a reason. Whoever scrawled it on the wall wants us to look at the case. The question is, when did the graffiti appear? Was it part of the attacker's remit or had someone unconnected to the murders left it there?'

An hour later, Rose drove past the Errigle Inn and headed on down the Ormeau Road, scanning the numbers on the buildings until she found 329. The Victorian terrace house had been divided up into offices, with Families for Justice situated on the top floor. By the time she had reached the third flight of stairs, she felt breathless and reminded herself that she needed to go on a run. Her body wouldn't thank her for slacking off workouts just because she'd had a change of routine. She had stopped at the landing, to give herself a moment to catch her breath, when she heard, 'Dr Lainey,' from above.

Rose looked up and there, peering over the bannister from the next flight up, was Joel Ellis.

'Hi Joel. These stairs must keep you fit,' Rose said as she resumed her climb.

He was wearing a plaid shirt over a T-shirt despite the heat. She followed him into his office. It was a small room in the eaves of the building with a sloping ceiling – little more than a glorified cupboard – and lined with books. Stacks of files sat in the four corners of the room. Her eyes scanned the titles on the spines of the books: *Lost Lives* by David McKittrick et al., *The Fight for Peace: The Secret Story Behind the Irish Peace Process* by Eamonn Mallie and David McKittrick, *Bandit Country: The IRA and South Armagh* by Toby Harnden and a selection of novels by Eoin McNamee, Kelly Creighton and Anthony Quinn.

'So, you're not going away and the Mulligan case raises its head again,' he said, taking his chair behind the paper-strewn desk.

Rose sat opposite him and caught a glimpse of the tall trees in the Ormeau Park through the window behind him.

'Yes, as I told you a couple of days ago, I'm part of a team carrying out a review.' She didn't care to share with him the Iona Gardener connection yet. If the murders at Dunlore had something to do with the Mulligan case, they needed to be careful and not let any information slip out. The press would love it and only make matters worse.

'Families for Justice has taken an interest in the case on behalf of the Mulligan family before. I thought we should talk, see if there is anything in particular you can share with me.'

Joel smirked. 'You think we are going to hand over files of confidential information just like that? To the PSNI? Nah, I don't think so.'

'No, I don't assume you'll do anything. But if you care about the case and the family then surely it's in all our interests to work together.'

Joel leaned forward. 'Listen, I don't *have* to cooperate. My job is working on behalf of the families. I put a lot of time into the Mulligan case. The PSNI weren't so forth-coming with helping me then, so I'm sure you can appreciate my reluctance to roll over and play nice now, just because they've suddenly decided it's worth looking at.'

Rose nodded. 'Yeah, I get it, but times have changed. Maybe this time we can all work towards the same outcome.'

'And what outcome would that be?' he asked, sitting back again.

111

'To find out what happened in 13 Moss Street that night, and to get some answers for the family.'

Rose could see Joel considering her words. She glanced around the room. 'I've done my homework. I know the Families for Justice files are full of bleak miscarriages of justice: teenagers gunned down for painting graffiti on gable walls, a school boy left brain damaged after being hit by a rubber bullet, a grandmother hit by sniper fire as she tried to get her teenage grandson out of the midst of a riot, and young men and women wrongfully arrested. You must be wondering why the Eden Mulligan case has come up for review, when there were so many other cases waiting in the wings which could be more easily solved?'

He shrugged and waited for Rose to go on.

'For all the media interest in Eden Mulligan's case over the years, no one has ever managed to formulate a concrete scenario explaining her disappearance. Say what you want about the cops, but they don't like mysteries that refuse to be solved.'

He shuffled in his chair.

'Tell me, what was it about the case that got under your skin?' Rose knew if she was to persuade him to cooperate, she would need to understand what it was that had made him want to work on the Mulligan case in the first place.

He sighed. 'When I left Queen's, I was fired up with a misplaced sense of wanting to make a difference. I didn't want to spend my life in a downtown solicitor's office, with the BMW and a nice house in Malone and the obligatory family. Families for Justice had advertised for a case worker and I applied, thinking I would be too inexperienced. Little did I know that all they really wanted was someone with a bit of intelligence and ability to trawl through reams of papers and befriend the families the organisation represented. Someone to whom the families could turn for support, advocacy and, above all, someone to listen to them when the police, and the rest of society, had moved on to the next injustice.' He shifted in the chair as if he was uncomfortable.

'The Eden Mulligan case was my first proper case. I read up on the history, checked out the many blogs and websites detailing the events, and submerged myself in the facts as they stood. All of which was of no use to me when it came to meeting with the family. The first meeting was with Cormac. He's so fucking damaged that you can see the gloom sit round him like a halo of smog.'

'Yeah, I've met Cormac. He wasn't forthcoming.'

'Can you blame him?'

'No, but what's the alternative? To do nothing? If they refuse to work with us, then whoever took Eden – *if* someone did take her – wins. The original police investigation had failings; I'm not denying that. We have a second chance to put it right, but I can't do it on my own. I need the Mulligan family on side, and to get that, I need you, Joel.'

She could see something shift in his features. His guard was coming down. Maybe she could find a way in and make him see that solving this case was in all their interests.

'Joel, work with me. Don't let Eden's case die with her children.'

CHAPTER 20

Rose sat in the office with the overhead light bulb casting a jaundiced glow all around. The Mulligan file was spread out on her desk as she was trying to make sense of the original witness statements, and the more recent pages of testimony that had been gathered by Joel in his investigation on behalf of Families for Justice. There was no evidence gathered on the night of Eden's disappearance as her absence wasn't reported straight away. The facts as they stood were: On 17 July 1986, in 13 Moss Street terrace, five children lay sleeping upstairs. The house consisted of one downstairs living room, a small kitchen, and two upstairs bedrooms – barely enough room for a couple, let alone a family of seven. The mother tended to have the two girls sleep with her, as their father was often absent, working in England. The three brothers shared a double bed in the bedroom to the back of the house.

According to the document Rose was reading, sometime between 3 a.m. and 5 a.m. the oldest child, Cormac, woke. He can't say for sure what woke him, but he thought he may have heard voices in the alley way at the back of the house. He decided to check on his mother and siblings, as was his usual habit when he woke. There had been trouble around the twelfth of July celebrations, and there had been talk of Catholic families being burnt out of their houses during the night, so he had been on high alert. Checking on the family was not an unusual occupation for the young Cormac though. As the oldest child, he felt a sense of responsibility, especially when his father was away.

Rose imagined her thirteen-year-old self having to get up in the night to check the family home. She didn't need to be reminded that Belfast was a dangerous place back then.

She read on through the notes.

When Cormac checked his mother's room, he found his two sisters, Eileen and Lizzie, asleep in the bed. Thinking his mother had gone downstairs to check on the same source of his waking, he headed down, only to find the house empty. No sign of his mother, and no sign of a break-in.

It was a week before the family reported their mother's absence to the authorities.

Why had they not gone straight to the police? Rose wrote in her notebook.

When the family were questioned by the police, Cormac reported that he had heard a car drive away slowly and didn't see any headlights when he looked out the window.

Rose looked back over the notes from the original statement and read how Cormac was described: *Young boy of thirteen, unkempt and unwashed. Upset about the suggestion his mother had left the family.*

There appeared to be little concern or sympathy. It was as though Eden had conjured herself away, vanishing in a puff of smoke like a magician's final trick. The showstopper.

Accounts from the neighbours appeared to offer nothing

more than rumour and gossip. Eden Mulligan was not disliked as such, but there was a sense that she was snobby, that she considered herself to be superior to her neighbours. For this reason, she wasn't particularly tolerated. Within weeks, there were rumours that she had eloped with a British soldier. Other stories circulated that she had been an undercover operative working for the British government. Another told that she had been seen getting the boat at Larne and was thought to be living with the children's estranged father in England.

Rose continued rifling through the box of papers that had come from Joel Ellis's office and found a transcript of an interview carried out with Eamonn Mulligan, the youngest of the children.

Eamonn Mulligan, speaking to Joel Ellis, 25 June 2015.
'I was six when it happened. Only a nipper. The night itself doesn't haunt me. No, it's the days and weeks later, when the realisation seeped in that she was gone and wasn't coming back. The finality of it was what hurt most. I wouldn't see her again, feel those hands cup my face or feel the chide in her voice if I did something wrong.

'Jesus, she could scold when she had to – you didn't want to be caught doing anything wrong. That was the type of her. She used to say, don't bring shame on our name. Don't ever do anything that gets you into trouble. It was as if she thought we should be extra good, us being without a proper Da about the place. She sort of held us up to be perfect, as if anything less would make the neighbours talk and prove them all to be right.

'Didn't matter what they said about her – she didn't care. But us? We were another story. Our Eileen always said that Ma's style needled them all. She'd a way about her, you know? Like a film star. Something you'd see in the pictures. She carried herself a certain way. Always dressed well, had her hair styled just right. The other women about here didn't take too kindly to that, I'd say. Jealous bitches, the lot of them. You could hear the tongues click in disproval as we walked down the street. The net curtains twitched, everyone wanting to catch a look of her.'

Rose searched through the files, looking for the photographs that had been kept. In the first one, a small, four by six faded snapshot, Eden Mulligan stood, hand on hip, head tilted to the sun with a wide smile. She was wearing a purple, form fitting dress that accentuated her small waist and cut away at the shoulders in a Bardot style. It was like something Sophia Loren would have worn, Rose thought. It looked dated for the time, but Eden carried it off. Her dark hair was mid length, worn in loose curls, reminding Rose of Madonna in the Like A Prayer video. The second photograph showed Eden surrounded by her children. While she looked straight at whoever was taking the photograph, the children were all looking at her, as if she was the centre of their world. Eden liked the camera and the camera liked her.

There was a folder of old, yellowing press cuttings. Rose picked out one, an old broadsheet-sized *Belfast Telegraph* page, and unfolded it. The article was on page five and consisted of two columns at the bottom of the page. The accusatory headline blazed out:

Sharon Dempsey

Runaway Mother Abandons Children
Mrs Eden Mulligan, from Moss Street in the Markets area of Belfast, was reported missing two weeks ago. It is believed she may have left to go to England, where her estranged husband, Geordie Mulligan, is working. Her five children wait anxiously for news, as neighbours rally round to support them.

A second newspaper cutting suggested that the missing mother had been suffering from depression. The implication was that she had committed suicide, leaving her children behind to fend for themselves.

Rose wondered why the disappearance hadn't been taken seriously and why initially there was no investigation. Vital information could have been lost before they even began looking for her. She folded the yellowing newspaper page and placed it back in the file.

CHAPTER 21

The next day, Rose was surprised to find a message from Eamonn Mulligan saying he was willing to meet her. Joel had obviously spoken to him and presented Rose's interest in the case in a favourable light.

'Thanks for coming to meet me, Eamonn. I'm sorry if it seems a bit formal to do it here,' she said, as she led him into a meeting room in the station. 'We need to make sure we follow procedures and record everything. I want to make sure that this time, everything is done right.' She didn't need to tell him that the initial investigation had been flawed, that while none of the current procedures had been in place at the time, even common-sense approaches had been neglected. This was a man who had been let down before. Who had experienced the worst kind of abandonment by all those who should have protected him.

'When I see cop shows now and realise that every conversation and bit of paper has to be documented, I could laugh at the importance they gave to us back then.'

'I appreciate that the initial investigation was lacking. I

know it can't be easy for you to talk about your mother and the past.'

'No, it's not easy, but sometimes I think it's harder not to. At least if I'm talking about her, it means she hasn't been forgotten.'

Rose registered the haunted gauntness of his face. She could tell by looking at him that life hadn't been easy. Pain was etched in every line under his eyes. Even his shoulders were hunched forward, as if a heavy weight was bearing down on his thin body, but he had the muscular leanness of a runner, which made Rose think of a panther ready to pounce.

'Please take a chair and we can make a start,' she said, moving through the doorway into the pale yellow room furnished with a teak desk, a small sofa and two chairs. Recording equipment sat on the table and a camera sat discreetly in a corner of the ceiling.

He eased himself onto the chair and leaned back in an exaggerated way, as if to appear relaxed, before placing his hands on his lap. The room was stuffy and smelt of something sweet and yeasty. Rose took her jacket off and placed it over the back of her chair before sitting down and reaching to activate the recording device. She spoke the time and date and then commenced.

'So, what do you want to know? There's not much I can tell you that I haven't told the police before.'

'How about you tell me what your mum was like?'

Eamonn lifted his head and smiled. 'I didn't expect you to ask that.'

He took a minute as if to gather his thoughts. 'Well, she was my world. When you're young, you think your mother can do no wrong. That she knows everything.' He sighed and laced his fingers together, cracking his knuckles as he did so.

'She loved us all right. I never doubted that for a minute. Her hugs were enough to swallow you up. At the same time, she was strict. Whatever she said was the law. You didn't step out of line for fear she would find out.' He looked past Rose as if he couldn't meet her eye.

'Go on,' Rose said.

'I'd say she was smart too. She wanted the best for us. She believed that we should try hard at school. I remember her bringing me down to St Colman's on my first day.' He laughed at the memory. 'God, I was a skinny wee skitter of a thing, in short trousers with scabby knees. Didn't want to go to school at all. My brothers had told me the master was a right hard man, and that I'd get the strap for every freckle on my face. Scared me half to death they did. She had to drag me there. When I started to cry she held me by the shoulders and told me off. Said I was a big boy and had to go to school. Well, I told her I didn't want to be strapped for my freckles. She laughed and promised me that the master would never, ever, strap me for my freckles and she said, "*If* he ever threatens to, you're to run home, and get me and I'll soon sort him out."' He tried to smile, his mouth twisted with emotion.

'Of course, Master McKee loved her. All the men did. She was a beautiful woman. Even as a child I sensed how the women treated her with caution, looked her up and down, and how the men were always extra nice to her.' He shrugged, as if proud that his mother's beauty was worth something in the eyes of others. Rose thought of the photographs and how elegant and glamorous Eden had looked.

'Afterwards, when she was taken, everything I did was

121

wrong. The one person in the universe who cared enough to stop me, was gone. One word from her and I'd have behaved myself. I never liked to make her angry, not because I feared her, but because all I ever wanted to do was to make her happy. See her smile and feel the warmth of her approval. After she was gone, no one cared enough to stop me.'

Rose could see he was close to tears. He put his head in his hands, the taut sinews of his forearms standing out like cords as he took a couple of deep breaths to steady himself.

'It must have been very hard on all of you.' Rose couldn't imagine the pain and fear those children must have felt. The sense of abandonment and a lifetime of questions unanswered.

The puffy pouches under his eyes showed a lack of sleep, but his clear complexion, and the tight wound-up spring of his body, all spoke of a man who took care of himself. His life had been about survival. Getting by and doing whatever it took to numb the pain. But there was something endearing about Eamonn. Rose couldn't say what it was, but he made her think of a lost child. A seeker endlessly looking for a part of himself that had been stolen away. Yet, he was entirely without self-pity, whereas Cormac carried his grudges like a weapon, ready to strike out at everyone every chance he got.

'Sorry, it still catches me out. One minute I think I'm doing okay, then the pain of it just crushes me. We all lost so much. Our mother, our childhoods, our home. All gone.'

'Do you keep in touch with your brothers and sisters?'

'Not really. Our Eileen does keep in touch. She's doing okay. Has a family of her own now. Three girls. They're all pursuing nursing careers or something similar. And Lizzie, she's done all right for herself. She's a nice house and the fancy car but all that means nothing. There's still pain there, hidden beneath the make-up and the nice clothes. I'd have hardly known her, if it wasn't for the Mulligan eyes, dark and dead-like. We go for the odd cup of coffee, talk about old times, the days before.'

'Do you need a break?' Rose asked.

'Nah, I'm just reminiscing. Lost in the memories. Trouble is, we all have so much hurt inside that if you try to share it, you just bring the other person down with you. Some of them have tried to move on with their lives. They've tried to make a go of it – life, I mean. I never managed that. Too damaged. Tried to cure myself over the years with drink and drugs. None of it worked though. Only made me worse. But I'm clean now. Trying to get by without any of that stuff. All those pills wreck your head and, believe me, my head's scrabbled enough as it is.'

He gave a wry smile. 'I always think of her, my Ma. Not a day goes by when I don't think, what would she have been like now? What would we all be like? Whoever took her that night altered six lives forevermore, not one. They handed us a lifetime of heartache.' He rubbed his hand across his stubbly shaved head, recalling memories gilded with sorrow.

'Every now and then you'd glance up to see her on the news. They would be talking about new enquiries, new sightings, possible leads – all for nothing in the end – and every time they would show that old photo of her standing in the field with us kids all around her. I was only a toddler, sitting on the grass with my face screwed up against the sun.

'Our Eileen told me that we were on holiday when it was taken. Somewhere near the Mournes, she said. Might be Murlough Bay caravan park. She couldn't remember. Still, it was nice to think that we had gone on our holidays all together, like. Once upon a time we were an ordinary family, with a screw-up for a father, but sure, they were a dime a dozen back then. Nobody had everything. A good Ma was what made a family.'

Rose nodded. She thought of her own mother and her complicated feelings towards her.

'Over the years there were promises of new enquiries. We even got as far as a dig once. Some farce that turned out to be, they found nothing but old relics.

'At first, there was a lot of attention from the press. It was on every anniversary, then every ten years, until they all lost interest. Funny how I missed the press attention when it was gone. I always thought, at the back of my mind, that one day someone would care enough to get to the truth. If the peelers didn't solve the mystery then maybe some trench coat wearing journalist would.' He snorted.

'Eileen used to say maybe she'd run away to Kilburn to be with our Da. That she'd had enough of our complaining and set off for a new life in London,' he said, half-amused. 'Wishful thinking. We would have forgiven her anything, just to know she was alive. When I realised that she was gone, and what I had lost, there was a hole inside of me as deep as a canyon. Nothing or no one could ever fill it. Now all I'm left with is nothing. Blank and empty. Spent and used.' He paused and stared straight ahead. Rose let the silence envelop them. She knew she had to let the story unfold in its own time.

'The Mulligan babies – that's what the press called us. We were their creation. The pitiful five. At first people were good. We were fed and clothed in hand me downs. We never complained, we knew it was better than nothing. In the end though, they had to split us up. No one family could take on all five of us. The big ones probably had it harder at the beginning. Cormac and Eileen. They were sent to a home in Downpatrick. At thirteen and eleven they were deemed too old for adoption. Paddy and Lizzie, the twins, they were lucky enough. A couple of teachers who had never had kids of their own, took them in. For a while it looked like they had it made. Until we found out what it was really like for them.' He stopped again and cracked his knuckles.

'And then there was me; six years old and ready to fight the world. I was an angry wee bastard. Hard to place with any family. The few that tried to take me in ended up sending me back to the nuns. I hung around the convent for a couple of years with the nuns on my back every five minutes. I could do no right in their eyes. And then the priest would call, or some rich benefactor, and I'd be scrubbed up and wheeled out like a performing monkey to recite the catechism. Six of the best if I slipped up.

'Eventually they sent me to the Christian Brothers home. You can imagine how that turned out.' He turned his head, as if he didn't want to meet Rose's eyes.

CHAPTER 22

Katy Carberry appeared fit and spritely for a seventy-year-old. She welcomed Rose and Danny into her bungalow, and told them to make themselves at home while she bustled off to put the kettle on.

'I haven't had anyone round here asking about Eden Mulligan for years,' she called out from the kitchen.

'We're doing a review of the case and your name was on the list of neighbours from that time,' Danny said.

'Oh, aye, we lived beside them, all right. Right next door. We were in the row of wee kitchen houses. Jesus, they weren't big enough to swing a cat in, but sure we were all in the same boat in the Markets in those days. We didn't have much, but we all looked out for each other. That's how it was back then. Not like now, when nobody hardly looks at you.'

She returned with a mug of tea and sat it down on a side table next to Rose. 'Would you like a wee biscuit? I've Jaffa cakes or some of them fancy ones, what do you call them? Viennese Swirls, that's it.'

'No, thanks, the tea is fine.'

Katy sat on the sofa opposite Rose and Danny. She appeared eager to talk, all wide-eyed and expectant, as if this was the highlight of her day.

'Well, what do you want to know? I can't tell you anything I didn't tell the police and the family back then.'

'You lived in Moss Street, what was it like?' Danny asked.

'Awk, what can I say? We lived in the house facing the bigger parlour houses. Ours was a wee two-up two-down, same as Eden's. Everyone looked out for each other. The boys all went to St Colman's school, and in the summer months they played out on the street. Not like nowadays, when you can't let them out the door.'

'Was it a good place to live?'

'We'd our problems, like everywhere in Belfast at that time, but it wasn't a bad place to live and bring up a family if you can discount the Troubles.'

Rose felt something sink in her stomach. The Markets community was small. Everyone knew everyone else. She couldn't help thinking of her own mother, who came from the same area. The chances were that Katy knew Rose's family.

'Tell me, what was Eden like?'

'Oh, Eden Mulligan was a beauty. She knew it, too. Loved herself they all said, but sure for all the good it did her. I think her looks were her downfall in the end.'

'What do you mean?' Rose asked, taking a sip of the weak tea.

'When you look like Eden did, gorgeous figure and style to match, you can attract the wrong sort of attention.'

Rose said nothing. She knew in certain situations, it was best to hang back, let the subject revel in the telling. The less she intervened, the more Katy would say.

'The thing was, Eden had a bit of glamour and mystery about her. For a woman bringing up her five children, she managed to dress herself like something out of a magazine. God, the style of her.' Katy smiled, remembering.

'She had this one dress . . . Oh, we all loved it. Navy it was, with white polka dots and a little red belt that pinched in at her waist. She was gorgeous in it. Like something out of that programme, *Dallas*. I remember asking her where she'd bought such a dress. You wouldn't have seen the likes of it round our streets. It was like something sent from America. Well, Eden just smiled, the way she always did – a slow, sleek sort of smile – and said she'd picked it up from the sale rail at Anderson and McAuley's, the big department store in the town. I don't know, I never believed her. For starters, where would she have got the money?'

Rose let Katy continue.

'She had a way of walking that drew attention, made you aware of how she carried herself. If it was a dreary day, she seemed to brighten the room. The type of woman who, given different circumstances, could have had a life of luxury. You could almost believe she had been born for it. Instead she ended up with Geordie Mulligan. He was a good-looking fella, don't get me wrong, but mean with the drink in him. You wouldn't want to cross him. That's why, when Eden disappeared, plenty thought he had something to do with it.'

'Did you suspect him?'

'No, not for a second. Geordie hadn't been around for a while. When he came back the whole street always knew about it. We only seen him when he had a bit of money. Liked to flash it around, as if he was a big fella. Of course, it never lasted long. He'd go down to Mick Mooney's pub and buy drinks for all his old mates, roll home drunk and cause a right merry carry on.'

'Was he violent with Eden?'

'Listen, I lived next door, and the walls might as well have been made of cardboard. I could hear all her records. She loved a bit of music: Madonna, David Bowie, Queen and the likes. Even the older stuff like Bob Dylan and the Stones. I could sing the lyrics along with her if I wanted to. Come nine o'clock, when the kids were all off to bed, the CD player would go on. I expect she was lonely without Geordie when he was away.

'So sure, they had their fights. The odd plate smashed and plenty of f-ing and blinding, but he wouldn't have hit her. If you ask me, Eden had the upper hand. Geordie worshipped her. Trouble was, he worshipped his whiskey just as much. Sometimes the drink won.'

Rose thought of the young wife dealing with a drunk husband. Maybe he had got heavy-handed. 'Were there any rumours about Eden and Geordie? Anyone say that he was violent?'

Katy set her cup down on the tray. 'Oh there were plenty of them but none of them ever involved Geordie beating her. The stories that were told were more concerned with painting Eden in a bad light.'

'In what way?'

Rose could see Katy was enjoying the reminiscing. 'People said there was an inevitability about it all. That she'd brought it on herself with her stuck-up attitude. They'd say it was the way she talked, her accent – softer than the ones round here – the way she dressed as if she'd style oozing out of her every pore. Watching her walk down the street was like catching a glimpse of one of them supermodels of the time – Cindy Crawford. That glamour, sophistication, and self-assuredness. Afterwards, I noticed no one was rushing to paint her as a saint. Funny how they didn't say much to her when she was alive, but they had plenty to say about her once she was gone. It was like a mantle to protect themselves. It was as if she'd brought the disappearance on herself; as if she was getting what she deserved. That way then they'd be safe.'

She lifted her teacup and took another mouthful.

'Belfast back then was nothing but a broken landscape of red brick terrace houses, but there was beauty beneath the façade of grime. If you knew where to look for it, you could find it. For some it was in music. Back in my day, there were backroom clubs where bands played, and you could see the likes of Van Morrison, starting out on his career, for a few shillings. Others found it in a boxing club; no one caring what religion you were born into, only that you followed the rules of the sport. Eden, well, she found her own way out.

'Some said she'd a married man on the side, others said she got all dolled up to stand on street corners, but when you live right next door you get to know a person. If she'd been up to anything I'd have known it. There was never anything to suggest that she had another man on the go. My husband Charlie, God rest his soul, used to say that no good could come from a woman looking like that living without a man. I suppose he was right in the end.'

'So, you never saw anyone of interest coming and going from the house? What about extended family?'

'No, from what I heard, she came from Portadown or somewhere. There was talk of her being Protestant, but she brought the kids up in the Catholic faith. There was no contact with her family, as far as I know.'

'What about friends?'

'None that I knew of, apart from Father Ryan, that is . . . if you could call him a friend. He was a lovely priest. He was from Sligo originally. He was like a breath of fresh air coming into St Malachy's Parish.' She took another sip of her tea and settled back into the sofa again.

'Right, where was I? Oh yes, Father Ryan. He took an interest in all the kids, set up a boxing club and had a dance organised for the last Friday in every month. Really brought people together. He would call into Eden's house often enough. Take a cup of tea and talk to the wee ones. I thought he took pity on her being without a husband, and that maybe he was keeping an eye on her. Many a time she'd say what a great priest he was, how he made the mass worth going to. Even if it was true that she was from the other side, she went occasionally for the kids. We all loved him. He moved parish eventually.'

'Where did Father Ryan move to after he left St Malachy's?' Danny asked, making a note.

'There was talk he had gone to America, some parish in Boston, but I couldn't say for sure.'

She sat forward suddenly. 'Hang on a minute, I have an old box of stuff from back then. There might be some photographs in it.' Katy left the living room and Rose could hear her opening and closing cupboard doors in her bedroom.

'Here it is.' She returned carrying an old biscuit tin and sat it down on the sofa between her and Rose.

'Oh look, them's my wee ones. Angela, Michael and Bernie; all grown up now with families of their own.' She showed Rose the old photograph of her children. She rummaged through the tin, discarding photographs, newspaper cuttings, and other snippets of her life – a memorial card, a legal document of some sort, a receipt.

'Look, here it is. This is what I was looking for.' It was an old St Malachy's parish newsletter.

'There, that's Father Ryan,' she said, pointing to the priest, who was standing with a group of young children around him. 'That's one of Eden Mulligan's children there.' She pointed to the smallest boy, standing in shorts and knee-high socks. 'Yes, that's wee Eamonn, standing beside Father Ryan.'

Rose looked at the black and white photograph. The priest stood in his black vestment, smiling to the camera, with his arms spread wide around the huddle of children.

'Who are the other children in the photo?'

'Let me see, that would be John-Joe Conlon, Sean Healy and Shirley McMullan. They must have all been on a trip or something. Every now and then the parish council would take the youngsters away for the day to a park or a local beach.'

Belfast had been a pit of savagery and subterfuge in the seventies and eighties so there was something unnerving in looking at these photographs of normal life. Rose forced herself to bring her thoughts back to Eden Mulligan and focus on the case.

'Was Eden very religious?' Danny asked, handing the photograph back to Katy.

'No, I wouldn't say she was. No more than the rest of us. She took the children to mass the odd Sunday, like I said, but we all did. It was expected of us back then. You felt that you had to pray to God to keep your family protected. You did the right thing, took them to make their first holy communion and the rest of it. It was our safety net. Not like nowadays, where the young ones hardly bother crossing the chapel threshold.

'I'd say Eden wasn't particularly religious. It was more that she liked to be seen chatting to the priest in her doorway, making sure all the neighbours got a good look. Being seen with him gave her a bit of respectability, especially with her coming from the other side, but I'd say she liked him too. He wasn't like the others. More down to earth and involved in the community, like.'

Danny looked up from his notepad. 'Can you think of any reason Eden would have been frightened for her safety?'

'No, I can't. If she had been in trouble I'd like to think she would have asked for help. None of us would have seen anything happen to her. We were a tight wee community. That's how it was back then. Everyone looking out for everyone else.'

Except when they needed to turn a blind eye, thought Rose.

CHAPTER 23

Rose slipped into the conference room as the briefing was being wrapped up, hoping to go unnoticed. Danny was at the front, pointing to the timeline board and holding the attention of his colleagues. Glancing around for somewhere to sit, Rose clocked a free spot next to Malachy Magee and made her way over to him.

'All right?' he said under his breath.

Rose nodded and took the chair next to him.

'As you can see, we have our work cut out for us,' Danny said, giving his best impression of being in charge. 'Keep the channels of communication open and ensure DS Lumen is updated every day with what you're doing.'

Rose had thought that, given his personality type – conscientious, with intuition playing a major part in how he responded to the world – Danny would be more comfortable playing the wingman role, happy to give the lead to whoever he was working with. She was glad to see him stepping up. He was a good copper. One of the best, she'd bet, though no one was perfect.

The room cleared, leaving Rose and Danny alone.

'How's it all going?' Rose asked.

'Oh, you know, the usual. Chasing up forensics, dealing with the boss . . . Same old shite.'

'How's it working out with you and Malachy Magee?'

'Ack, he's all right. Gets the job done, but he's not much fun. Knocks off the minute the clock hits seven and runs home as fast as he can to his family. I can't blame him for wanting a life outside of the job, but cases like this can't be run watching the clock. You know what it's like, Rosie. Some of our best work has happened over a pint.'

Rose smiled.

'Speaking of which, how are you fixed this evening for a catch-up? We can talk cop shop all night if you like.'

'Sure, but shouldn't you be getting home to Amy?'

She noticed him flinch ever so slightly, just enough to alert her that something was up.

'She's over at her sister's tonight. No need to hurry home.'

'Okay then. I could do with bouncing around a few ideas about the case. I'm curious to know what the SOCOs have come up with as well.'

By the time they called it a day and settled down in Madden's pub in Berry Street, it had gone nine o'clock. Rose was glad of the long hours. Sitting in the soulless apartment all alone wasn't good for her. It was nice to have someone to talk to instead of settling down with a cheese and ham toastie and nothing but her laptop for company. She wasn't in the mood for trawling through Netflix.

'I am starting to get to grips with Eden Mulligan. Who she was. What made her tick. From what Katy Carberry told us, it seems that she was stylish, good looking and liked to keep herself separate from her neighbours but not meaning it in a stand-offish way. I think she was out of their league. Someone with a bit of glamour who dreamt of a different kind of life than the one she had ended up with.'

'And has any of that thrown any light on what happened to her?'

'Unfortunately, no. I'm ruling out more than I'm ruling in. Tell me about the cottage case, any leads yet?'

'Still sifting through the debris. Nothing concrete.'

'What about the victims' background and their families?' Rose asked.

'All met at university and have recently graduated. Henry appears to be the only one who is close to his family. The others had less interest in going home in between terms. From what we can gather, they were pretty much inseparable around campus. Lived in the same rented house from the end of first year, and although they all studied different subjects they were often seen in the library studying together. A tight wee unit from first year is how they were described by one of the lecturers.'

Rose took a sip of her drink. 'You've been up to the main house and talked to the owners?'

'Of course I have. What do you take me for? The owners of the main house are Elsie and Oliver McGoldrick. They must be in their late sixties, totally traumatised by the murders happening in their property. They were staying with family in Newry when the murders happened. They were pretty shaken up, but more than keen to answer questions and be of assistance. They rent the cottage out to try to cover the upkeep of the place. They had no idea why "Who Took Eden Mulligan?" was on the wall either.

It certainly hadn't been there before the friends had taken on the lease. There's no connection that I can identify, yet. Maybe you would like to have a look around and have a chat with the McGoldricks?'

Rose nodded. 'Yes, definitely.'

'I'll go with you tomorrow, if you like. It would do no harm for me to have another word with them.'

'And the background of the victims? No disgruntled ex-lovers hanging around?'

'No exes of significance and no stalkers reported. Seems that the group of friends liked to keep to themselves, by all accounts.' He placed a group photograph of the five friends on the table.

'This one, Henry Morton,' he said, pointing to the tall, curly haired man. 'He's the one that rented the cottage. Seems that his family has plenty of money and he was planning on going into the family business – some sort of packaging company based in Dungannon. Theo Beckett was doing a funded PhD in some rare engineering topic.'

Rose looked at the young man sitting in the picture. He was wearing round rimmed glasses and smiling, looking every inch like a young professor in training.

'And Olivia Templeton there' – he indicated to the good-looking blonde draped over Theo – 'had just bagged herself a graduate job with one of the big accountancy firms in town. She was to start her new position next week.'

Olivia's blonde hair was tossed back and her face was tilted, posing for the camera. She looked vibrant and mischievous. Nothing like the bloodied corpse Rose had seen on the bed.

'Iona Gardener, our confessor, was into journalism, writing for blogs though she was studying social work.

137

Looks like she was working for a new multiplatform website, whatever that is. Dylan Wray was the only one without some sort of plan for the future.'

Dylan was a handsome guy. The type who wore his good looks with ease. Dark haired with swarthy skin and intense eyes.

Five bright graduates. Sparkling lives ahead of them.

Rose lifted the photograph. 'And there's nothing on any of them? No minor possession charges, no drunk and disorderly?'

'Nada, not even a library fine. Even their previous land-lord sang their praises. Said he'd never had better tenants. Left the house in better nick than when they'd moved in.'

There was something attractive about them as a group and the idea of their tight-knit circle. Rose had never belonged to a group like that. At uni she had clung to Danny, and had been happy to be part of whichever group he favoured.

'Why had they rented the cottage?'

'Apparently they wanted to continue living together after university. The rent was cheap and it is near the motorway for easy access to Belfast or Dungannon, where Henry Morton was going to be working.'

Danny took a sip of his pint. 'We had a word with some other students on their courses and they all said largely the same thing – they were never rude or stand-offish, but that they kept to themselves. They were rarely seen at parties, and if they did attend, it was always as a unit. We were told they never really mixed with anyone from their courses. Just polite chat before lectures.'

They had no need to, they'd each other, Rose thought. She envied them their exclusivity, their sense of belonging. Rose had never been the popular girl, and if she hadn't had

Danny she'd have been a loner. By choice though. She had learned to keep herself contained and apart. It was safer that way.

They finished their drinks and ordered more.

'Right, no more shop talk.'

She looked at Danny, sitting there, so keen to hear how her life had turned out. If he knew the truth, that she had little in her life beyond work, he'd be horrified. The odd one-night stand didn't amount to enough to talk about. It certainly wasn't pulse racing stuff. She needed something more but had lost the will to look for it.

She'd come close once, with Leif. He was Danish. Blond and charming. Too nice for her liking. The chasm that lay between them was too great to surmount in the end. The trouble was, he was in her field. He could read her and saw that parts were hidden. He knew that she carried damage and secrets; had told her to sort herself out, seek help. But there's no fixing without tearing open some wounds and she had little interest in that.

She took a long drink of her gin and tonic. Her relationships were all doomed from the beginning.

'Not much to tell, really. I'm one cat away from being a crazy cat woman.'

'You know you can talk to me if you ever need someone to listen,' he said, moving in close to her.

He looked at Rose with such earnestness that all she could do was laugh.

'What's so funny?' For a second he looked like a petulant child, ready to stage a tantrum because he had been embarrassed.

'You are, you dickhead. Offering me a shoulder to cry on, as if I'm going to wallow in self-pity.'

'I just mean I'm here as a friend if you need one. Aww forget it, I thought we were mates.'

He looked sad now, as if she had hurt him, and she instantly regretted her flippancy.

'Ah shit Danny, don't go all moody on me. We are mates. If I need you, I promise I'll cry on your shoulder, snot and all.'

'Well, if you're sure.' It sounded hollow, as if he knew she'd never expose herself in that way, let herself be too involved with him on an emotional level.

'So, what about you?' she asked, turning the tables on Danny. 'How's married life treating you?'

'Awk, you know me, old boring married man now.'

Rose laughed. She knew Danny was far from being a player, but she didn't see him being happily settled into married life either. She needed to readjust her image of him. Life had changed them both. Maybe when she met Amy she would accept that the Danny she knew from before had grown up.

He swallowed the last of his beer. 'Sure, drink up, Rosie. It's time I hit the road or Amy will be sending out a search party.'

CHAPTER 24

Elsie and Oliver McGoldrick's house was easier to find than the cottage. It was the type of estate you expected to be turned into a wedding venue to help with the cost of the upkeep. Rose drove up to the main house and parked the car to the side.

'Maybe we should go around to the servants' entrance,' Danny said, doing his best downtrodden impression.

Rose sighed. 'Come on, let's see what we can find out.'

Oliver McGoldrick opened the door almost as soon as Danny rang the old-fashioned bell. He was every inch the country estate gentleman, from his fraying tweed waistcoat to the worn-in brown brogues.

'I'm not sure if we can be of any help,' he said, having shown them into the living room. 'The cottage has been part of the estate for as long as I can remember. Every now and then we threaten to sell if off, but we don't like to think of breaking up the estate. Instead, we rent it out. I've passed the details of the rental agreement on to your colleague DS Magee. The young people who took it on seemed responsible. The rent was cheap in exchange for them making some improvements.'

'Yes, thank you for that. It appears the cottage had been unused for some time before Henry Morton had rented it. Do you know who would have had access to it?'

'Just our staff. We have a groundsman, Brian Martin. He keeps an eye on the outlying buildings.'

'Good morning.'

Rose turned and saw Elsie McGoldrick standing in the doorway. She had steely grey hair cut into an austere bob, and was dressed in wool skirt with a cotton cream blouse. 'I apologise for not being here to greet you sooner. I was sorting out the dogs.'

'No problem at all,' Rose said. 'We were just discussing the cottage and who might have access to it.'

'Brian sorts all that out. He's worked for us for years and we've never had any cause for worry,' she replied, sitting down on the sofa opposite Rose.

'We will be speaking to Mr Martin. Anyone else who would routinely call to the house?' asked Danny.

Oliver McGoldrick looked irritated. 'No, only family and friends. Really, detectives, we have been over all of this with your colleague. We are certain that whoever has committed this crime has nothing to do with us.'

'Do either of you have any connection to the Mulligan family?' Rose asked.

Elsie shook her head. 'None whatsoever. We can't think why that graffiti would have been put there. It wasn't there when I last checked on the cottage just before the new tenants had arrived. The whole thing is most upsetting. I can't bear to think of those poor young people murdered on our property. It is a horrendous ordeal altogether.'

'Can I ask what your occupation was before retirement?' Rose asked Oliver.

'I was a barrister.'

'Must have been interesting work,' Rose said.

'Yes, at times.' He didn't elaborate.

'And yourself, Mrs McGoldrick?'

'Oh, I looked after the family and ran the estate. There was plenty to do, believe me.'

'I don't doubt it for a second.'

'We may need to speak to you again, but that should do for now,' Danny said. 'If it's okay with you, we would like to take another walk around the cottage grounds.'

'Certainly. If you head out the side hallway you can take a left past the stables and the lane will take you to the cottage.'

They made their way along the dirt track that Oliver McGoldrick called a lane.

'This place is huge.' Danny stopped and looked around, taking in the view of the house behind them.

'It's fairly isolated, too.'

They walked on in the direction of the cottage grounds.

The efforts to tame nature around the main house began to fade as they reached their destination. From this angle, the cottage looked less fairy-tale and more run-down out building. The police tape was still marking the area a no-go zone. Danny hopped over the tape and Rose lifted it to duck under. The cottage was all closed up and looked peaceful. Even peering through the dirty windows into the gloom of the living room gave nothing away.

The tree where the hanging dolls had been found stood solid and reassuringly permanent, making Rose think of the decades of people passing through it must have been witness to. There was still something otherworldly about the setting. Something that made her skin crawl.

'So, Rosie, do you think old man McGoldrick could have had background in military intelligence? He has that army look about him. All straight back and stiff. The barrister stuff could be a cover.'

Rose shrugged. 'I didn't get that vibe, but we should check him out. He may have made a few enemies in his time as a barrister. Maybe someone has come along seeking payback. It's worth digging to see if he has any skeletons hanging in his closet.' Rose paused. 'Listen.'

They stood still, hearing nothing but birdsong.

'It's just occurred to me that no one would have heard their screams.'

CHAPTER 25

That evening, Rose let herself into the apartment. The sleek, modernist feel of the space suited her better than the old Edwardian terrace flat she had in London.

She'd survived another day in Belfast.

She kicked off her shoes and threw herself down on the sofa. In London, the place she had called home for so long, she had felt like an outsider. Now, after the death of her mother, everything was alien and draining. She couldn't see a way to make life better. Maybe this posting offered her a way out. A chance to start over.

Connecting with her family didn't have to be as bad as she feared. She loved her work, even being in the 'basement of doom', as Danny called it. It suited her to take a step back from the research and policy and to experience the energy and excitement of regular police work. The careful, methodical examination of the facts, the unearthing of new information, and the need to formulate a narrative of the events surrounding Eden's disappearance held an academic quality that suited her. Maybe she'd never get to find out the whole truth, but she was determined to find at least part of it.

The evening was warm and muggy, so she had a shower, stretched out on the sofa and lay letting her skin dry in the warm air. Eden was on her mind. She couldn't shake the feeling that maybe Eden had known her abductors, had been taken to her death by people she trusted in some way. People who lived among her community. What must the walk to the car have been like in the dead of night, knowing that she was possibly not going to see her children again?

Rose resisted the urge to pick up her phone and check her emails. Instead, she dragged her hair out of her face and tried to put it in some sort of knot to keep her neck cooler. She thought of how her mother would have admonished her for her not worrying about her appearance, but the truth was it was hot and she didn't care. Thankfully, the temperature had dropped a little and the promised storm seemed to be on its way.

Her thoughts turned back to her family. All those years spent in exile. The tug of home had pulled at her sometimes, but it was more out of sense of duty to the others. Especially Kaitlin, who had every right to feel resentful that Rose had abandoned her, yet now, following their mother's death, her sister was being so welcoming. She had to admit, she liked being home. Even if it did bring up questions that needed to be answered. Ever since Kaitlin rang telling her that Evelyn had died, Rose had been tormented by memories of her childhood. Snatches of conversations that didn't make sense, late night knocks at the door, her mother disappearing only to return in the dead of the night.

There was one person outside of her immediate family

who could throw light on what had gone on: Aunt Josie, Evelyn's sister. Rose could remember the two of them being close when they were younger. Josie had been at the funeral. She had nodded hello to Rose but that had been the extent of their interaction. Now though, Rose felt it was time to pay her a visit.

Josie hadn't aged well. Her once dark hair was streaked with coppery highlights, probably added to hide the grey, and her skin looked as if it had been ravaged by time. She seemed smaller, slight even, and the delicate features, which were so typical of the women in their family, now made her look wizened and haggard.

'Josie, thanks for seeing me.' Rose hugged her aunt and felt the bones of her shoulders through her flimsy blouse.

'Come on in. This heat's powerful. I'm sure you could do with a cold drink.' Rose followed her into the hallway of the red brick semi-detached house off the Rosetta Road. It was a tidy house, furnished to look like something straight out of a Laura Ashley catalogue, all cowslip sprigs and duck egg blue with plumped velvet cushions and pretty lamps sitting on side tables. Josie returned from the kitchen with a tray of glasses and a jug of lemonade. 'I didn't make it but it's that nice stuff from the deli on the road.' She poured Rose a glass and added a sprig of mint.

'Thanks, it's lovely.' Rose sipped at the drink, glad of the coolness.

'You must still be in shock about your mother. Terribly sad altogether. Sorry I didn't get talking to you at the funeral, but I thought you needed to be with the family.'

Rose nodded. 'I'm sorry I didn't ring you more and keep in touch. It just seemed easier that way.'

'No need to apologise, you have your own life to lead. Sometimes it's better not to look back.' She peered at Rose, as if drinking in the details. 'You look like her.'

'My mum?'

'Yeah. You've her eyes and the cheekbones. Oh, how I envied her those cheekbones.' They both smiled.

'You're here to ask about her, aren't you?' Josie said.

'Is it that obvious?' She tried to make her voice sound light and casual.

'I've been able to see through you since you were no higher than my knees. What do you want to know?'

Rose paused. She didn't know how to frame the sentences, to put into words what she needed to know but didn't want to hear.

'Tell me about her. What she did. Was she *involved*?'

'It didn't start with your father, if that's what you've been thinking.'

Rose looked up, surprised.

'No, her heart was hardened before then. He got shot because he was a Catholic, in the wrong place at the wrong time. Any political leanings she had had formed well before that. You can have three girls grow up in the same house and each one of them has a different interpretation of what's gone on. That's what your granny used to say. There was no explaining our Evelyn. She was one of a kind. A fire-cracker, reckless and passionate. Given a different situation, she could have done something totally different with her life. As it was, she found a purpose in politics, but talking shop was never enough for her.'

The reality was that if Rose kept poking around in the detritus of Evelyn's life, she knew she was going to find out things that would make her uneasy. Ashamed, even.

'The thing is, I'd rather know who she really was than try to mourn my idea of who she was. Does that make sense?'

'The truth is I can't tell you anything you don't already know. Honest to God.'

'I know she was connected in some way.' That word – *connected* – held a power all of its own. Shorthand for so many things that covered up the brutal realities of what it meant to be involved with the paramilitaries.

'Let the past die with her. There's no good to come out of digging through the dirt.'

'Tell me what she was like. How did she end up the way she did?' Rose said.

'When we were growing up in the seventies, everything was changing. The world was finding new ways to be. Our Evelyn loved to read, and every time she read something that incensed her or excited her, she would inevitably cast her eye around this place and see where we fell short.' Josie laughed. 'She was an idealist. Always seeking that something to make the world a better place, whether it wanted to be or not.'

Rose sighed. 'It probably doesn't make sense, but I feel like I never really knew her. My own mother and I can't say I had a handle on what made her tick.'

'Do we ever really know our parents?'

'I just thought if I asked what she was like back then, before we were born, then maybe I could understand her a bit better.' Rose hesitated. 'Sean Torrent, did you know him?'

'We all knew *of* him. He was one of the lads, one of the "volunteers", as they called themselves. Thought of themselves like the leaders in the Easter Rising, brothers in arms and all that carry on.'

'He used to send for my mother, and she'd be at his beck and call.'

'I'd say she probably worked as one of their couriers at first. Running secret messages between houses for fear of phones being tapped, and there was always money or guns to be moved around.'

'He had some kind of a hold over her. I don't know if it was fear or what, but if he came calling, we all knew to stay out of the way.'

'Men like Sean Torrent positioned themselves in the community like overlords. They acted like they owned the place and everyone in it. Called themselves heroes of the cause.' Josie looked Rosie in the eyes. 'Don't waste your energy on someone like him.'

But Rose believed Sean Torrent was more than a cold-eyed commander to Evelyn. He either had something on her or they had been in a relationship. There was an energy about them that suggested either fear or lust. Rose just didn't know which.

In the end, she left Josie's none the wiser. If Josie knew anything, she wasn't saying.

CHAPTER 26

The air in the office was stagnant. Someone's significant birthday had called for birthday cake and the sweet, cloying smell of icing and marzipan was tickling the back of Danny's throat. It was all off kilter. He could never accept the need to be joyful and over familiar in the office, especially in the midst of a big case. When his head was full of autopsy reports and evidence bags, he had little space or tolerance for colleagues blathering on about being fifty and nifty. He'd signed the office card and stuck a tenner in the kitty, but he sure as hell wasn't going to sing 'Happy Birthday'.

He glanced around the office, willing himself to give them ten more minutes before losing his shit and telling them to all get back to f-ing work. At least Magee seemed to be working. He was talking intently into his phone and taking notes. Danny went back to his computer screen and tried to block out the cake sharing.

A few minutes later, Malachy sat down in front of him.

'A new lead. It looks like one of the victims, Dylan Wray,

had history with a known drug dealer, Conal Brady. According to our inquiries, they went to school together and were good friends up until Dylan went to university and Conal launched his career as a DJ, with an active sideline in dealing.'

'And nobody picked this up before now?'

'Dylan was clean. We'd no reason to think he'd been using – or any of them in the cottage, for that matter. Their toxicology reports came back clear, and we found no traces of drugs in the house.'

'So, how did it get flagged up?'

'Conal Brady had been reported as mouthing off in a club in Belfast, suggesting he knew who did the stabbings and that it was at his instigation for drug debts not paid. And he's form too. He was arrested last year for assault but got off with a slap on the wrist. There had been some sort of altercation outside the Hatfield bar. A student ended up with half of his ear bitten off, but Brady's barrister argued that there was no evidence he was the one responsible. There were five of them involved in the scrum.'

'Bring the wee shit in.'

'Already on it.'

Conal Brady was a big lad, bulky, with a tough attitude that could be seen in his walk. All slouched shoulders, rough gingery stubble and a snarl, his bearing suggested he'd been disturbed from his sleep to come down to the station at the ungodly hour of 1 p.m.

'Mr Brady, good of you to come in.'

'I haven't done any fucking thing, so I don't know why I'm being harassed. I've rights, you know. Rights to be left in fucking peace.'

Danny stared at him. The big fecker was mouthing off before they'd even begun. He didn't need this.

'Mr Brady, there's no need to take that tone. This is a friendly chat to help us with our inquiries.'

'No such fucking thing as friendly when it comes to coppers. Am I going to need to ring my solicitor?'

'That's your right to do so, Mr Brady, but for now all we want to do is ask you how you know Dylan Wray?'

'X-Ray? I knew him at school. That's all. We're not mates or anything. We used to hang out together back in the day, but that's it. I'd nothing to do with him ending up in hospital, if that's what you're getting at.'

'We're going to need to know where you were on the night of the twenty-eighth of June.'

He took out his phone and opened up his Instagram account, hit the profile icon and turned the device around to show them a video of himself behind a mixing desk, bass heavy, the thumping music and flashing blue strobe lights whipping a crowd of drunk teenagers into a frenzy.

'Doing a gig at Red Star nightclub. I've five hundred odd party goers who can vouch for me.'

'You like to do a bit of under the mixing desk dealing, I hear. Good business strategy to sell to the revellers. They can't get the stuff past the bouncers, but you can.'

'Nah, not me. I don't touch the stuff.'

'Word on the street says otherwise.'

'Well your sources are wrong. Ask anyone – I'm clean and I'm not stupid. Dealing is for wasters. I'm building a career, not playing.'

'A career out of busting people's heads with that dance crap music. Should be a crime against good taste. Bet you've never even heard of Nirvana.'

Conal Brady smirked. 'Showing your age there, old man.'

'We have it on good authority that you were heard slabbering about the Dunlore murders and that you're involved.'

'Seriously? Come off it! You shouldn't listen to crap like that. If someone is trying to muddy my good name, then I want to know who it is.'

Danny looked at him with derision. 'Your good name? Don't make me laugh.'

'I'd nothing to do with those murders. Fuck sake, I'm telling you the truth and the video proves my whereabouts.'

'If you are found to be withholding anything of significance relating to the stabbings we will come down on you so hard that you'll wish you were still sitting on your mother's knee.'

'Seriously man, I haven't seen X-Ray for years. Not since school. We don't mix in the same circles. Besides, I'm not into hurting people. My kind of rampage involves a party vibe.'

They let Brady go and headed back to the office.

'Well, what are you thinking?' Malachy asked.

'He seems legit. Like a legit dickhead. Check out his alibi with the club and look into who was trying to make him look dirty. Might have been a ruse to take our attention elsewhere.'

Malachy nodded. 'Leave it with me. I'll speak to Henderson from undercover. He works a snitch known to frequent the kind of dives that pay Conal Brady to play his wee dance tunes.'

CHAPTER 27

Rose woke just after dawn, slick with sweat. The bedroom was suffocating. She got up and opened the window, but even the morning air felt stagnant. The heat wave didn't seem to be breaking. The news was full of reports of threatened hose pipe bans and warnings not to leave dogs in cars. She was more accustomed to experiencing four seasons in one day in Belfast, not this interminable choking heat.

Returning to bed, she lay considering the case. Katy Carberry's account painted Eden in a pretty good light. There was nothing beyond rumour to suggest she was anything other than a dutiful mother trying to care for her children without the support of her husband. Single mothers in a working class, conservative Catholic community would have been frowned upon. There was no doubt that in the eighties, Eden would have been a source of ridicule and gossip.

Then there was the priest Katy talked about, Father Ryan. Who was he in all this? A concerned man of the cloth looking out for a parishioner? Or was there anything more to his interest in Eden? Priests were bound by their vows to protect dark secrets whispered in confessional boxes. Maybe the priest knew Eden's secrets. Had he revealed what she had told him and somehow put her life in danger? Maybe, given the passage of time, he would be willing to share his take on what happened to Eden. His leaving may have been a timely coincidence, but Rose needed to check it out. If the priest was still alive, that is.

She thought of the house at Dunlore and the remains of the half-burnt papers in the fireplace grate. She needed to see if Danny had anything back from forensics to help identify what the papers contained.

Oliver McGoldrick didn't flag up on her searches of security and intelligence handlers. He seemed to have been a legitimate barrister working mainly medical negligence cases. Still, she wanted to make sure there was no possibility of someone carrying out the murders as a way of coming after the McGoldricks.

Her mind turned to her mother, Evelyn. She had last heard from her when she was nineteen. Rose had sent a letter to Kaitlin and Evelyn had intercepted it. She had written to Rose, calling her a traitor who had turned her back on her family. Hate-filled words that made Rose surer than ever that her leaving had been the right thing to do.

They were never going to have a close relationship. Whatever tenuous bonds they'd had, had been broken when Rose left. The memories had been hard to shake but she had worked hard at keeping them buried.

Now, though, the talk of the old Markets area in Belfast, where her mother and father had come from, had been needling at her. The idea that the close-knit community was a hive of shadows and secrets made her curious to know who Evelyn really was, and if she was as bad as Rose believed her to be.

She shut off all thinking about her messed-up origins and decided her next step was to track down Geordie Mulligan. If he had nothing to do with Eden's disappearance then why had he never returned to look after his children? For the first time in her career, Rose felt that she was solving a mystery as much as a crime.

She tracked Danny down in the conference room, where he was busy covering the old-fashioned whiteboard with information pertaining to the case.

'Hey, Danny, got a minute?'

'Sure, what can I do?'

'It's about Geordie Mulligan. I think he sounds dubious.'

'You know what they say, it's usually the husband.'

'I think it's more than a bit suspect that he never returned to Belfast after Eden vanished.'

He turned around and set the pile of papers on a desk. 'What would his motive be?'

'That he was jealous of Eden. She was a good-looking woman who would have attracted attention whether she wanted it or not. Maybe Geordie suspected she was having an affair and in a drunken rage he killed her. The kids could have covered for him.'

'Didn't the initial police investigation say Geordie was working away at the time of Eden's disappearance?'

Rose leaned against the wall. 'Can we trust any of that though? The timelines are murky. It could be that someone said he was away and it became embedded in memory. We don't even have an actual date for Eden's disappearance. And he never returned to Belfast. Not even to take care of his children. Surely that has to raise questions.'

Danny agreed that she should get the go ahead to contact Geordie Mulligan, to see if he was still alive and to decide whether or not he had a hand in the mystery. If Katy Carberry was right, he could be still in England.

Back at her desk, she fired up her computer and checked her emails. It was full of the usual stuff from human resources about training opportunities.

It had been six days since Rose had walked into the station and become involved in the Dunlore and Mulligan cases. News of the graffiti left on the living room wall had been leaked to the press, and all hell had broken loose. The Stephen Nolan radio show had everyone and his granny phoning in with their opinion on what had happened. Some claimed that the murders had been the work of paramilitaries cracking down on drug suppliers, others claimed collusion and retaliation for Eden Mulligan's disappearance. Funny how, in Belfast, nobody liked to talk to the police but plenty had an opinion they were happy to share on a radio show. An immediate inquiry had shown that the information had come from outside the force, most likely from the McGoldricks or their groundsman.

McCausland had scheduled a meeting with Rose, primarily to review her work to date. She was keen to press on and to be allowed to play a bigger part in the investigation. If her role was limited to interviewing an unreliable witness, she really didn't need to be hanging around.

Rose knocked on the opened door of the ACC's office and walked in. McCausland was sat reading a file of notes and didn't look up. She stood for a moment, waiting for him to acknowledge her, and when she got no response, she spoke.

'Sir, we have a meeting.'

He put his hand up to silence her as he read on.

'Sit,' he said, finally giving her his attention.

Rose knew it wasn't necessary to get on with your ACC, but it would have been helpful. She disliked Ian McCausland. He had the air of a man convinced of his own importance, and it was clear he liked to be treated with the respect he believed he deserved. Rank wasn't enough for Rose to bow down to him. She had yet to feel he deserved anything other than polite courtesy. Once again, his neck spilled over his collar in a pink roll, and she wondered how he could stick the tightness of it cutting into his flesh.

'Lainey, I gather you have been down to the Dunlore cottage?'

'Yes, Sir. It's useful to see the scene and to understand the larger issues at play.'

'What issues would they be?'

'I'm referring to the graffiti. It suggests that the stabbings were in some way connected to the previous missing persons case. I'm sure you know my background. I have experience in missing person cases and unreliable testimonies.'

'And you think there is some sort of link between these brutal murders and a cold case going back thirty odd years?' His tone let her know that he didn't believe the two were connected.

'That has to be established, Sir, but I'm sure you agree it must be looked at and there's enough of a connection for me to be involved in a more all-encompassing role, don't you think?'

'Lainey, I think our missing woman is unlikely to turn up at this stage. Some cases are never solved. We do a review, satisfy our sense of duty, and move on. I'm sure you'd like to be doing some real work instead of sitting in that basement office, reading over old interview transcripts.'

Rose noticed tiny beads of sweat gathering on his forehead like little blisters. The heat was insufferable.

'To ensure I do a full and proper review I need resources and support. If there's a link between the Dunlore deaths and the Mulligan case, I need to be able to investigate freely.'

McCausland looked at her, fixing her with his steely gaze. 'You *are* the support, Lainey. The answers needed to solve the Dunlore case won't lie in the past.'

'Sir, for all we know, the answer to Eden Mulligan's disappearance lies in the present.'

'Conduct your inquiry with due diligence and care, but wrap it up as quickly as possible. Then write a report and move on. Danny Stowe and his team are capable of ruling out any Mulligan connection with their case and they don't need you trampling all over their crime scene and muddying the waters. That leak to the press shouldn't have happened. I don't want the Mulligan case being stirred up in the papers any more than it already has. There's nothing to be gained in getting the family's hopes up.' He went back to his reading, effectively dismissing Rose.

'One more thing, Sir, I need clearance to trace Geordie Mulligan, Eden's husband. He never returned after Eden's disappearance and I want to follow up on him. Iona Gardener is still off limits, so my hands are tied there. I can make better use of my time by helping DI Stowe review the Mulligan connection.'

He sighed. 'Fine, do it, but cases from the past are never black and white. Sometimes we have to be prepared to leave the past behind.'

CHAPTER 28

Secrets rarely stay hidden unless those keeping them have something to lose. Rose had worked with enough victims and perpetrators to know that the worst kind of secret can burn deep and become a burden that few people want to carry to the grave. In Rose's mind, whoever had taken Eden had murdered her. They wouldn't be sleeping easily. Sooner or later, the shell of protection would fracture into tiny fissures and the murkiness below would ooze out into the light. Rose wanted to be the one who cracked it. She also knew that the best keepers of secrets were family members. A sense of loyalty often ensured silence.

Tracking down Geordie hadn't been too difficult. He was living in north London, renting a small flat on the outskirts of Chalk Farm. Long since retired, he was claiming benefits and trying to make it through to his next birthday. The flight to London was brief and uneventful. It would be a quick turnaround, a meeting with Geordie Mulligan, with a return flight at seven in the evening. A quick visit to her flat before her appointment with Geordie had allowed her to collect some extra clothes and had been a chance to empty the fridge.

The meeting was scheduled to take place in a police station on Chalk Farm Road, north London, rather than at his house. She arrived early and found a café to sit in, sipping a coffee while people watching. A dark-skinned man with a shaved head and bright pink Adidas trainers was reading Haruki Murakami's *Norwegian Wood* at the table beside her. An American tourist was talking loudly into her mobile phone and an elderly woman was secreting sachets of sugar into her pocket. The vibrancy, the hustle – it all allowed for anonymity. A city of millions was easy to hide in.

At eleven, Rose made her way to the station. She wasn't sure what she was going to get out of Geordie, but his absence from his children's lives needed to be explained. She introduced herself to the desk sergeant and was shown into an interview room where Geordie was waiting. He had the look of a drinker, a man of slight build, almost entirely bald, with inflamed, scabby skin that looked as if he picked at it on a regular basis. A lifetime of labouring work and drinking had taken its toll and he was obviously in bad health. A junior constable was sitting with him.

'Hello, Geordie. Dr Rose Lainey.' She reached out to shake his hand as she approached him. As she sat back down Rose noted his spittle flecked lips, and rheumy eyes that gave the impression he was on the verge of tears.

'Thank you for coming to meet me. Can I get you a coffee or tea?'

'I'll take a tea. And it's not like I had much choice. Scared the life out of me when that police car pulled up outside my house. Didn't know what they wanted.' His Belfast accent had mellowed and was tinged with a London dialect. The constable offered to do the tea run and returned quickly with a tray set up.

'Milk?' he asked.

'Aye, please.' Geordie accepted the mug of tea and stirred it, waiting for Rose to start.

'I'm sorry about the police car, but I'm conducting the investigation from Belfast, and it was easier to send an officer round to verify you were the correct Geordie Mulligan before I hopped on a plane to come over here. We need to make it official, so I will be recording this interview.'

The constable pressed the record button. 'Interview conducted with Geordie Mulligan at 12.20 p.m.; Constable Khalid in attendance with Dr Rose Lainey acting on behalf of the PSNI.'

'Fair enough. So, this is about Eden, isn't it? After all this time, have they found her body?' His voice cracked as he spoke.

'No, we haven't found a body, but I'm looking into her disappearance. There was never any evidence to say she was killed, so what makes you think there's a body to be found?'

'Oh, come on. What else could it be? In those days, people disappeared for looking in the wrong direction. I always figured that Eden had crossed someone – someone connected – and she paid the price. Either that or she was killed because someone had the wrong idea about me. I thought maybe someone had pointed the finger. Marked me out as a tout or something.'

'When did you first know Eden was missing?'

'Not for a while after. I was never in one place long

enough to settle in those days. Went wherever the work was.

'A fella, originally from Antrim, who worked the building sites with me said he'd heard about it when he was back in Belfast. He'd seen the story covered on the local news. Knew she was my wife. I was always the one to phone home from whatever digs I was staying in, so the kids didn't have a number to get hold of me.

'At first, I didn't know what to do. I thought about the kids, but selfish bastard that I am, I didn't have it in me to go back and look after them. Seemed too big a job for me.'

'Did the police or social services never track you down?'

His head dropped to his chest. 'Yeah, eventually they caught up with me. Asked me what I wanted to do about the children.'

'What did you say?'

'Told them they weren't my concern any longer. That I wanted nothing to do with them and that they'd be better off in care.' He lifted his head. 'Then one night, must have been five years later, I saw it on the TV. They were doing some programme about the Troubles and the Disappeared. Christ it stopped me in my tracks all right. They had a photograph of Eden. God, she was a looker.' He stopped to wipe at his eye.

'By then I was living in the Isle of Man. Belfast seemed like another lifetime ago.'

'Neighbours on Moss Street said you always returned to see the family regularly. That is, until Eden disappeared. What made you suddenly stay away?'

He leaned back on the chair and sighed. 'A couple of months before Eden disappeared, I received a letter telling me not to return to Belfast, and saying that if I did, I would be executed. No reason given. Signed P. O'Neill. Just in case I hadn't got the message loud and clear, they'd sent a bullet along with it. For a while, I thought Eden was behind it, thought she'd gone to the paramilitaries and told them I'd beat her, or worse, raped her. God knows I never put a finger on that girl without her say so. She'd a way of making me feel like I didn't deserve her but I loved her. Loved the bones of her. The trouble was, she knew she could have done better than me. Much better.'

Rose knew that it wasn't unusual for letters of the type Geordie described to be sent as warning to anyone falling on the wrong side of the paramilitaries. P. O'Neill was a cover name for the IRA army council.

He stopped for a moment and took a sip of his tea, cupping his hands around the red mug.

'Eden could've had her pick of men and she deserved more than I could give her. It was easier to lose myself in the drink, or run away to work, than to live with the fear that one day she'd tell me to go for good.'

Rose nodded to encourage him to keep talking.

'I always carried a photo of her, showed it to the lads on the building sites, made them all jealous. God, she was a beauty.' He looked away, as if embarrassed by the force of his feelings.

'In those days, if you were warned to stay out of the country you heeded that warning. As far as I was concerned, there was no going back. I would have risked a bullet in the back of my head.'

'What about your children?'

'You think I didn't miss them? I regret every day that I wasn't there for them. When I heard about Eden going missing, well, I thought they had taken her instead of me.

It had crossed my mind on a few occasions that maybe the letter hadn't been at Eden's request. Anyone could have pointed the finger at me – said I threatened them, or that I was passing information on to the army. I never did, though.' He stared into Rose's eyes intently.

'But I knew if the suggestion of informing had been made, I had no way of disproving it. The threat was enough to scare the life clean out of me.' He scratched at his neck, the skin red and raw. 'If they took Eden and I was out of the country, well then, I figured it was best for the kids if I stayed away. Suppose I justified it to myself. I was a heavy drinker in those days. I've often wondered if I had said something I shouldn't have when I was on the beer and whiskeys. Insulted someone who wears the balaclava and the beret. Who knows? Whatever it was over, it cost Eden her life and me my family.'

She studied Geordie. He was an old man transposed to another country, exiled from his family by the hold the paramilitaries had over his community, with a lifetime of regrets and nothing but theories as to how he had ended up there.

'Do you still have the letter?' she asked.

'No, burnt it long ago. Threw it into the fire one night when I was morose from the drink and the memories. Watched it go up in flames as I drank myself into a stupor. I woke the next day and told myself to put it all behind me. Tried to get on with making a living. Didn't forget the threat or my children, but did my best to move on.'

He paused and looked down into his tea.

'Do you believe in ghosts, Miss Lainey?'

'No, can't say I do.'

'Well I can tell you, I've seen Eden's ghost many times. She's always watching, waiting for me to slip up. She's the only thing that keeps me away from the drink. I know beyond all certainty that if I give in and down a whiskey, she'll get me. I wasn't the husband she needed me to be.'

Rose saw fear and sorrow in his eyes. A life spent on the run from the ghosts of his past was no way to live. His revelations hadn't moved the case along any, but it had at least clarified in Rose's mind that he had nothing to do with Eden's disappearance. He had been a worthless husband and an absent father, but he wasn't a murderer.

CHAPTER 29

Danny woke from a bad dream with a feeling of dread. He couldn't recall what he'd dreamt about but knew it had been something unnerving and most likely relating to Amy. He turned over and checked the time on his phone. Only 6.05 a.m. and it was already warm. He'd another full-on day ahead of him, but for now he wanted to close his eyes and chill before the work of the day took over.

He thought of his father, out working on the farm from dawn, and how he would've chided Danny for lying in his bed when the day had already begun. It had been a few weeks since he had gone to visit his parents. Lately, he couldn't face it. The long drive home, the forced small talk, and the pretence that he was interested in farming, were all too much. He'd avoided telling them about him and Amy. It wasn't as if they loved Amy exactly. They had grown used to her. Liked her, even, but she had never really fit in. Her sophisticated ways, her need for constant reassurance and her fragility had meant that they had never had a chance to really get to know her. She seemed like a mystery to them. Danny blamed himself for this. He had never really helped them understand their delicate flower of a daughter-in-law, preferring instead to keep them pretty much separate in his life and in his head. Sure, she was brought along at Christmas and special family events, but by and large his Belfast life stayed in Belfast. This applied to his working life too. He knew they worried about him, scanned the news for any bombs or dangerous cases, but the less he mentioned work, the less they asked.

Since his marriage had ended, he'd preferred to spend his weekends working. The extra hours on a case as complex as the Dunlore one were necessary. No one was going to give him a gold star for knocking himself out, but if he didn't get a result soon, he'd have to answer to his superiors.

The demands of the job were both a salve and a torture. Danny appreciated the ability to lose himself in a case, to become entranced in the evidence, the data, the findings and the procedures. He knew only too well that every case brings with it new possibilities for fucking up. Ever since the Lennon case he'd felt the potential for failure keenly. He may have led investigations in the past, been successful in bringing them to a close, but he had no certainty that he would be so lucky again. And he did think of it as luck, to a degree. There were many variants at play. Yes, he knew how to carry out his duties and follow protocol to ensure that the investigation was thorough, legitimate, and he had allowed no unconscious bias to damage his work. But he realised that people fucked up and in the depths of his despair he feared he would do so again.

He'd failed in his marriage too. He wondered, if he had

known marriage to Amy was going to be so fraught, would he have run for the hills or would he have signed up anyway? It was hard to tell. Back then, he'd loved her enough to think it would get them through any dark times. Now he knew different.

But still, he missed the companionship. The shared rhythm of living together. He wasn't made to be single. All of the nightclub trawling, looking to meet someone, was never his thing. Even when he was a student, hanging out with Rose was how he preferred to spend his time. The en masse pub crawls and drinking until you were off your face didn't get a look in compared to a night of playing Scrabble with Rose while listening to Radiohead.

The heat of the last few days was alien and intrusive. It made him think of cheap summer holidays, cocktails drunk under parasols, and bodies slick with sun cream. Belfast wasn't itself at all. Everyone was talking about the inconvenience of having to work in hot weather, as if they should have a reprieve in honour of the surprisingly high temperatures.

The basement office offered a welcome coolness. Rose seemed to have become accustomed to the gloom and found it a productive place to work. He could still hardly believe she was here working alongside him.

'Hey, boss. I've heard back from Henderson about Conal Brady,' Malachy said, as he stuck his head through the door frame.

'And?'

'He said Brady has a reputation for ambition both within the drug and music scene. Unless Dylan Wray was a rival dealer, it's unlikely that Brady would have gone after him.

Also, the nightclub alibi checked out – he was indeed standing on a stage playing shite dance tunes to a bunch of headers. But that's not to say that there wasn't something going on between them. Brady could have paid someone else to do his dirty work.'

Danny blew out a breath. Malachy was right. Conal Brady's alibi may have checked out, but he was worth keeping an eye on.

'Let's do a bit of digging on Dylan Wray, see if anything turns up that would implicate Brady. Have they had any contact recently, any shared connections? Check Dylan Wray's phone. It was found at the cottage.'

'Right, Sir, on it,' Malachy said leaving the office.

The week's itinerary was laid out on the screen in front of him, of which the most pressing event was a meeting with the ACC to go over the findings to date. Before that, he had plans to speak to the former investigating officer on the Eden Mulligan case. He had long since retired, happy to have his handsome pay out and to spend his days on the Malone golf course. In advance of the meeting, Danny looked over the spreadsheet Rose had created detailing the timeline of the interviews that had been conducted during the original investigation. The initial reluctance to treat Eden's disappearance as anything other than a runaway mother had prevented vital information being gathered at the start. That reluctance to initiate a proper search and inquiry needled Danny. Identifying the reasons for this, and speaking to the officer who had made that call to not follow up concerns voiced by the family and neighbours, was important. It could help clarify certain issues that had played on Danny's mind.

* * *

Former Detective Inspector Victor Mason walked with a brisk step for a man in his seventies. His upright, rigid posture suggested a military background, but as far as Danny knew, his service had only ever been with the Royal Ulster Constabulary, the old Northern Irish police service, not the army.

'Mr Mason, thank you for meeting me,' Danny offered, standing to greet him.

'Not at all. I'm honoured to be of service, even after all this time.' He sat on the plastic chair and arranged himself until he was comfortable, then rested his hands on the table, a gold signet ring on his little finger.

'This is about the Mulligan case. You want to talk to me about the investigation, I believe?'

'Yes, I am conducting a review of the case, trying to shine some new light on what happened.'

'Good luck with that. In my opinion, for what it's worth, cases like that one are best left well alone. Waste of valuable time and police resources. I'm sure there are plenty more pressing cases for you to look at.'

'No doubt we could say that the case doesn't merit our time, but we owe it to Eden Mulligan's family to do our best,' Danny replied, disliking how the man had pursed his thin lips in disapproval.

'Well, if the case needs to be re-examined I am certain you will find no wrongdoing on the part of me or my colleagues, but please keep in mind they were different times we were working in.'

Danny reached for his file to look at his notes. He wanted the older man to feel the weight of officialdom. To know that he wasn't having a cosy chat with one of the boys.

Victor sat back in his chair, as if to brace himself.

'Shall we begin? Can you tell me what you remember about the Eden Mulligan case?'

'After she disappeared, most people thought she had simply gone to England to track down the husband. Geordie, I think he was called. A worthless drunk, by all accounts. That seemed to be the most likely scenario.

'The papers at the time described her as a good time girl. For a mother of five she certainly kept herself well clothed and all dolled up. There was no shortage of money for the latest fashion and trips to the hairdressers. You have to ask where did that money come from? I did wonder, was there a fancy man on the side? Someone with a bit of money who was slipping her a few pounds to help stretch the money the husband was sending home. We never identified him, the fancy man, if he did exist, but if you ask me there was something going on.' His mouth was twisted into a grimace, his disproval of Eden Mulligan and how he assumed she conducted her life was clear.

Danny sighed and cocked his head to the side. 'There was no proof that she had a lover or that she was involved in anything, was there?'

Mason stiffened his shoulders back, as if asserting his superiority. 'Not as such, but we never had the opportunity to dig too far. Maybe something had occurred to bring her into contact with the paramilitaries. She could have inadvertently rubbed someone up the wrong way. You have to understand that in those days the hold they had over the place was powerful. People were scared to be seen with the wrong person. Frightened to say the wrong word. Communities kept to their own. It was safer that way.

Maybe Eden had a lover from across the barricades, so to speak. And then there had been the incident six months before she went missing.'

'What incident?' asked Danny.

'A house of a known paramilitary man was to be raided and somehow, as so often happened with those things, the IRA got wind of it. Their priority was to move a weapons stash that had been housed in a stable in the Markets area. In those days, there were a few stables down that end of town. There was even a blacksmith's up until the mid-seventies. Anyhow, the women of the street were called on to hide guns in prams, and to push them through the town, on to another location – somewhere up the Falls Road, I believe.' He worried at his chin, tapping his fingers in an odd way. 'Sorry, Parkinson's. Plays up every now and then.'

Danny nodded.

'Where was I? Yes, the weapons. It was thought that Eden could have been asked to take some of the guns and refused. That wouldn't have gone down well within the Markets area. Not enough to see her killed maybe, but enough to see her threatened, taken away and taught a lesson. Perhaps something went wrong and she was killed accidentally.'

'Victor, if you don't mind me saying, what you have told me is all conjecture. Was there no evidence collected?'

'DI Stowe, please understand that Northern Ireland in 1986 was in the midst of a terror campaign. I don't mean to be obtuse, but a runaway mother wasn't high up on anyone's agenda. Even public pressure for a satisfactory outcome was absent. In those days, things happened in communities that were best left alone. I suppose that you need to have lived through those times to understand. Some cases just have blind spots. Not every crime is committed in full view of witnesses or CCTV cameras.' His body twitched, as if attached to invisible electrodes. Danny noted the defensive tone, that sense of being blameless, because that was how the system worked back then. Self-important wanker.

'Still, I would have expected a more thorough investigation. People don't just disappear into thin air without someone knowing something.'

Mason lifted his chin and gave Danny a stern look. 'I agree, but again, you need to keep in mind the RUC were a credit to their Queen and country. We served under extreme circumstances and were disciplined, dedicated professionals. A young one like yourself can't possibly know the strain our force was under. Communities were tight. Even if someone knew something, it was in their best interest to keep quiet. People were killed for passing on less,' he added.

Danny had become accustomed to this reticence. This sense that the past was an intransigent place that had to be treated with deference.

Mason placed one hand over the other to steady the tremors. 'Remember there was no CCTV in those days and we had no witnesses to say that they saw Eden Mulligan being taken. For all we know, she could have decided to throw herself into the Lagan. No one would have blamed her. A young mother trying to scrape by with five kids to feed and clothe. That would be enough to break anyone's spirit. We can't even be sure that there were nefarious elements at play. She could have died by her own hand or left home freely of her own accord.'

Danny listened to his assertions and wondered what it was about Eden Mulligan that made her fair game. Victor Mason's attitude towards the mother and his lack of concern for her welfare made Danny more curious than ever to know who Eden Mulligan really was, and to find out what set of circumstances brought about her disappearance.

CHAPTER 30

Rose wasn't expecting anyone but when the buzzer went, she was sure it could only be Danny.

'Whiskey?' she said, raising her eyebrows at the sight of him carrying a litre bottle of Bushmills. 'It's that kind of night, is it?'

Danny said nothing and followed her into the apartment.

'What is it with these places? They all look out at nothingness. A blank expanse of stagnant water. Soulless living at its best.' He gestured towards the window, his reflection looking back at him like a distorted fairground mirror.

'Somebody's in a bad mood. What's up?' Rose asked, retrieving two glasses from a cupboard in the kitchenette area.

'Nothing. Everything. I just wanted company. Someone to talk shop to.'

Rose sat on the little sofa beside him. He was leaning forward with his hands raking through his hair. She could tell he had already been drinking. The rosiness of his cheeks gave him away – that, and the scent of smoke. She knew he used to smoke when he was drunk. A habit he had blamed her on. A bad influence he had called her, on more than one night out.

'So, what's going on? Is the case getting to you?' Rose knew that pressure had been building for the team to get a result. She knew enough of policing to know that the job got under your skin. You couldn't help taking home the stench of death and the only way to find peace was in doing a job well and seeing the culprits put away. But that pressure, that need to see justice done, was like a boulder chasing you down a hill, ever present and ever threatening. That was part of the reason she had never pursued a career in the police in the first place.

Danny threw himself back on the sofa and placed his long legs up onto the glass coffee table. 'Make yourself at home, why don't you?' Rose said, not annoyed, just concerned. He seemed out of control. Not like his usual careful, considered self. She could see the exhaustion on his face. The shadows of lost sleep and the strain of a complex murder case. Occupational hazards. He passed a hand over his hair again, which Rose noticed was beginning to thin a bit on top. She'd have to slag him about that when he was in better form. She was used to Danny being the one to pick her up, to keep the mood light. Tonight, he gave the impression of a man ready to cry, or to punch someone's lights out for no particular reason. Either would be the release he looked like he needed.

Rose leaned back beside him, handing him the glass with a measure of whiskey. 'Talk me through what's bothering you.'

'My wife has instructed a solicitor to oversee our separation. I suppose this makes me a free man.' His words sounded bitter.

Rose waited. She had always been the one with a reluctance to let him in, and Danny respected this. But Danny, well, he was usually an open book. He downed the whiskey and handed her the empty glass to refill.

'I'm surprised. You didn't say anything,' Rose eventually said.

'What like, hey Rosie, good to see you after all this time. By the way, my marriage has failed. I fucked up.'

'You could've talked to me.'

'Yeah, like how you've talked to me over the years.' His tone was bitter.

Rose looked away. She could hardly blame him.

'Talk to me now. I'm here. You must have known this was coming, so why has it hit you so bad?'

'Because I never wanted the divorce in the first place. None of this was meant to happen.'

His voice cracked with emotion and Rose placed her hand on his back. 'Tell me, but only if you want to. Why did it all go wrong?'

'It's fucked up, the whole bloody relationship. Fucked up from beginning to end.' He leaned forward with his head in his hands.

'You think when you're young that if you love someone that will be everything. That all they need is your love and if they love you back, well, you're made for life. Funny how when you grow up you realise all that love is a load of bollocks.'

Rose didn't respond. She waited for him to continue.

'All the love in the world couldn't have fixed Amy. She's anorexic.'

179

'I'm sorry,' Rose said, not knowing what else to say.

'She's had it since she was a teenager. There's times when she can't eat. When it's physically impossible for her to let food pass through her lips. Jesus, it was worse than if she'd been having an affair with the lies and the secrecy. Avoiding food was like a full-time job for her. I've been there for her during those times, but we all thought she was getting better. We were planning a family. She had to maintain a good weight in order to get pregnant, and we thought this time it was all behind us, the secrets, and the lies about food.' He took a drink of the whiskey and set the glass back on the table.

'I wanted kids. We both did. I thought that if she had a little one to live for, to love, she would stay well. I figured if she can't do it for me then hey, she'd do it for our baby. That probably sounds messed up.'

Rose shook her head. 'No, it doesn't. I can see why you'd think like that.'

'Yeah, well, Amy got pregnant. In spite of all of the starvation, her body managed to function enough to allow the pregnancy to take. For a few weeks, we were delighted. Amy seemed to be doing okay but then she had a miscarriage.' He dragged his fingers through his hair.

'Or at least, that's what she told me. Turns out she had gone to London and had an abortion. She'd lied to me, said she was on a weekend trip with her sister to see a show. Instead, she had gone to a clinic and paid them to get rid of the baby. Just like that, no need for me even to know, let alone give consent.'

Rose groaned. 'Danny, no wonder you're a mess.'

'Yeah, and before you tell me it's her body and all that feminist stuff, I *know*. I know she was the one having to carry the baby through the nine months of pregnancy, give birth and all the rest, but Jesus, I would have been right there alongside her, doing whatever the hell I could for her.'

'Did she tell you why she did it?'

'She didn't need to. Her anorexia, it screws up her head.' He gestured at his temple. 'She has this mortal fear of her body changing. I know if she had been well, things would have been different. But after what she did, well, I couldn't stay with her. I couldn't look at her without thinking about what she'd done, so I left.'

'Why didn't you say something sooner? You could've told me,' Rose said. She couldn't help feeling hurt that he hadn't talked to her. She felt sad too, that she had let him down by keeping her own defences up. How could she have ever expected Danny to lean on her when she never allowed him to see the vulnerable parts of herself? God, at times she could be so selfishly wrapped up in her own problems.

'Shame, I suppose. What kind of woman aborts her wanted child, and what kind of man abandons his sick wife? Told you it was fucked up.'

Rose took her hand away from his back. 'Hey, you know me better than that. I wouldn't judge either of you. Life's complicated. Amy needs to deal with her own issues. You can't fix her.'

'I felt that I should have been able to help her. I was embarrassed that she couldn't get a hold of herself and then for her to get a termination, well, she went too far. There's no coming back from this.'

'I'm sorry Dan, but you have to see that it's Amy's body. She was the one having to carry the child. She couldn't cope with that and we can't sit in judgement. But you have to go easier on yourself, too. You're not to blame for any of this, and maybe you couldn't have saved your marriage even if this hadn't happened. Sounds to me like it was doomed from day one.'

Danny shrugged his shoulders. 'It was good in the beginning and in the bits in-between.' His voice was low and filled with hurt.

For a while he rested his head on her shoulder and they sat staring out across the city lights. Gradually the night drew in around them. When they'd drunk enough whiskey, they ordered in Chinese food and the conversation drifted back to work as they ate.

'The wounds were consistent with a frenzied attack. The pathologist's report says that the assailant was probably male, owing to the depth and force of the wounds. He was manic in his approach.'

Rose forked a piece of sauce-glistened beef. 'Yet, he had arranged the bodies. He went to great care to carry them up to that bedroom and place them into the bed. That doesn't suggest a manic approach – more of an ordered, planned out strategy. For some reason, he wanted the three bodies to be found together. So, what does that tell us?'

'I don't know. Not yet.' Danny said.

'The McGoldricks didn't seem nervous or particularly stressed. Just concerned. I don't suspect them but that doesn't mean we won't find anything to implicate them.'

'And Conal Brady – the druggie DJ – while he knew Dylan Wray at school, we can't link them now. Tania checked Dylan's phone. There were no unusual call patterns and the most interesting thing to flag up was that outside of the friends in the house, he didn't phone anyone.'

Danny got up, walked over to the kitchen area and poured

himself a glass of water. 'Maybe their final movements might hold some clue of what was to come. I don't think this was random. The killer had to know the victims, he had to have had some sort of connection with them. This wasn't a burglary gone wrong, or a domestic dispute. This was the unusual – a cold, calculated murderer creating a bloodbath.'

Rose thought about what Danny had said about the Dunlore murders, cold and calculated, yet the scene was a bloodied massacre. There was an art to the killings, a choreography of death played out within the confines of that old cottage, so far removed from the type of violence associated with Northern Ireland's past.

In the past, the opera of violence that was conducted by terrorists every day was replicated in every living room via the local news and it was all consuming. Programmes were interrupted by police reports asking key holders of businesses to return to their premises to look for incendiary devices. A new language evolved to express the chaos of violence: knee-cappings, pipe bombs, shrapnel, collateral damage. Deadlock, insurgency, paramilitary. The language of war cloaked in officialdom. A whitewash from Whitehall. The official words owed more to police reports than to local people but they adopted the words as their own and were soon fluent in the language of political violence. That had been life for the Mulligan family in 1986.

CHAPTER 31

Despite working in a clinical environment for part of her career, Rose hated hospitals. The endless corridors punctuated with illness-inspired art. It was designed to make the spaces better yet only served to remind you of your own mortality. It made her want to run. The antiseptic smell made her feel queasy and there was always something of the apocalypse about the endless hallways and a sense that they'd be the place you would find the zombies waiting for you in times of danger.

They took the lift to the third floor, following the directions to the intensive care unit where Dylan Wray was being treated. At the entrance way, an upset family of three stood in a tight huddle crying softly, their arms wrapped around each other. Rose apologised as she moved past them to press the intercom buzzer on the wall.

The ICU nurses had been informed that they were coming so when they gave their names, they were allowed through to see Dylan. The ward was eerily quiet and populated with bays of beds with patients hooked up to machines, ventilators and IV stands. Dylan was in the third bay to the left. His eyes were closed and he was receiving a blood transfusion. A male nurse sat on a stool in front of a monitor taking notes.

'How's he doing?' asked Rose quietly.

'He's still critical, but stable. His white blood cells are up, which means there's an infection to deal with, and he's lost a lot of blood,' the nurse replied before turning to adjust a line running the length of Dylan's bed before snaking under his arm. Rose noted the deep lacerations around his face and neck, neatly stitched with black thread. He was wearing a cotton hospital gown that gaped at the top, showing yet more stiches and staples on his shoulder, running to his collar bone.

Danny walked around to the side of the bed. 'Dylan, are you able to hear me?'

The male nurse turned. 'He's out of it, mate. We're keeping him in an induced coma to stop the swelling in the brain. It's possible he can hear you, but he won't be able to respond.'

Danny bent down and said directly into Dylan's ear, 'We are going to get whoever did this to you and your friends. Hang in there.'

'The family are around if you need to speak to them. You'll probably find them in the visitors' waiting room.'

'Thanks,' Rose said.

They found the visitors' waiting room and approached the lone couple sitting holding hands.

'Mr and Mrs Wray?' Danny said. 'DI Stowe. We met a couple of days ago. This is my colleague, Dr Lainey.'

The man stood up and then sat back down quickly, as if he couldn't trust his legs to take his weight. 'Any word on who did this?'

'We're working on it,' said Rose.

'We were in seeing Dylan. This must be so hard for you both. If we can do anything, please just let the family liaison officer know.'

'The only thing you can do for us is to find out who did this to our son and why,' the mother said, her voice quiet and low. She stared straight ahead, as though making eye contact was too much effort.

It was obvious that they could do nothing more, so they left and walked back to the car park. 'How do we make sense of this for the families? They look at us as if we can give them all the answers, and the truth is, even if we catch who did it, we still may never truly know why.'

'Can't say I blame them. It must be the most awful pain to cope with,' Rose replied, fastening her seatbelt.

'The post-mortems should be back later today, so we'll review them in the briefing with the team tomorrow morning. It might be useful to have your input, if you're around. Care to join us?' Danny said, pulling out onto the roundabout where the two huge metal spherical sculptures stood, known locally as the Balls on the Falls.

'Sure, I'll be there.'

Danny turned on the radio to hear a commentator on Radio Ulster asking why the mass killer hadn't been found.

'Back in the day, at least you knew who the bad guys were. This here is something else. Young people murdered in their beds. Honestly, you've got to ask what are the PSNI doing?' Rose leaned over and switched the radio off.

CHAPTER 32

The morgue was a good ten degrees colder than outside and Danny welcomed it. The good weather was continuing, surprising everyone, and making the Democratic Unionist Party talking heads look exceptionally stupid, when discussing their belief that climate change was nothing more than a huge con, concocted by the Green Party. They were more likely to attribute the heat wave to a surge in heathenish activity than global warming.

Danny buzzed the inner door of the pathologist's lab and was greeted by Siobhan, the receptionist. 'Back again?' she said, greeting him as she carried a sheaf of paper from the printer. 'He's expecting you.'

'Thanks, I'll go on through then.'

Lyons was leaning against his desk and talking into a Dictaphone when Danny entered the office. He looked up and indicated *one minute* with his free hand. Danny took the liberty of walking to the window and peering into the lab. The three bodies lay on separate steel tables, covered by long paper sheets.

'Sorry about that,' Lyons said. 'Come on through.'

The antiseptic smell mingled with the cadaver scent prickled Danny's nostrils, making him switch to breathing through his mouth. He was well versed in decomposition – the breakdown of the body's tissues and process of putrefaction – and he had to admit that thanks to ventilation and good cleaning practices, modern mortuaries didn't smell half as bad as they could. Attending to a rotting corpse was a different story. Danny had been new to the force when he found the decomposing, maggot-riddled body of a woman who had lain dead and rotting in her bed for over a month while her learning impaired brother had sat playing video games downstairs. He had told the complaining neighbours that the bad smell was a blocked drain. That vile and sickening sweet-rot had stayed with Danny for much longer than he had cared for. After that experience, he knew to be thankful for the clinical mortuary setting.

'You've seen the initial report but sometimes it's good to talk through everything with the bodies in situ,' Lyons said, wasting no time getting to the job. Danny got the impression that he was the type that relished the opportunity to talk through his handiwork. It occurred to Danny that like some doctors and surgeons, Lyons possessed a bit of a god complex, and was lacking in bedside manner. He had found his calling working with corpses, that was for sure.

The lab room itself was windowless, cool and airless, with only the drone of refrigerators and the ventilation system filling the silence.

The first body they came to was Olivia Templeton's. The strong LED lights stripped the last remnants of dignity that the white tissue sheet had provided. She looked younger on the table than she had in the bedroom. Too young to be lying on a mortuary slab with hairy arsed men poking around and making notes on her. Her skin had that ghostly bluish-whiteness, with patches of lividity collecting around the right-hand side. The Y-shaped opening running across her chest and down the torso had been neatly stitched together, but it did little to stop the image of Lyons' hands rummaging inside her from tormenting Danny.

'She died from exsanguination, bleeding out. This incision here was the likely culprit. I've noted a blow to the side of the head. She could have fallen against a piece of furniture during the attack, or maybe she turned quickly to avoid the knife attack and fell. You can also see some grazing around the eye socket. Indications are that she was lying prone when the assailant's knife entered her thorax. When she was unconscious, she was placed in some sort of plastic woven bag and transported to the bedroom. We've found some fibres on all three of the bodies.'

'What kind of woven bag?'

'If I was asked to guess – and a guess is all I'm offering – I'd say some sort of builder's merchant bag. Something to carry rubble or logs in. It would need to be big enough to place a body in, making it easier to carry it up the staircase. I would suggest that the three were killed in the downstairs of the house, then placed one at a time into the bag, and carried up to the bedroom before they were laid out on the bed.

'You can see here' – his gloved hand lifted Olivia's slender finger – 'it was clear that she fought. Some of the nails were broken and the index finger on the right hand is at an odd angle, clearly broken.'

'Any sexual assault?' Danny asked.

'No. No evidence of rape, bleeding or abrasions to the genital area, although there was semen present, suggesting she had sex within the twelve hours previous.'

'So, do we know any specifics other than size of weapon we are looking for? There wasn't anything found at the scene.'

Lyons held up his gloved hand to silence Danny.

'We'll get to that. The amount of force needed to inflict the injuries, and the extent of internal injuries will help me establish the type of knife used.'

He pointed to the hands of Theo Beckett, the second victim, where Danny could see puncture wounds, and a clean slice across the palm. 'The defence wounds indicate capability of the victim to act. These sorts of details allow me to reconstruct the sequence of events and to distinguish between self-inflicted wounds and involvement of another party. There is evidence of metacarpal fractures as well as incision wounds to the hand on this victim. I think we can say this one put up quite a fight.'

'I don't think we are in any doubt that the wounds weren't self-inflicted,' Danny said.

'No, but we can't make assumptions. A multiple murder-suicide has to be ruled out. When dealing with deaths of this kind I am looking specifically at the type of injuries, the number and anatomical distribution of those injuries, and the shape, size, length, and depth of each.' He held a small metal ruler against one of the slashes to show Danny what he was measuring.

'You can see here that by examining the wound itself it is possible to determine the type of instrument used to inflict the injuries. As you'll no doubt be aware, a neat wound indicates the use of a sharp object, such as a knife, whereas ragged wounds would suggest a blunter instrument. In this case, we are looking at the same knife being used on all three victims.'

'Anything else you can tell us about the weapon?'

'Trying to gauge the dimensions of a knife from the wounds can be tricky. There can be problems with skin shrinkage and elasticity of skin when the knife is withdrawn. This can lead to inaccurate approximations of knife size and blade width. Sometimes the blade has entered the skin at a slanted angle, making the length of the entry slit wound longer than expected.'

'If you had to wager a guess?' Danny asked.

'Slender filleting knives penetrate more easily than thicker blades. My opinion would be that it was sharp, fit for purpose. What we can see in many of the incisions is a blade with an approximate thickness of two millimetres that is perhaps around twenty-five centimetres long. My best guess would be some type of carving knife with a laminated steel blade. But like I said, there are many vari-ables in the wounds.'

Danny looked at the neat incision before walking around the three bodies. He could tell Lyons was enjoying his work. Pathologists gave him the creeps. He was sure they were only one step removed from being psychopaths.

'One interesting aspect to note is that the number of stab wounds is higher than necessary to kill the victim. Overkill, as we call it. This may point to a strong emotional conflict between the perpetrator and the victims.'

'Interesting.'

'From looking at the angle and the depth of the incisions, the perpetrator appears to be left-handed and at least five feet ten in height. And yes, he is male.

'The bodies were checked for signs of rigor mortis and lividity at the initial crime scene examination to determine time of death and whether or not the victims had been before or after death. In this case, the bodies were moved post-mortem and deliberately staged by the killer.'

'So, the perpetrator was playing out a precise scene or perhaps wishing to convey some sort of message.'

'That's for you to work out, Detective.' His smugness irritated Danny.

'What else can you tell me about the murderer?'

'In a frenzied case such as this one, it is impossible for the murderer not to leave behind trace elements of their DNA and even fibres of their clothes. We do have some traces for you to run through the system but considering the nature of the attacks and the feverish pattern there are surprisingly few.'

'An absence of data can often be significant in itself. Shows how prepared and precise the killer was. Are we certain that there is only one attacker?'

'One knife man, but I would guess he could have had someone to help him move the bodies.'

Had Iona been the accomplice? Could she have aided the killer in moving and staging the bodies on the bed? She was slightly built and didn't look like she'd the strength for the job, even as a helper, but Danny knew that in times of high stress people can find reserves they didn't know they had.

He left the morgue knowing that despite their best efforts, they were left with a crime scene that gave little away. The killer had been thorough and particular in the staging, despite the murders themselves being feverish and furious. It was a contradiction that bothered Danny.

CHAPTER 33

Danny sat nursing a hand-warmed glass of whiskey. He'd made the mistake of going into McCann's before going home. There was something niggling at him about the case and he couldn't put his finger on it.

The bar was filling up. Too many cops and too much work talk for his liking, and now Constable Tina Ward was making a beeline for him.

'So, Sir, how's it going on the slasher case?' she asked, lifting herself onto the barstool beside him. She was a constable with high hopes of making it into the Serious Crime Unit. Attractive, tall, slender and blonde, she kept her hair in a neat pleated construction at the back of her head that made him think of sexy librarians.

'Now Tina, you know what they say. Say nothing, in case you put the scud on it. What are you drinking?'

'I'll have a prosecco if you're buying.' Her perfume made him think of something sweet and cloying, like fairground candyfloss.

'Is the case going well for you, though? I hear there's

no weapon found, and that the slasher arranged the bodies.'

'Never believe what you hear in the canteen. Unless you're working the case, all the rest is pure speculation, so it is.'

She nodded and took a sip of her drink, her fingers stroking the stem of the glass like she was thinking.

'I'd love to be working a murder case. Is it as cool as they say?' she said, sounding very young and inexperienced to him. He could remember that feeling of being on the outside looking in though. When working on the Serious Crime Unit was the pinnacle of his career dreams. That anything else was just chasing road traffic accidents, burglaries and paperwork.

Danny shrugged. 'It isn't exactly a bed of roses. It's not like on the TV. These are real lives we're dealing with.'

'Sure, I know. I didn't mean to sound disrespectful. I just think that it would feel like we're making a difference. Going after the really bad guys, you know?'

'Sometimes the bad guys win.'

Danny drank the last of his whiskey and decided to call it a night.

'You'll get there one day. In the meantime, keep your nose clean and learn on the job.'

'You're not sticking around? Go on, let me buy you another.' It was tempting. She placed her hand on his and he felt that flicker of connection, that desire to lose yourself in someone else for a while. Sadly, the only relationship he was in these days was with a bottle of Jameson's, and he was determined he wasn't going to complicate matters by bringing a woman into it, even if she was as attractive as Tina, with those blue eyes imploring him to hang around.

'Sorry Tina, I've a big day on tomorrow. Another time, maybe.'

He left her to it, heading out into the still night air and walking towards his apartment building. The whiskey sloshed around in his stomach, reminding him that he hadn't eaten since lunchtime. He knew he'd have to knock the drinking on the head soon. He didn't want to end up being a walking cliché – the divorced cop with a drink problem. No, he knew his limit and it was somewhere close by. He resolved to get cleaned up and hit the gym the next day. A few rounds sparring in the ring would clear his head and help him think. It would be good to sweat the hangover out and hang out where no one gave a shit about his job or his failed marriage.

In the meantime, he had to find what was connecting the Dunlore murders to Eden Mulligan. Why had the killer directed them to re-examine Eden's disappearance and what did that tell them about what had happened at Larchfield?

CHAPTER 34

With Iona still under the auspices of the psychiatric unit, Danny had suggested Rose focus on the Eden Mulligan case.

'See if you can uncover some new angle,' he said. 'There must be something we haven't seen yet.'

Somewhere in the recesses of her brain she remembered Katy Carberry mentioning Father Ryan and the hold he had over the community. How they loved him. A charismatic figure of authority like that could influence someone as lonely and vulnerable as Eden. The parish priest had seemed like a good place to start but she knew that the chances of tracking him down were slim. He could be dead or based anywhere. She knew priests rarely stayed in one parish for too long.

An hour later, she pulled into a church car park with neat hedging all around and a statue of some saint standing in the centre of a mini-roundabout, surrounded by a well-kept flower bed of brightly coloured plants and shrubs. From the church, she drove down the adjacent Carlisle Street until she pulled up at number forty-nine. The parochial house was a large, red brick double fronted Victorian building. It stood in a mature garden alive with bees and the odd bird flitting around in the early morning sunshine. The forecast had warned of thunder and heavy rainfall, but it was hard to believe the heat would dissipate any time soon. Rose rapped on the front door with the huge brass knocker and was greeted by a woman in her sixties with wiry grey hair and a bustling demeanour. She had a yellow duster in her hand and smiled at Rose. 'Hello, come in. *Dominic* is expecting you.' She said Dominic with a kind of emphatic hushed reverence, as if she was at once both honoured to be on intimate first name terms with him and also respectful of his status as priest.

'Father Dominic is just through here in his study. He'll be delighted to see you. He loves to get visitors.'

There was something over-friendly about the way the housekeeper spoke to Rose and she kept touching Rose's arm as she guided her down the hallway.

Rose followed the housekeeper into the book-lined study, where she found Father Dominic working at his computer. The shelves held books of a philosophical nature, tomes on Descartes and Kant and Thomas Aquinas.

He looked up as they entered.

'Detective Lainey, is it?'

'No, Dr Lainey, actually. I'm consulting on this case as a forensic psychologist.'

'Dr Lainey it is then. Please come in. Forensic psychologist – that must be interesting. You might be surprised to hear I'm partial to watching murder mysteries myself.'

'I can assure you that my job isn't as exciting as the TV shows may portray it.'

'Still, it must be interesting. Isn't this weather something else? Simply amazing. We don't know ourselves at all having such a great summer. Trouble is we will be expecting the same again next year.' He laughed.

Rose agreed with him. She didn't like to mention that the spike in high temperatures had given rise to a spike in so-called recreational rioting. The good weather seemed to bring the worst out in the youth of Belfast.

He got up from his desk and shook Rose's hand. 'It's like being in the south of France. Hannah, could you bring us coffee? Or would you prefer tea, Dr Lainey?'

'Coffee is fine, thank you.'

'Why don't we sit in the garden? Hannah, could you bring the coffee out to us, please? And some of those lovely biscuits you buy me.'

Hannah nodded and left them to it. He opened the French doors that led out to a large walled garden. A massive willow tree stood in the far corner, draping its long branches over the lawn, while neat borders of rhodo-dendrons, roses, azaleas, and other shrubs and bushes Rose couldn't name, all fought for space, teeming with colour and life. A painted, green, cast iron table and two chairs sat on a stone patio.

A few phone calls making enquiries about Father Ryan had led Rose here. While she wasn't sure what she would discover she still felt it was worth having a conversation with him.

He pulled out a chair for Rose. 'Please rest yourself here. Now, isn't this better than having a chat at your police station?' He'd been reluctant to meet her at the station and she'd no reason to insist.

'We may need you to speak to us in a more official

capacity at a later date. A visit to the station could be unavoidable.'

Rose sat and took in the view. It was a beautiful spot.

'Isn't this a beautiful place?' the priest said, almost as if he'd read her mind. 'I just love to spend part of my day contemplating the beauty of God's creation. How fortunate am I to find myself here?'

Indeed, thought Rose. She had an innate distrust of the clergy. That self-righteous do-gooding didn't sit well with her, but she did envy their faith, that certainty of knowing there was something beyond this world.

'So, Dr Lainey, Father Ryan brings you to me, I believe?'

'Yes, I was told that you and he were friends.'

'Colleagues, religious brothers, even, but I wouldn't say friends.'

Rose made a note of that.

'I was a young priest when I first met Edmund. He would have been in his fifties by then. You see, my work brought me into contact with priests who had been involved in the Troubles.'

Belfast loved its euphemisms, thought Rose. She'd spent the previous evening trawling through old cases of disappeared women, trying to find a connection with Eden Mulligan, and had found herself reading about the notorious 'Romper Room', where victims were taken to be tried at a kangaroo court and beaten to death.

'I was tasked with correlating and recording the part that the Catholic Church had to play in orchestrating peace. We were there at the table, helping to ensure that the church and the people worked together for the greater good. Life in those days was difficult. Sometimes people were compromised, or, morally conflicted, shall we say. Demands were placed upon them that in normal circumstances they would feel strong enough to avoid. Father Ryan found himself caught up in such a dilemma, playing devil's advocate. A treacherous path to take, no doubt.'

He swatted a wasp away and turned, smiling, to Hannah as she returned with the coffee. A jug of cream and a pile of chocolate chip cookies, arranged on a decorative china plate, were placed in front of Rose.

'So, you were saying Father Ryan was compromised? In what way, exactly?' she asked.

'Yes, well, Edmund was one of the priests I undertook interviewing about the Troubles. Normally this information would remain protected by the auspices of the church. In this case, Edmund left instructions that in the event of his death I was free to share his part in the war.' He clasped his hands together as if he was about to pray.

'Make no mistake, it was a war of sorts. History will judge these men less harshly than those of our own time. Anyway, I shall hand a copy of the transcript of the interview over to you to read, under the understanding that it is not released to the press. Edmund died a good few years ago so I am permitted to share this, but we don't want this falling into the wrong hands.'

He handed Rose a brown A4 envelope.

'Now, coffee first, and then you can take that away with you.'

It was an hour before Rose was able to return to the coolness of her office to read the transcript held within the brown envelope. She unfolded the two pages and began.

I, Father Edmund Ryan of Boston's Saint Aloysius Catholic Church, wish to confess to my sins. This document is my sworn testimony, which should remain confidential in the hands of the Roman Catholic Church until such time of my death.

In January 1975, I was moved from the Holy Trinity Parish Church in Newcastle, County Down to St Malachy's, in the Markets area of Belfast. It was an area of much impoverishment. Unemployment was high and housing needs relative to family size were not being met by the local authorities. The existing housing conditions were substandard. I found my parishioners requiring political and economic support as much as moral guidance. They needed social justice as much as religion and, inspired by our liberation theological brothers in Latin America, I sought to help them achieve this. In my quest to help the people I worked among I engaged in somewhat morally questionable activities, namely storing weapons and allowing the sacred confessional box to act as means of passing on vital information. Occasionally, I was requested to provide safe passage for comrades needing to cross the border.

During one episode of particular difficulty, a young man of sixteen years was caught, tried and held accountable for trying to rob IRA funds from a local public house. I was called upon to give him the holy sacrament of penance and the last rites. When I arrived at the designated location, I found the lad on his knees, his hands placed behind his head. I had been instructed to attend to him, counsel him in his final moments and to hear his final penance before he was executed.

When he had told me his sins, admitting to stealing from the IRA-owned bar, he was told to say the Lord's Prayer, before a gun was held to the back of his head. The impact of that pulled trigger will stay with me to my dying days. I am not afraid to admit that I was a changed man having witnessed that young man's death.

The following evening, I was called to the home of Eden Mulligan. One of her children had been in trouble at school. Eamonn was a handful for her and the headmaster had summoned her to his office. Eden, in desperation, had asked to see me. I arrived at her home that evening hoping to offer some consolation and guidance, and perhaps to talk to the boy and set him on the righteous path again, so to speak.

That evening came at a time when I was facing much turmoil. The impact of my pastoral work in such a difficult time was wearing me down. Instead of me comforting Eden that evening, I found myself drawn to her and unburdening myself. I didn't tell the details of what had occurred the night before, but like everyone in that small community, she had heard of the execution and knew the young lad by sight. Eden became a great source of solace to me.

In time, well, we became close friends. She was struggling to raise her five children during a difficult winter. Her husband was a worthless drunk who, under the guise of looking for work, left her at regular intervals, sometimes for up to three or four months at a time. We both had needs that our current situations could not meet, and I have to say we found refuge in each other.

Rose put the page down. It was half a story. She checked in the envelope to see if she had missed some pages, but it was empty. Father Ryan's relationship with Eden was intriguing. The testimony seemed to suggest that it was more than platonic without categorically saying so.

He was involved in paramilitary activity and he had a close friendship with Eden. The priest had navigated dangerous territory.

Rose's mind trawled through the various scenarios where a priest would be called on to hear confession. There were so many dark stories relating to Belfast's troubled history. In taking lives, how many men had turned to their priest to lessen the weight of their transgressions?

She thought about Eden's children, left to fend for themselves, and the sense of abandonment that they must have felt. How they had been dealt a lousy hand in life. As bad as Evelyn was, at least she'd been there for Rose and her siblings.

CHAPTER 35

When Rose arrived at her office the next morning, Danny was already sitting at her desk reading the *Belfast Telegraph*.

'Have you nothing better to do than read about what a terrible job you're doing on the Dunlore case?' she asked, throwing her bag on the desk and taking off her jacket.

'Very funny, Rosie. If you must know, I was reading about Eden Mulligan – they're dredging up all the old stories again. Going back over the files. There's even talk of a new site being excavated. Have you heard?'

'Yes, I got wind of it yesterday from Malachy Magee.'

'Apparently, the Independent Commission for the Location of Victims' Remains – the ICLVR – is going to announce that a new site has been identified. It's on Tyrella beach in County Down,' Danny said.

'I know it well. We used to go there as kids.'

'Aerial footage taken by a drone has shown a scorched plot. Lots of prehistoric sites are being rediscovered but they could tell that this site was created more recently. Plus, they've had a tip-off that there could be one of the disappeared buried in it.'

'Do you think it could be Eden?'

'Who knows? I've set up a meeting for tomorrow with Nigel Rankin. He heads up the Commission. After I find out what's going on, do you fancy taking a run out there to look around the proposed dig site, before it kicks off?'

'Sure, like we've nothing else on. In case you hadn't noticed, you're up to your eyes in corpses.'

'Ah, stop your complaining. It's all connected. One way or another.'

'So you keep telling me,' she said.

Rose noticed Danny pulling at his ear. It was an old habit she recognised, something he did when he was thinking. 'We need to find a connection. Something that draws the two cases together. There must be some commonality that we're missing.'

Rose sighed. 'The cottage keeps bothering me. Why there? What is the significance of that place?'

'And why those five individuals? It doesn't feel random. With a case like this you have to work with what you have.'

'What, no suspect and no evidence?' She almost laughed.

'No Rosie. Even though there's no immediate or obvious connection yet, there will be. We just have to know where to look.'

'Whatever the motivation for the murders, the killer had a personal connection. I'm sure of it.'

Beyond drug dealer Conal Brady, they couldn't find a connection to any of the friends that would link them to someone capable of such a crime.

'There was no sign of forced entry. Could the killer have

been in the house? Hiding out and listening in on the friends?' Rose asked.

'No, SOCO checked out the attic. The dust and spider webs suggest no one had been up there in decades.'

'How long did it take Iona Gardener to get to the police station?'

'Approximately thirty minutes. She was on foot and looking at the route we suspect she took, that's the time frame we're working with.'

'So that gave our murderer time to put distance between him and the crime scene. There were no track marks other than the car used by the five in the cottage.'

'Yes, that's right. So, what about the priest's testimony? What do you reckon was going on there?' he asked.

'I don't know yet. Something dodgy, that's for sure. The priest's story doesn't add up. The transcript says he was working on the sidelines for the IRA, turning a blind eye to the moving of weapons, protecting members, that sort of thing. He seemed to be some sort of counsellor to some of the older men. He allowed them to offload their guilt and absolved them of all responsibility and sin by saying a few Hail Marys. Disgusting, really. It claims that Ryan was embroiled in the execution of a teenager caught robbing from an IRA bar. But maybe he was more than just a silent bed partner.'

'What, you mean a fully paid up active member heading up a cell in the Markets area?'

'Yeah, why not. There's a fine line between supporting their activities on the side and turning a blind eye when weapons need storing, to being a strategic driving force. He could have been calling all the shots for all we know.'

'Why was he transferred to Boston?'

'Father Dominic suggests it was because of his relationship with Eden Mulligan. It had crossed the line from friendship to something else. But maybe they were protecting him from being caught? Or perhaps Ryan was privy to Eden's secrets. Did she know something that put her in danger?'

'Where does Eden's disappearance fit into all this?'

'That, my friend, I still don't know.' She sighed.

'Right, I'm off to shake a few trees upstairs and see what falls out. Keep me posted,' Danny said, swinging his legs round and getting off her chair.

When he left, Rose picked up his discarded copy of the *Belfast Telegraph*. The headline called for a fresh dig following new evidence that a body had been buried by the IRA near Tyrella beach. The feature speculated that it could be Eden Mulligan's remains. Rose noted that the report failed to say what the new evidence was. The heat wave had scorched the surrounding land and the burial site had been exposed, discovered by aerial surveyors. It wasn't the first – there were reports of ancient settlements, burial sites and waterways having been revealed in different spots throughout Ireland. Rose thought about how the dead don't always remain silent. It can take years, decades even, but bodies can always be found. The earth throws back that which has been hidden.

She knew that any evidence obtained directly or indirectly by the Commission was deemed inadmissible in court proceedings, and any remains discovered were not allowed to undergo forensic examination, except to establish the identity of the dead person or how, when, and where they died. That information was then supposed to remain secret, with only the family being privy to it. If somebody was leaking information about the discovery to the press, then the question was: why now?

McCausland's assumption that the case review should be a tidy summation was becoming more outrageous. Rose knew that when bodies are dug up, secrets come with them.

Rose had read through the autopsy notes Danny had given her. The killer was determined and brutal. It was likely that Dylan's survival and Iona's escape had been down to someone interrupting the murder spree. Who had that person been? Why had they not raised the alarm? Iona's escape still weighed on Rose's mind. There was a possibility that her escape had been orchestrated to make her look innocent.

The blood patterns report had made for interesting reading. Arterial spray had been evident in the living room. When a major artery is severed, the blood is propelled out of the damaged blood vessels by the pumping of the heart and often creates a pattern consisting of large, individual stains, with a new pattern created each time the heart pumps. Expirated spatter – caused by blood from an internal injury mixing with air from the lungs being expelled through the nose, mouth or an injury to the airways or lungs – was found in the bedroom. Olivia had been alive when she had been placed on the bed and she'd slowly bled out.

From Lyons' report, Rose could see that she was dealing with someone who had so much hate in them that when it was unleashed, it had come out in a torrent. The repetitive, overkill nature of the stabbings suggested a high level of anger. Rose knew that overkill – the infliction of massive injuries by far exceeding the extent necessary to kill the victim – can have an association with sexually motivated murders. This wasn't the case with the Dunlore murders, so what had led the killer to feel such rage in the first place? Rose was drawn to the notion of the killer expressing sadistic sexual pleasure in the overkill and the organisation of the bodies. But she was reluctant to see it as a solely sexual crime. This was more complex. Sexual murderers plan their killings in order to make them as consistent as possible with their fantasies whereas the non-sexual murderer's modus operandi is the result of an explosion of anger. The Dunlore murders felt reactive, impulsive and extremely violent, with an internal sexual tension.

Initially mystified, she was starting to get a sense of who they were dealing with. Someone with deeply embedded issues so complex and disturbing that when they unleashed their fury, the result was a massacre.

CHAPTER 36

Danny looked across at Rose as he walked her home. She was wearing her hair different from their uni days, it was longer than usual and swept back from her face. Her eyes still held that magnetism. When he checked they seemed grey, fading to green around the edges, reminding him of a stormy sea. They were walking through the town, back to her apartment block, enjoying the balmy feel of the night. He hated himself for it, but he couldn't help compare her to Amy. Rose had a cool, quiet strength that Amy could never possess. They looked a million miles apart too. You only had to look at Rose to know she was tough, could handle anything life threw at her. She was dependable and capable. Whereas Amy was fragile and unpredictable. A ticking time bomb. Any perceived slight or hardship could send her over the edge. He couldn't go on living like that, trying to contain the damage. Trying to fix her.

'So, what's bothering you, Danny?' Rose finally asked. 'You're terribly quiet for a change.'

'Awk, it's this bleeding case.' Danny pulled at his ear. 'I

keep wondering what I'm missing. I'm like a broken record but there has to be something beyond the graffiti that draws the two cases together. Or am I looking for something that's not there? Perhaps the message had nothing to do with the murders.'

Rose sighed. 'The cottage keeps bothering me. Why there? What is the significance of that place?' They walked on through the Titanic Quarter, passing under the flyover, the cars roaring overhead.

'You ever see anything like this before?' she asked as they crossed the road at Custom House Square. A lone taxi drove past with a long-haired girl hanging out of the window, looking like she was about to throw up.

'Nah. Not in my time. Not since the Troubles ended. Of course, there was the Shankill Butchers back in the day. They went about cutting throats and carving people up under the guise of defending God's own country. All that political violence shite was nothing more than a cover for psychopaths on a mission to spill blood. Nothing as clinical as a mercury tilt switch placed under a car for them. They wanted the real deal. Blood and guts.'

'Gruesome, wasn't it?'

'In those days, the nastier the murder the more it frightened and intimidated people. It kept everyone in the cycle of tit for tat and ensured mouths stayed shut out of fear. This feels different. The victims have to have been known to our killer and specifically targeted. He knew where to find them so one of the five must have a connection with the killer, and the message in the cottage suggests one of them had a connection with Eden Mulligan.'

'What about the burnt papers in the fireplace?' Rose asked.

When Danny had asked for the ashes in the grate to be examined by forensics he had been nearly laughed out of the station.

'You're hopeful,' DS Joanne Wilson had said, as she used a hair tie to pull her blonde hair back into a ponytail. 'Have you seen what was collected from that grate?'

'I know it's a long shot, but it's worth checking out.'

'Hey Malachy, your man here is hoping for a signed confession to be found in the ashes,' she'd shouted across the office. Magee had given her a grin as if to say, sure he's an eejit, but what can you do?

Danny threw a rolled-up ball of paper at him. 'Away on, Joanne, check it out. You'll be eating humble pie if it throws up something.'

She'd rolled her eyes and smirked. 'I can't promise anything, but I'll make sure we tell the lab people to give it an extra good look, just for you, Danny boy.'

When she came back a week later she wasn't so cocky.

'So, the ashes from the grate in the cottage are back in,' she said, grabbing a chair and bringing it over to Danny's desk.

'Please give me something good and juicy. This case needs a kick up the hole to get stuff moving,' Danny said.

'Basically, when paper is burnt, the content written on it becomes charred and impossible to see, but the laboratory uses an infrared reflected photography technique to essentially see what has been burnt away.'

'So, get to the point, do we know what was on the papers?'

'We have a random sample of rescued words.'

She handed a ten by eight photograph to Danny. He looked down and saw the endangered handwritten words:

Shelter from the Storm

'What's that? A book or a film?'

'No, it's a Bob Dylan song, apparently. I can't think of any reason why it would be relevant to the case, can you?'

Danny shook his head. He looked at the words. Fuck, no further forward.

Now, walking along with Rose, he recounted the words and started whistling the tune.

'Not much of a Dylan man myself,' Danny said. 'I reckon the ashes burnt in the grate were just lying around, and were of no significance.'

'Hang on,' Rose said. She stopped dead in her tracks and put a hand on Danny's arm.

'Katy Carberry, the old neighbour, she told me that Eden loved music, and would play her records all the time. She could hear them through the wall, Bob Dylan, David Bowie and the Stones as well as more modern stuff.'

'So what? It doesn't have to mean anything. They were the big names back in the day, before Eden's time.'

'Maybe there's something in it.'

The day's heat had drained away, leaving a stillness over the place that felt menacing. They walked on.

'Anything your end?' Danny asked.

'What, with the Mulligan case? It's wrapped up tightly under a code of omertà.'

'Yeah, I'm hoping you're going to crack the connection for both of us.'

'Dream on. Has no one ever told you the most important thing about cold cases is that they take time and patience?'

'Well, I don't have the luxury of either.'

'No, you sure as hell don't.'

'Nightcap?' asked Danny, as they approached Rose's building.

'Better not,' she said, giving him a wry smile before turning away and keying the security code into the door.

As he left Rose, Danny checked his phone messages. One from the lab people, a DNA profile from the under-nail finger scrapings, but unfortunately there wasn't a match in the system. Still, it was good to have something on standby should they find a suspect to haul in.

CHAPTER 37

Being adopted had always been Rose's go-to childhood fantasy. She'd daydream at the back of Miss Buckle's class that her real parents were trying to track her down. One day they'd find her and she could leave Belfast and her mother behind. If she was in a good mood, she'd allow Kaitlin to go with her, but if her sister was annoying her, she'd say so long and climb in the fancy car sent to pick her up before driving straight to a mansion house in the country.

Being home had begun to unfurl something in Rose. Lost or latent sensations of shame, guilt and horror now struggled against blame, anger and a need to set right that which was done. There had been times when she had tried to understand her upbringing, tried to excuse it even, but no matter how Rose tried to frame it, she still felt the heat of anger. Now, when she thought back to her childhood, she felt nothing but resentment. There were few light moments. Life was all about sticking it to the Brits, her parents' devotion to the republican rhetoric, attending rallies supporting the Hunger Strikers, and worse. The dead of the night rap at the door. The secretive conversations held in front room. The awareness that neighbours were over friendly to her parents, while still keeping their distance. How they'd been respected but feared.

Returning to Belfast was never going to lead to a long-lost family happy ending.

Now, the Eden Mulligan case was dredging up all sorts of associations to her own childhood and making Rose feel uncomfortable.

Evelyn had been reckless in her pursuit of the dogma. She revelled in the injustices against her idea of Ireland, spouting chapter and verse from famine history to partitioning. Like a fanatic, it was her succour and salvation.

From the age of thirteen, Rose felt that Evelyn was always on the attack with her. Waiting for the next fight and relishing the power and control she had over her. It was all, *where are you going, who are you hanging out with, watch what you say*.

Rose parked her car outside the row of terrace houses, shielded her eyes from the glare of the sunlight reflected from the small rectangle windows, and made her way up to Kaitlin's door.

It opened before Rose had a chance to ring the bell.

'Roisin, you made it. Come on in.' Kaitlin stood dressed in a cotton summer dress and wedged sandals. She looked as if she'd caught the sun, freckles covering the bridge of her nose. She smiled widely and seemed genuinely pleased to see Rose.

They moved down the hallway and Rose caught sight of the tidy living room before Kaitlin directed her into the kitchen.

'We've the house to ourselves, well, apart from Buddy.' She indicated to a black dog in the corner of the kitchen on a bed that was much too small for him. It lay sound asleep with its tongue lolling out the side of its mouth.

Rose offered the bottle of wine she'd picked up from the WineMark on the corner of the road and they hugged awkwardly. She did feel some sort of connection with Kaitlin, she couldn't deny it. She could see traces of herself in her sister's face, in her bone structure and shadowy grey eyes. Self-preservation had meant cutting herself off from her family and she was okay with that, but it felt good to have a renewed connection to where she had come from, and to know Kaitlin and her brothers were doing okay.

'I'm glad you came to see me. Is everything all right?'

'Everything is fine. How are you?'

'Awk, I can't complain. The usual annoyances from the kids, but you just have to get on with life, don't you?'

Rose nodded her agreement.

'Here, I'll open the wine. Tony has gone to see his Ma and the kids are out with their friends.' They sat at the large kitchen table. Everything was meticulously tidy and clean. Kaitlin handed Rose a wine glass and set about opening the bottle. She poured a generous glass for herself and then one for Rose before reaching for her electronic cigarette on the kitchen counter.

'So, tell me. How's life for you in London? Do you have a fella?'

'Nah, it's just me. Never met the right one.'

'Aren't you the lucky one that's still single? I'm sick of washing Tony's boxers and cooking his dinner. What I wouldn't do to trade lives for a week.' She laughed and then fell quiet before saying, 'She used to talk about you, you know.'

Rose gave her a look. She didn't believe her.

'She did, honest to God. She'd say a whole load of shite like, but she'd also say our Roisin was a beauty with brains. She knew you could do anything with your life. I think that's why she resented you so much. You'd choices.'

'Can you imagine if she knew I was working for the PSNI?' They both laughed. The idea of one of their family working for the police was so out there. Growing up the RUC and then later the PSNI were the sworn enemy.

'Oh you got one over her in the end, that's for sure,' Kaitlin said, taking a sip of the wine.

They both fell quiet for a few minutes, listening to the tick of a clock close by and a car passing down the street.

'It always felt like there was danger in the air,' Rose said. 'We were on high alert, always waiting for the next thing to happen. I didn't realise how hair-trigger it was until I left and breathing seemed easier somehow.'

'I know what you mean. It was all we knew. It had to be over before we realised how awful it was.' Kaitlin sighed. 'It wasn't all bad though. We'd happy times too. You never seemed to appreciate that.'

Rose sighed. 'I couldn't forgive her as easily as you did, or maybe I just didn't want to. I expected more. Wanted more.'

'Did you find it?'

'What?'

'Whatever it was you went looking for?'

'Jesus, Kait, it's not that simple.'

They both sat quiet, in their own thoughts, Rose contemplating her life in London, and how she felt about being back in Belfast.

'I'm glad you're staying for a while. I've missed you, you know.' Kaitlin reached out and took Rose's hand.

Rose felt it, that tug of guilt. She had saved herself but left Kaitlin behind. Funny how she never felt the same about the boys. They were too young and annoying to have that kind of bond with.

'What are you thinking?' Kaitlin asked.

'I don't know. I suppose it's this case I'm working on. Do you remember talk about Eden Mulligan? She was from the Markets area.'

Kaitlin shrugged. 'I knew of her, but I didn't know any of the family. Why?'

'Working on her case, talking to people from the area and that time, has made me curious, I suppose.'

'Curious about what?'

'Ma.'

'Don't go there. She's gone. No point dragging up the past.'

Rose shivered despite the warm sun shining through the window.

'I'm sorry. I don't mean to cause you upset,' Rose said. 'I'm surrounded by documents, newspaper reports and transcripts all connected to the place I grew up. I can't help thinking of what she was really like. Wondering how far she was in. I don't think I ever really knew her. Do you know what I mean?'

'She was our Ma, what else do you need to know? Children never really know their parents, not as separate people. Besides, you don't need to go raking over old history connected to us. Leave well alone.' She looked directly at Rose with fear or menace in her eyes. It was hard to say which.

'What have you heard about Eden Mulligan over the years?'

'Not much really. Only what was said in the papers and on the street. That she vanished into thin air. It's those children we all felt sorry for. There was talk that she'd run away with a soldier, but we knew that she wouldn't have done that. That's just the kind of stories that people put about, wanting to create a bit of mystery and gossip or blacken her name. There was no truth in it. God love her, she probably topped herself. Jumped into the Lagan or else she was taken away and met a sorrowful end at the hands of the Provies.'

'If she had jumped into the River Lagan then her body would have turned up eventually. It looks more likely that someone was responsible for her disappearance.'

'I dare say.' Kaitlin drew on the vape and blew out a puff of strawberry-smelling steam. 'People vanished in those days for all sorts of reasons. Some ran away to England or America, others found themselves mixed up with the wrong sort and were told to get out of the country. Others didn't get the choice. They were taken away in the back of a van and met their fates in some deserted waste ground and buried in an unmarked grave.'

Rose sighed. 'If Ma was operating for the IRA in the area at that time, then I need to know.'

Kaitlin stared out the window. 'You know what she was like, meetings and people calling. It's hard to say what she knew or what she did. Community worker was the job title, as I remember.'

'I know that, but if she had anything to do with the Mulligan case then I need to find out.'

Running Evelyn's details through the system had occurred

to Rose before. Something stopped her though. Apart from the system recording her search, there was a sense of dread and fear. She wasn't sure if she could handle what she might find. Her mother had been a difficult woman. Whatever she managed to find out, she was certain it wouldn't be good.

CHAPTER 38

Until she could get full access to Iona, Rose was concentrating on Eden Mulligan's disappearance. She had put it to Danny that the key in the Mulligan mystery had to lie within the tight-knit community of the Markets.

'It's a small enclave where everyone knows everyone's business, so someone had to know what happened to Eden. People talk but, when it suits them, they also hold secrets close,' Rose said.

Danny leaned back on his chair. 'Don't forget that people were frightened of loose talk in those days. One wrong word and you could find yourself implicated, or worse, on the receiving end of a punishment shooting.'

'Yeah, that's true, but someone knows something and the best place to start is with the family.'

Getting the Mulligan clan together for a meeting was difficult. Eamonn was the key. They hoped he would persuade the rest of them into hearing Rose out. Cormac was still hedging his bets, preferring to abstain from any gathering, but Joel Ellis, from Families for Justice, had persuaded him that he needed to hear what they had to say.

Rose had convinced Danny to let her lead the meeting and they had agreed to meet in a safe, neutral venue. A police station wasn't going to work, so a meeting room had been booked in the Europa hotel – its claim to fame being that it was the most bombed hotel in Europe. Rose had to accept that they would always see her as the outsider and to a certain extent, the enemy. To the Mulligans, the police had let their mother down and disappointed them on many occasions. The hurt they still carried and the damage inflicted on them growing up was largely down to failings in the police investigation. Rose could see that and it made her even more determined to do her job to the best of her ability. She couldn't let them down again. Rose hoped they appreciated that she was working with them, trying to make this process as easy on them as she could. She wanted everything documented and carried out with diligence.

Rose arrived early and waited while the staff at the hotel set up a conference table, complete with a jug of water and glasses for each of the five siblings. She had yet to meet the daughters, Eileen and Lizzie, or Paddy, the second youngest son. She hoped they would all turn up. It was important for the entire family to be kept up to date with the investigation and to know that she had the best of intentions in pursuing what had happened to their mother. The Mulligans had been smothered in assumptions, lies and fear. She hoped that she could help them gain insight and some degree of closure.

Joel arrived carrying a copy of the *Irish News* and a folder of papers. 'All right?'

'Yes, everything is set up. I'm just waiting on them to arrive.'

'I spoke to Cormac last night. He'll be here and he says the rest of them will turn up, too.'

'I hope so,' said Rose straightening her folder of notes. She was nervous. The full weight of the failings of her predecessors was bearing down on her, making her feel anxious. She had to win their trust, and to do so she had to convince them that she knew what she was doing. She had to make them see that she wouldn't let her superiors get away with whitewashing the truth this time.

Joel took a seat at the far end of the table. So much for providing support, she thought.

'You don't like the police much do you?' she asked.

'Let's just say I have my reasons. Where I grew up, the police weren't exactly your neighbourhood friendly bobby on the beat sort.'

'They're not all bad you know.'

'Aye, so I hear.'

Eamonn was the first of the Mulligans to arrive. He looked unsure of himself and anxious, scratching at his head, his eyes darting from Rose to Joel.

'Eamonn, good to see you,' said Joel, standing to welcome him. They shook hands, and Joel gave the older man a pat on the back.

'Am I early?' he asked.

'No, right on time. Hopefully the others will be right behind you,' Rose said. 'Can I get you tea or coffee or a glass of water?'

'No, I'm grand, thanks.' He sat next to Joel and stared down at the mahogany table.

Cormac arrived next, followed closely by Eileen and Lizzie.

Rose introduced herself and thanked them for coming.

'Shall we wait on Paddy?' asked Rose.

'I doubt he'll come. Paddy's not exactly sociable these days. Keeps to himself,' Eamonn said.

'I spoke to him on the phone yesterday, and he said he'd come,' said Joel.

'Then let's give it a few more minutes,' Rose offered. She straightened her notes again, and took a sip from her glass of water. She was thirsty and nervous. The assembled family were watching her with a mixture of expectation and hope, tinged with distrust. She could feel it in the air and see it in the sideways glances they gave each other.

Rose drew a breath, glanced at her notes, and was about to begin when the door opened, and Paddy entered. He appeared disorientated, slightly out of it, with a slovenly look about him. He was tall and whippet lean.

'Sorry I'm late, had a quick half pint in the Crown, and then couldn't find this here room.'

Rose watched him as he ambled over to the table. His jawline was saggy, and he had the appearance of someone who didn't dress to please others – a lived-in look, like an ageing rock star, Rose thought. Someone who's lived one too many lives.

'Don't worry, you're here now. Come sit beside us, Paddy. I haven't seen you in ages. How have you been?' Lizzie spoke with such a tenderness in her voice that Rose felt for her. She was an attractive woman, elegant and well dressed. Their twin bond had probably sustained them through their rough childhood. She knew from the case notes that Paddy hadn't lasted long with his adoptive parents. He ran away on several occasions and was eventually placed back into foster care with a different family, following his claims that he had been physically abused by the original adoptive father. Lizzie was to remain with the family for the next ten years. Their separation was just one more fallout of this entire case.

Paddy looked sheepish and embarrassed and took a seat next to her and Cormac.

Rose cleared her throat and stood, before starting the recording device she'd brought to document the meeting. 'Now that we are all here, I'll make a start. I've brought you here today to give you an update on your mother's case, and to go over previous statements.'

She looked at them and could see unease, a defensiveness in the set of their shoulders, the way they avoided making eye contact with her. She couldn't blame them, but she needed to win them over if she was to make any headway.

'I know you have been bitterly let down by previous investigations. That you were treated badly by the system from the moment your mother disappeared.'

'Disappeared, ugh. I hate that word,' Cormac spoke. 'She didn't just disappear, she didn't skedaddle, or vanish in a puff of smoke. Someone *took* her.'

'Yes, I appreciate that,' Rose said. 'In order to clarify the details, we need to work together. This is a complex investigation. The trail is cold but within each of you there could be some seemingly inconsequential piece of information that could make all the difference.'

'We've been through this before. It's all promises and lies.' He sighed.

'Cormac, hear her out. Maybe this time they mean what they say,' Joel said.

'Yeah, Cormac, come on. It's better than doing nothing. At least if they are going over the case there is a hope that something will turn up,' Lizzie spoke in a measured tone and rested her hand on his arm. 'We have to keep trying.'

She turned to Rose. 'I think what Cormac is getting at is that we need to know we won't be let down again. If we agree to being involved, you have to understand that. We've had enough disappointment and humiliation to last us ten lifetimes. Every time the papers go over the case, they drag up all sorts, saying our mother slept around, kept bad company. But she wasn't like that at all. Every time they rewrite who she was, a bit of who she really was vanishes. We can't afford to lose any more of her.'

Rose nodded. 'All I can promise each of you is that I am doing my utmost to examine the facts of the case as they stand, without pre-judgement.'

Paddy took a deep breath and shuddered. Rose turned to see him wipe at his eyes, flustered and anxious.

'I shouldn't have had that pint.' He attempted to laugh, but his words came out in painful gurgles, hesitant and broken. He pulled an inhaler out of his jacket pocket and shook it before sucking in the medicine like his life depended on it. His hair was receding in the same pattern as Cormac's, leaving his face looking exposed and vulnerable. His clothes looked cheap and old. The sleeves of his shirt cut into his muscular arms and Rose noticed the top button was missing.

Eileen turned to him. 'You're pathetic. You can't stand to see any of us having a normal life. We could have all wallowed in self-pity. Cried for the rest of our days and said poor me. But no, we picked ourselves up, we educated ourselves, got jobs and tried to build a life. Sure, it would be nice to down a bottle of vodka and think about the days before they took her. But we don't allow ourselves that luxury.' Her dark eyes were alight with rage. 'We had to move on. Otherwise, we'd all end up like you.' She looked at him with scorn, like she was disgusted by him.

'Come, Eileen, that's enough,' Eamonn spoke as he tried to take her gently by the arm and lead her away from Paddy, who had placed his head in his hands.

'I'm only saying what the rest of you are thinking.' She looked at Eamonn, her eyes blazing. 'Somebody has to put him right. Let this here doctor do her job. If there's stuff to be found, information or whatever, let her find it.'

The room was quiet. No one moved or spoke.

Paddy pushed back his chair, walked over to the window and stared out at the traffic below. 'If the rest of yous want to do this, then go ahead. I won't stop anyone. We've got to do whatever it takes to get to the truth if any of us are ever to find some kind of peace.'

Rose wondered what Eden would think if she could see her children now. How would their lives have turned out if their mother had been around to raise them and guide them? Instead, her vanishing had damaged them in all kinds of ways.

'In the last few years, since the cease fire, more information has been uncovered about the so-called "disappeared". We don't know if your mother was taken by paramilitaries but we do know that there was a secret IRA group tasked with taking people in this way, called the Unknowns. Their remit was to abduct, kill and bury in secret anyone who had supposedly crossed them.'

Joel leaned forward. 'Families for Justice never found

any information which led us to think that the Unknowns were responsible for Eden's disappearance.'

Rose looked at them all. 'The main thing is, if we are to unearth anything new, we need to have all known connections brought to the table. No holding back from any of you.'

CHAPTER 39

'Well, how do you think that went?' Rose asked Joel later, when they had finished the meeting.

'As good as it could've. They seem to be open to working with you. Even Cormac and Paddy.'

She could feel the tension in her shoulders ease a bit. The inquiry could have continued without their support, but she wanted them to know that she was on their side, and that she would do her best by their mother.

'What did you make of Paddy?' Joel asked.

'He looks broken.'

'Aye, I'd say, out of all of them, he's the one that has suffered the most. He had a bad time. They all did one way or another, but I think he's the most damaged.'

'You mentioned when we first met that your involvement with the case nearly cost Eamonn his life. What happened?'

'It was early on. I'd been pushing him to go public, speak to the media to raise awareness. I thought if we made enough noise something would be done by the assembly and the police to really investigate the case properly. Word on the street was that with the Good Friday Agreement in place, the IRA were going to hand over information about the disappeared. They were protected from prosecution so the feeling was: what did they have to lose?'

'So, what happened?'

'Eamonn got taken for a trip over the border. It was October, a good few years ago, and he was walking home when a black car pulled up and three men invited him in to go for a wee drive.'

'Did he go?' she asked, incredulous.

'Rose, when you're brought up under a regime that breeds terror and fear, you simply act as you are expected to. There's wee lads the age of sixteen on these streets that have been given the word to meet masked men up entryways to get knee-capped, and they go. Lambs to the slaughter. Some of them have brought their mummy's tea towel to staunch the bleeding. Eamonn knew if he didn't get into that car, they'd come back for him another time and next time they wouldn't be asking nicely.'

'So, what happened?'

'He was blindfolded and taken to a house a few hours away. He was held for five days. Denied food, only given sips of water, and beaten over and over again. On the last day, a new captor arrived. He calmly explained to Eamonn that the beatings had been for his own good. They had been designed to help him realise that the media campaign was not in his or his family's best interests.' Joel paused and pressed his fingers against his temples, as if trying to alleviate a headache.

'Eamonn was told that out of respect for the family's loss of their mother, they were not going to execute him, but should he continue with sharing his plight, then they would have no option but to finish him off. His face was a bloodied mess. Cheekbone broken, nose wrecked, one ear drum exploded, never mind the cracked ribs and Ribena-coloured bruises. His own sister, Eileen, didn't recognise him when he was delivered to her doorway.'

If Eden had been an informer, then surely Special Branch and the security forces would have been desperate to know how the IRA had discovered her role. Had Father Ryan passed on information about her? The family were adamant that their mother had not been a tout. The RUC had denied it too.

Now, the Dunlore murders had muddied the waters further, but somewhere within the swamp of rumour and memory, the truth lay hidden, waiting to be revealed.

CHAPTER 40

Ten days had passed since the murder case had landed on Danny's desk and he was feeling the pressure. The press had continued to run with the story, and it had even carried across the water. The tabloids had also taken an interest, revelling in the brutal nature of the deaths and the idyllic location. All of which only heightened the sense that ACC McCausland was putting the screws on, creating a renewed sense of urgency to crack the case.

Danny had a meeting booked for twelve to update McCausland and he felt a frustrated knot in his gut. There was little new to tell, and he expected to get a bollocking. McCausland liked to flex his managerial muscle and the Lennon case fuck-up was never far from memory. He envied Rose, coming in fresh from the mainland, no history of messing up to overshadow her current case.

He could feel sweat gathering between his shoulders. He thought of his father out working on the farm, his tweed cap firmly on his head, a farmer's tan darkening on his arms. He loved that farm and couldn't for the life of him understand how Danny was prepared to give it all up to spend his days working for the PSNI. Never mind that every year it was harder to make a decent living from it.

But he knew his father spoke proudly of him in company, that he had some sense that what Danny did for a living was worthwhile and rewarding. Except on days like this, when he felt that he was making no progress and he longed to be out in the fields, with the feel of the heat on his back and nobody to answer to except the cattle and the sheep.

Annoyed, he grabbed a cold can of Coke from the vending machine and cracked it open in the hallway. He then checked around the office to see what the rest of the team were up to. Malachy Magee was on the phone, chasing up CCTV footage from the nearby motorway that led to the cottage. Jack Fitzgerald was focused on his computer screen, running through data. He was meticulous and one to get on with the job in hand. A bit lippy at times, but not a bad lad. Cases like this one weren't going to be solved by painstaking evidence trails alone though. It was going to take something out of the ordinary to point them in the right direction.

'Listen up. We need to focus our energies.' He spoke with attitude, a sense of wanting to smash their heads together, to make them care enough to push that little bit harder. He had stopped caring about being liked. It was about getting the job done and making sure he did everything in his power to make that happen.

'This case is proving to be difficult. The stakes are high with three dead and Dylan Wray hanging on by the skin of his teeth. We need to get something and fast. Dr Lainey has been given the go ahead to talk to Iona Gardener again so I'll be heading to the Shannon Clinic with her soon. I need one of you good for nothing eejits to bring me something worth looking at by tea time.'

He hoped it would be enough to shake them up.

Now, he had to deal with the boss.

McCausland was waiting on him, sitting watching the corridor with his office door wide open. He was one of those men who liked to assert his authority and managed the squad through a thin veil of intimidation.

'All right, Sir?' Danny said, walking into the office. A fan was sitting on the desk, whirring away and blowing the warm air around them.

'Sit down, Stowe, and get me up to speed on what's happening with the case.'

Danny folded himself into the chair and began. He ran through the forensics, the autopsy reports and the dire lack of theories.

McCausland's stony face said it all.

'I'm heading over to interview Iona Gardener now. I believe that she holds the key to all of this.' He wasn't sure if he really believed that or not, but he had to offer up something to make McCausland's face mobile again.

The ACC leaned back in his superior office chair, all black leather padding and special neck support. 'I shouldn't need to spell out what is at stake here. Your career is on the line with this one, Stowe.'

'Yes, Sir. I'm aware that I've a lot to prove.'

'What about the Lainey woman. How's that working out?'

'Dr Lainey has been a great help. She's the one who got the go ahead to conduct an interview with Iona Gardener.'

'Well, make sure she earns her keep. I don't want to be hauled up to justify extra spend on quacks.'

'I can assure you, Sir, that Dr Lainey is proving her worth,' Danny said.

Danny knew that every witness was different, and every trauma left its own mark. Iona Gardener was his last hope. What he had told McCausland could be true. While he didn't for a minute believe she could've carried out the murders alone, he knew she had been present and had valuable information. He respected the need to treat her with care, but he was past the stage of making allowances and he had given enough special consideration to her state of mind.

Solving this case was the most effective way of helping her. She had to talk.

He hesitated before he picked up the phone. He hoped he was doing the right thing. Some cases seemed to yield results quickly, one lead turning into another. But this one was brick walls all the way. He needed a sledgehammer to break through and that sledgehammer could be him. Rose could provide the back-up. For now, he wanted to see how Iona reacted under normal police interrogation.

CHAPTER 41

On the way to the Shannon Clinic, Danny filled Rose in on McCausland's pep talk.

'He's out to make a point. If I don't get a result soon, I'm screwed. You know that the Lennon case didn't exactly go as it should've and I've paid for that with the move into HET. The move back to the Serious Crime Unit with this case is a probationary one.'

'What happened on the Lennon case?'

'I missed a valuable piece of evidence and cracked the perp's head against a wall. My mind wasn't on the job. Shit was going down with Amy and I let it get in the way. Lesson learned.'

'I wasn't sure if I should ask.'

He looked straight ahead and changed the subject.

'This is a tricky beast of a case. We need to make Iona talk, find out what she's hiding and why. If she had a hand in the murders, we can't be restricted by medics. We need to question her.'

'I've been in contact with her doctor, Angela Duffy, again.

She told me Iona is making progress, but they are reluctant to push her. While she's happy for us to speak with Iona, we have to do it in situ at the hospital,' Rose said. 'And that means playing by their rules.'

Rose looked out at the sun-dappled houses as they drove up the Saintfield Road. 'Emotional injuries can be as profoundly debilitating as physical injuries. Whatever happened that night, Iona has been psychologically wounded. We have to tread carefully. The collateral damage of what she has experienced is post-traumatic amnesia. It may not be simply a matter of making her talk. Her memories of that night could be wiped.'

'No, we have to hope it's all there for the picking. It would be a bit too convenient to say she's had her brain wiped. That's like the type of defence you see on an American crime drama. We're not buying into that. How else would she be affected by the trauma of what went down in the cottage?'

'Anything from confusion, agitation, distress and anxiety through to acting out in uncharacteristic behaviours such as violence and aggression. In some cases, the patient may present as being quiet, docile and compliant,' Rose said.

Danny nodded. 'Go on.'

'It's likely that Iona has been in a heightened state of fear and panic. Her body will have been filled with adrenaline and this has several effects. The hippocampus is a part of the brain that processes memories. High levels of stress hormones, like adrenaline, can prevent it from functioning as it should. Often, we find that flashbacks and nightmares happen after the event because the memories of the trauma can't be processed in the normal, expected way. When the stress levels fall, the adrenaline levels get back to normal and the brain is then able to repair the damage itself. The symptoms that Iona is presenting with can occur as soon as the traumatic event occurs, or after a delay of weeks or even months.'

'I'm relying on you to cut through all of that. Flash her that Rosie smile, the sympathetic nod of the head, and see what gives.'

Further up the Saintfield Road they saw the sign for the hospital and pulled into the long driveway of the vast grounds. A sign listed the names of the buildings and units – Inver, Copeland, Divis, Donard and others, obviously named after Irish mountains, islands and rivers.

Tall, well-established trees populated the lush green grounds. Danny drove slowly up the hill and found the grey building where the Shannon Clinic unit was situated. When they parked the car and made their way into the unit, they came across a sign stating 'High security area. All visitors must sign in'.

Rose pressed on the buzzer. 'There's a risk that any information we get from her is actually only a reaction to placate us. The mind can turn on itself when it has been exposed to something traumatic. You saw that cottage. Anyone would be disturbed to have lived through that rampage. She's vulnerable.'

Danny sighed. 'The false confession only messed this case up even more. We have discounted her claim that she did it on the grounds that she couldn't have murdered them. According to the pathology reports, the force and entrance of the knife wounds mean that the killer was male and bigger than average. So, if Iona was involved, it was in some capacity of assistance. Plus, there's no motive yet that we can attribute to her.'

A voice came through the intercom, asking them who they were expecting to see.

'Patient Iona Gardener and Dr Duffy,' Danny replied.

'One minute please.'

'We can talk to her, see where we stand, and if she's willing, there's techniques the psychologists can use to help her recover memory. I've had a couple of conversations with Dr Duffy and she isn't so keen, so it may not be an option.'

'That's something we can fall back on,' Danny said as the automatic doors slid open.

The staff were more welcoming when they saw their credentials. It took a couple of nurses and questions before Danny tracked down Angela Duffy in her office. 'You found us, Detective,' she said, as she stood from her desk and reached out her hand to shake theirs.

'Aye, we did, so. You've spoke to Dr Lainey on the phone,' he said, by way of an introduction.

She nodded to Rose.

'I wondered, could we have a word before we go in to see Iona?' Danny asked.

'Of course. What can I do for you?'

'Have you seen anything like Iona Gardener's case before?'

'What, you mean a patient suffering from complex post-traumatic stress disorder?'

Danny nodded.

'Yes, we've seen cases like this before. The memory can be distorted when someone experiences a traumatic episode.'

'Yeah, I get that, but she has confessed to a crime that we know she can't have committed. She said she did it, not that she was involved or knew who had done it. Why would she do that?'

She leaned against the wall. 'You have to realise that recalling an episode from even the recent past may involve a blend of fiction and fact. There is a type of trauma-focused cognitive behavioural therapy that can help, but like anything of this nature, it can't be rushed.' She looked towards Rose, as if to say, this is all obvious.

'And can you tell if she is trying to fool us? Trying to hide what she knows by pretending she is so traumatised that she can't remember?' Danny asked.

'Detective, I can assure you we can tell the difference between someone who is presenting with clinical symptoms as opposed to someone who is putting on a show of pretence.'

'Aye, I'm sure, but you know, I have to check.'

'What's her recovery process been like?' Rose asked.

'We are working with her using a mixture of therapy and drugs, but it will take time to see progress and that's why you can't expect a breakthrough for your case any time soon. I'm sure you are aware of the need to be cautious of any information Iona may give you. She is starting to respond and to speak more, but I'm sure I don't need to tell you that it is a process. One that we can't force.'

'So, you're saying she isn't a credible witness in her present state,' Rose clarified.

'I'm saying she is at risk of giving you flawed testimony, that she can process the events and come up with a different version of the truth. She may have survivor guilt and may feel a huge sense of injustice that this has happened to her friends. Whatever she tells you, treat it with care.'

'Anything else we should know?' Rose asked.

'Iona was seeing a university counsellor before this happened. Mild depressive episodes. We've no reason to think that this was related to anything other than stress –

the pressures of modern living and exams looming – but I just wanted to mention it.'

They were shown into Iona's room and a Filipino nurse, who announced his name was Ernest, sat in with them. Danny took the chair near the window and spoke first.

'Iona, we need to talk to you again about the night before the murders. Do you remember my colleague Rose Lainey? She is a doctor, but she also works with the PSNI. We both want to help you. Can you go over what you all were doing that evening?'

Iona stared at him, her eyes limpid pools of nothingness. She was ghostly pale. Her skin diaphanous, the blue veins snaking across her wrist, which she kept rubbing with her other hand.

Rose put her hand out and reached over to take Iona's. 'I understand that this is hard for you, Iona. You have lost three of your friends. But I am also sure you want to help us find out who did it. Dylan is still seriously ill. If he recovers, he will be able to help us, too, but in the meantime, you are our only hope.'

She nodded ever so slightly. Enough to encourage them.

'Thank you for seeing me again,' Rose said.

'Sure, we're happy to see a visitor. Aren't we Iona?' Ernest said.

Iona didn't reply. She looked like she could hardly care where she was or who was speaking to her.

'Shall we have a wee sit outside in the courtyard?' the young orderly asked.

Rose nodded. It would be good for Iona to get out of the room with the pale green walls and sterile smell.

* * *

The walled courtyard was empty except for a table with a parasol and four chairs.

Iona sat first and Rose took a chair opposite her. The nurse sat apart from them in the shade of an overhanging roof.

Iona had that haunted look about her that only the grief stricken wore. Her pallor was greyish, and she had dark shadows in the hollows beneath her eyes. She looked like she hadn't seen the sun in years, despite only being here for two weeks.

'Iona, we need to ask you some questions. I am working on a particular angle of the case and have some questions of my own.'

She was staring down at her leggings, plucking the fabric repeatedly.

'Iona, in the cottage there was some graffiti on the wall of the downstairs living room.' Rose opened her folder of notes and passed a photograph of the wall towards Iona. Her eyes flickered to it for a second before looking away again and resuming the plucking of her leggings.

'It says "*Who Took Eden Mulligan?*" Do you know who wrote that on the wall?'

Again, that flicker of the eyes. A sharp darting, as if looking for an escape. Her eyebrow twitched involuntarily.

'Iona, we need to understand why that was written on the wall of the living room. Anything you tell us can help.'

'It was me. I wrote it.' Her voice was hoarse and whispery, as if she hadn't spoken for a long time. She looked directly at Rose, her eyes wide and suddenly brighter.

'Why did you write it? What connection do you have with the Mulligan family?'

The shutters came down, her face strangely passive and blank.

243

'Iona, did someone visit the cottage that night? Was there someone else there with you all?'

Her eyes flickered to the left. Danny noticed Rose taking note. It was a tell-tale sign that she was concealing something.

'Did you know the person?'

She nodded.

'Iona, talk to me. Tell me what happened.'

She swallowed hard. Opened her mouth slowly and then closed it again, as if she was unused to speaking. Then she began.

CHAPTER 42

'In the cottage, we were happy,' she said softly, barely above a whisper. 'It was like before, when we were all students, just hanging out, taking the piss out of each other and roaring with laughter. We had a shorthand together, everything was so easy.' Her voice was low and quiet with a raspy quality to it. Danny watched as she stared into the distance, looking as if she was viewing the scene unfold before her. She kept her hands clasped together on her lap, almost as though she was in prayer.

'It felt like a holiday at first. We had finished university and we were all about to start the next phase of our lives. We missed spending every day in each other's company just talking, reading, drinking and eating. At university, we would go to our separate lectures and then come home to study together, and spend the evenings hanging out. It was a golden time. We felt like it would never end. That's why when Henry suggested renting somewhere long term we all agreed.'

'Who was in the cottage with you, Iona?' Rose asked.

'Olivia, Dylan, Henry, Theo. The squad. That's what we called ourselves.'

She spoke as if she had all the time in the world.

'Can you tell me what happened on the night of the twenty-eighth of June?'

She shook her head, her whole body quivering in a quick, sharp shake, like a dog trying to avoid a leash.

Danny sat forward. 'Do you remember walking to the police station?'

'No. Did I walk?'

'We think so. There was no one with you where you appeared in the CCTV footage and you arrived on foot.'

'My feet were sore and cut up.' She reached down to rub at her ankle. 'That must be why.' She said it as if it had only just occurred to her.

'You were out of breath and upset when you got to the police station.'

'Was I?'

'Yes, they said you were distressed, in a state. Cuts on your arms and hands. Don't you remember?'

'Not really.' She avoided his gaze.

Rose placed her notebook on the table in front of them. 'Iona, on the night the stabbings happened, where were you?'

'In the cottage, I think.' Her voice was low with an edge of something like trepidation.

'And who was with you?'

'The squad. All of us.'

'That's Olivia, Henry, Dylan and Theo?'

She nodded.

'Do you recall what you ate that night?'

'Pasta, I think. Olivia and Dylan probably cooked. We had been out on a long hike, I remember that.'

'That's good. So, what time were you out on the hike?'

She shrugged. 'Early. Maybe ten in the morning.' She said it almost like a question, as if she wanted reassurance.

'And where did you walk?'

'Around the grounds.'

'Okay. That's good. So, when do you think you returned to the cottage?'

'Late afternoon. It was a really sunny day. We ate lunch while we were out. We had packed sandwiches and sat near a stream to eat them. Theo had sunburn along his shoulders. I can remember that.'

'And after you returned to the cottage, were you all together?'

'Yes, we were. I can remember Olivia saying she was going to have a shower. Dylan was reading in the garden. Theo and Henry were playing some card game,' She was staring straight ahead. 'I don't know what I was doing.'

'That's okay. You're doing great. You said there was someone else in the cottage. Who was that?'

'Me. But I wasn't me, I was different somehow.'

Rose leaned forward. 'Iona, there is something we need to know – do you have any connection to Eden Mulligan?'

She started and shook her head.

Eden Mulligan disappeared in 1986 and we think it might have something to do with the killing of your friends.'

Her bottom lip quivered, making Danny think of a child moments before it began to cry.

'I can't remember anything else. I'm sorry, but I can't.' Her voice was raised, panic creeping in.

She lifted her head and looked directly at Rose. 'There is only one thing I am certain of. I do know that I did it. I killed them. I just don't know why.'

CHAPTER 43

'So, Dr Lainey, making yourself at home?' Malachy Magee appeared at the doorway of Rose's office.

'Doing my best. Come on in. And you can call me Rose. I don't need a title.'

'In that case, call me Mal. Malachy makes me feel like my mother is around.'

Rose laughed. 'Take a seat.'

'How are you finding being back in Belfast?' he asked.

'In some ways it's like I've never left and then I'll walk through the Cathedral Quarter and see the place alive with revelry. The city centre was still pretty much a ghost town at night when I was a teenager.'

'Aye, the young ones don't know how good they've got it these days. So, how are you finding the case?' Malachy asked. He seemed genuinely interested. Rose had the impression that Danny rated Magee despite his tendency to clock watch and head home as soon as he could.

'All good. I'm dredging through the Mulligan case notes, checking to see if we've missed anything.'

'Bad business that case. What are your thoughts on the original investigation?'

'The family were fobbed off. Too many other demands on the RUC to justify a proper inquiry – that's their story, anyway. A disappeared mother didn't warrant too much attention.'

'And we're expected to pick up the pieces decades later.'

'The connection with the Dunlore murders certainly demands a full investigation. Something must connect them. So, what are you doing down here?'

'That would be my doing,' Danny said, coming in and closing the door behind him. 'Rose, I want you to talk Mal through Iona's state of mind. He's worked with forensic psychologists on other cases and has an interest in this kind of work. Look, here's the profile Rose drew up.'

He handed Malachy the file and waited while he scanned over everything.

Rose took out her notebook and pen for something to do.

'Before we begin looking at the report details on Iona, I need you to understand why someone would confess to a crime they clearly didn't commit,' Rose said.

'First of all, are you certain she didn't do it?' Malachy asked. 'We all know a confession can appear to be the golden ticket. Why go looking elsewhere if your case ties itself up for you? But we all should remember, a dodgy conviction is worse than no conviction. Sometimes it's just too good to be true. But in this case, there are just too many improbables. You saw the crime scene. Iona Gardener's build, height and strength all say that she couldn't have done it. But was she working with someone or covering for someone? Could she have a connection to Eden Mulligan that she is hiding? That's what we don't fully understand yet,' he said, leaning back in his chair.

Rose took that as her cue to jump in. 'To create the profile, I have examined the location of the crime, the method of entry, the weapon used, the nature of the attacks and the apparent randomness of the knife entry wounds. All of this helps to gain an understanding of the perpetrator and to give us a sense of what happened in the cottage. Evidence suggests that Iona could not have been our attacker and that she couldn't have moved the bodies on her own. But we have to ask: is she the accessory or co-conspirator? Was Iona the one to assist the killer?

'As for the graffiti, when Iona was brought to the hospital originally, she was examined thoroughly and there was no trace of charcoal on her hands or under her nails. And what's more, a handwriting expert says it was done by someone who is left-handed. Iona is right-handed so, with all of that in mind, we can safely say she didn't write it. Our next question has to be, what made her think she did it or, at least, why did she claim she did?'

Malachy sighed with exasperation. 'God, this case is doing my head in. Why is she lying? Who is she protecting?'

'My assessment of Iona is based on the interview and the reports from her psychiatric doctor and the mental health team. In a state of high anxiety such as fear or terror, the prefrontal cortex can be compromised. Sequencing information – the timelines, the place and layout of where she has been – is impaired, damaging her memories. It can take years for this to heal,' Rose said.

'We all know innocent people can get locked up for crimes they haven't committed and I'm not just talking about the Guildford pub bombings type of scenario.' Danny commented.

'Yeah, but usually it's following an old-fashioned Castlereagh-type interrogation, or they are coerced into it.' Rose looked at Danny, their eyes locking for just a second before she glanced down at her notebook.

Malachy walked over to the window. 'Sometimes people want the attention, or the notoriety of being involved in a big crime. Maybe Iona falls into that category. She's attention seeking.'

'In my experience, a lot of people say they committed a crime just to get out of the interrogation room, thinking they can retract their statement at any time – the complaint false confessors – or as you say, Mal, they just want the attention. We've all seen it in high-profile cases, where there's a lot of media attention. I have occasionally come across someone who truly believes they're guilty though. They internalise the crime, and persuade themselves that they are responsible. This is the category I think Iona falls into.'

She paused.

'In Iona's case, I believe she is confabulating memories. She has claimed responsibility for crimes she did not commit, without pressure from the police – no coercion or long, drawn out interrogation. She walked into the station, apparently unprompted, and said she had committed the murders. Our next questions have to be: is this out of a desire to protect the real perpetrator? Is she deluded and suffering from some sort of psychotic episode? Or is this some sort of self-punishment to pay for either real or imagined past transgressions?'

'Exactly where do we go from here then?' asked Malachy.

'We can assume that whatever happened in that cottage was traumatic for Iona to witness. Her memory of what transpired may be distorted beyond reality at present but, thankfully, this is usually not a permanent state. I think you will find that as the days go on, she will come to the realisation that she is not the murderer, even if she never regains a full understanding of what happened.'

Suddenly Rose turned to Danny. 'Maybe she knew him.'

'Who, the killer?' he asked.

Malachy put his hands behind his neck. 'Yeah, that could be why she wasn't so badly hurt.'

'It would explain her sense of responsibility. Her connection with the killer is the reason she is still alive,' Rose said.

'If she knew him, she could've let him into the cottage. She didn't feel he was a risk. But why spare her, and why is she taking the blame?' Danny said.

'The Mulligan case – did Iona say anything about it to you?' Malachy asked.

'No. We've nothing more than the graffiti, but there has to be something more. We just haven't found it yet,' Danny said.

CHAPTER 44

Rose felt the thin cotton of her T-shirt stick to her back. She longed for a shower to wash the grime of the day away, but she was hours from getting home. On her desk, she spread out interview transcripts from the Mulligan children. They had each given her their version of what had happened. When they realised that their mother was gone, they initially tried to cope alone, not informing anyone, hoping that she would be back, that she had just popped out for a minute. Cormac had been adamant that she had been taken and had begged them to contact the police. The others had persuaded him to wait. They had no means of reaching their father and Rose suspected that they didn't have an expectation of him coming back to care for them.

A half-eaten chicken and avocado sandwich, bought at lunchtime, lay drying up and curling at the edges on her desk. The air was still and the slice of sunlight that came through the high-up window had reached the far side of the office. Her stomach lurched, reminding her that she needed to eat. Her watch showed that it was gone 7.25 p.m. She thought of people with normal jobs, clocking off at six, going home to eat with their loved ones, spending a couple of hours catching up on rubbish TV or mundane chores, something nice like cutting the grass or dead-heading flowers. A night like this called to be outdoors. She'd thought of going to see Kaitlin, sitting on the patio, sipping a cool glass of prosecco with her family around. That would never be her life though. And she didn't know if that made her sorry or glad.

She had enough self-awareness to know that the job served as a handy out. An excuse to opt out of playing happy families, settling down and getting married. There was something she recognised in Danny that told her he needed the excuse as well. He drowned the pain of his disastrous marriage by clocking up hours on the job. That sense of being fully awake, present and ready, could only be achieved if you gave the job all you had. There was no room for anyone – or anything – else.

She thought of the Mulligans. How their lives had been consumed and damaged by the absence of their mother. The girls had made something of themselves. Lizzie, in particular, had done well for herself. She had forged a career as student counsellor and was married to a builder – a self-made man by all accounts, who specialised in commercial properties. But the boys were rudderless, each one finding their way through the murkiness of life without the relief of snatched moments of joy. She couldn't imagine what that would do to a person.

Paddy's testimony was the slimmest of them all. He held back in ways that Cormac and Eamonn hadn't. In the family meeting, he had appeared troubled, struggling to stay in the room and listening to the talk of the investigation. He hadn't wanted any part in the proposed dig. 'What would it change?' he had asked, his words slightly slurred by drink.

'Awk Paddy, come on,' Eileen said. 'It would at least give us some sense of closure.'

'Fuck closure. What in the hell good is closure to any of us? It won't bring her back and it won't right the wrongs of the past, will it?'

Eileen shrugged and looked away.

He had approached Rose when they were finishing off and leaving the Europa, putting his hand on her shoulder to catch her before she left. 'Look, I'm sorry about being late an' all. I'm not the best when it comes to these here type of things. Sometimes I think we'd all be better off just forgetting. If the doctors could give me a tablet to wipe my memories I'd take it. How fucking sad is that?'

Reading his transcript, Rose felt compelled to talk to him again. Of all the siblings, he was the one she had the least handle on. The sisters Eileen and Lizzie had been more forthcoming. They had been keen to follow through with the new dig and had been insistent on Rose pushing for more to be done. They had managed to salvage something after the wasteland of their childhoods. The boys hadn't fared so well.

Father Edmund Ryan's story also wasn't complete. Rose felt that she should at least try to pick up the lead and see where it took her. Father Dominic on the Antrim Road had been a bit of help. If Rose wanted to dig deeper she had to go to the source. Ryan may be dead, but the church he had sought shelter in and served in was still standing.

She dialled the number for Father Ryan's church in Boston and held her breath, hoping for the break she needed.

'Hello. I am calling from the Police Service of Northern Ireland.'

the secretary she would have ris to mean. In Boston

CHAPTER 45

The package bore a US postmark and had the word 'private' stamped across the top. Rose carried it into her office and opened it to find a typed letter from Marni, the secretary from the Boston parish house who Rose had spoken to on the phone. The letter stated that Marni had done some research on Father Edmund Ryan and had discovered he wasn't dead, but living in a retirement home somewhere in Bray, Ireland. Rose took in a sharp breath. If Ryan was still alive, she had a chance of questioning him.

But why did Father Dominic say he was dead? She paused, trying to gather her thoughts. Was Father Dominic protecting Ryan? Or had he been misled? Either way, she had to try to track down Ryan. The package included photocopies of documents showing that Edmund Ryan had resided in the parish in Boston for twenty-one years. He had assisted the parish priest, but never moved beyond that role. A priest as charismatic as Katy Carberry had painted him surely would have risen to the position of parish priest at some stage. Rose wondered if he had been blocked by senior officials in the climb to a more senior role, and what the reasons for keeping him contained might have been.

She wondered if her mother had known Father Ryan. The idea of a link between Evelyn and this case had niggled at Rose before but her suspicion was growing stronger now. Belfast wasn't a big city and it wasn't unknown for women to take up active roles with the paramilitaries, a role which may have brought her mother into contact with the priest. She wondered if her mother had been alive, would she have questioned her. Asked her if she had known Eden Mulligan. Rose shuddered. She had waited too long to do what she should have done from day one on this case – put Evelyn's details into the system and tell Danny about her mother's connection to the paramilitaries.

Before that, she had a meeting set up with Paddy Mulligan.

Convincing him to see her hadn't been easy. He had the same reluctance that Eamonn and Cormac had displayed, and there was also an edge of something else. Some undercurrent of resistance that Rose had put down to distrust of the police and the authorities. After all, he and his family had no reason to place their faith in Rose. She got that, but in the absence of anyone else fighting their corner, she failed to see what they had to lose by working with her.

They had arranged to meet in Bittles bar, a flatiron-style red brick building in the city centre. Rose walked through the narrow door and found it was a traditional pub, all dark wood and faux leather-topped stools sitting snuggly around wooden tables. It was one of those Belfast pubs that had managed to ride the dark days of the Troubles and even survive the hipster brigade. It has retained its worn-in pub vibe, not trying too hard to please anyone, offering food, a great selection of beers on draught and a cocktail menu. In spite of the balmy day outside, a fire was lit in the grate. A lone fiddler played diddly dee music to keep the tourists happy, while the rest of the crowd got on with their afternoon of drinking. Paintings of famous Northern Irish writers, poets, politicians and sports people decorated the walls, and the clientele looked to be regular fixtures, old men nursing pints.

She scanned the place and found Paddy standing at the bar.

'Paddy, how are you?' Rose said, moving in next to him.

'Aye, I'm grand. What are you having?'

'A tonic water will do me, thanks.'

He ordered their drinks and they carried them over to a corner away from the main bar area. Rose took the glass of tonic water from him.

'Thanks,' she said, taking a sip.

'That weather would give anyone a thirst. It's to change at the weekend. I heard thunder and lightning is the forecast. It'll clear the air.'

'Yeah, I heard the same. Still, it's been good while it lasted.'

He put the green bottle of Heineken he'd ordered to his lips and swallowed.

'I'm not used to being in a room with all my family at the same time. I find it all . . .' he paused, looking for the right word. '*Forced.*'

Rose nodded. 'Families are complicated at the best of times. Throw in what you have all gone through and it must be extremely hard.'

He nodded.

'We struggle. Keeping in touch is one thing, but we can't be doing with family occasions. It's never felt right. There was one Christmas we talked about spending it together, but by the time Christmas Eve came along we all wised up and realised it was a bad idea.'

'Yeah, I can appreciate it would be difficult. So, do you work, Paddy?'

'Aye, here and there. You got to have a bit of money to get by.'

'What do you do?'

'Gym work, mostly. Personal training, like. That, and sometimes I do a bit of maintenance on buildings for a mate of mine. He's a roofer, but he gets asked to do all sorts and I give him a hand for a few quid.'

'How old were you, Paddy, when your mum went missing?' She knew, of course, but it was a way in, to get him to talk about the past.

'I was eight. Only just made my holy communion the year before. Me and Lizzie were all dressed up for the occasion. That was the last happy memory I have of my mother and my family. Can you imagine what that's like?'

'Afterwards, you were adopted by Linda and Alan Atwood, isn't that right?'

'Yeah, they all talked like Lizzie and me were the lucky ones to get taken on by a married couple, and be brought up like their own. Teachers, they were. Supposed to be good, upstanding people. Went to mass on a Sunday and helped out at parish events. Well, let's just say it didn't work out for me.'

'Lizzie stayed with them, even after you had made a formal complaint of being abused?'

He shrugged. 'That was her choice.'

Rose made a mental note to follow up with Lizzie. See what her take on this was. Why had the authorities not intervened and taken Lizzie away, too, if the Atwoods had been abusive?

'What's your theory on all this?'

He downed the last of his bottle of beer. 'My theory?'

'Yeah, what do you think happened to your mother?'

'What da fuck do I know? She skedaddled, vanished into thin air, and there was nothing left but a black hole of where she'd once existed. *D'imigh sí gan tásc ná turairisc*: disappeared without a trace.'

'So, you don't have a sense of what might have happened?'

'Either my Da and us weeuns drove her to top herself, or someone whacked her. There's not many other likely scenarios.'

'Was there someone you thought would be likely to want to harm her?'

He stared at his empty beer bottle. 'I need a piss and another beer. What about you?'

She nodded. 'I'll have another – the same again – but here, take this. It's my round.' She handed him a ten-pound note for the drinks.

When he came back he looked agitated. His eyes had that glazed look and he had a sheen of sweat on his forehead. He'd obviously taken a snort of coke in the toilets.

'Here's your drink,' he said, setting it down in front of Rose.

Within minutes, he was rambling on about the state of the Northern Ireland assembly. The lack of quality politicians. 'At least back in the day people like McGuinness and Paisley had convictions. You knew where you stood with them. This shower of shites, well they're only interested in collecting their fat pay packets. To hell with the average man and woman on the streets. Don't you agree?'

Rose wasn't going to get anywhere with him. She decided to call time on their meeting.

'Paddy, I have to head off now, but if you can think of anything I should know about your mother, please call me.' She reached into her bag and retrieved a card with her contact details, setting it down beside his beer.

'Aye, right, no problem.'

She went out into the street, relieved to be out of his company.

CHAPTER 46

A few phone calls had led Danny to Iona Gardener's university advisor. She didn't appear to be too put out to meet him on a Saturday morning, so he headed to the university quarter, pulled into Rugby Road, and found a space to park. Come October, when the students were back at the university, parking would be a nightmare, but for now he was grateful that he didn't have to abandon his car a mile away and walk. He didn't have time to waste.

He intended for it to be a quick chat before heading back to the station to give the rest of the team a bollocking. If they were clocking up overtime, he wanted to be getting the most out of them. Managing the team was a challenge. Instinctively, he wanted to be liked, to be everyone's mate, but he knew that was professional suicide.

The university area was peaceful. The tall sycamore trees provided shade as he made his way past the red brick Victorian houses, each identical except for the colours of their doors. He couldn't help peering in through their sash windows and catching glimpses of bookcases and comfortable armchairs.

It all looked genteel and academic; a million miles away from his rural upbringing of pig shit and turf.

Professor Danielle Wheeler met Danny at the entrance to the school of social sciences – a modern addition to the Gothic style of the main Lanyon building – situated within the quadrangle overlooking an immaculate grassy square. Professor Wheeler was in her fifties and looked trim and fit. Her platinum grey hair was cut short and spiky and she was dressed in jeans and a faded green T-shirt with a slogan proclaiming something about the climate crisis.

'Detective Stowe, come on up to my office.'

Danny followed her up the two flights of stairs. She offered him a glass of water but he declined and took a chair next to her desk, the surface of which was clear except for a laptop and a few text books.

'Professor Wheeler, I know my colleague, DS King, spoke to you on the phone, but I felt it might be useful to meet in person.'

'Yes, such a tragedy. Iona is due to graduate from her post-graduate diploma in the autumn. I've checked her exams and she is sitting on high marks. She still has her dissertation to submit, but I was her supervisor and know that she was producing exemplary work.'

'Forgive me, but what was it she was studying? Social work, was it?'

'Social work and policy studies. It's a professional certi-fication. I've no doubt she will find work straight away. She has a nice way about her. Very capable, with the right attitude, too. Not everyone is cut out for clinical work, but I'm certain Iona would manage to deal with whatever the job threw at her.'

'What area of study was she interested in?'

'Her dissertation was based on cross-generational trauma – the notion that even in a largely peaceful time, young people in Northern Ireland are affected by the violence of the past.

'The theory behind it was that we have a whole generation of young people born after the cease fire, yet they still feel compelled in some way to express their identity in terms of the culture inherited from their parents. She was keen to understand how the conflict of the past affected young people and her work was making a study of how some young people in socially deprived areas continue to perpetuate the sectarian prejudices that have marred our society.'

'Sounds worthy.'

She nodded. 'We are only beginning to understand the full impact of the conflict on our communities. The trauma, the crisis management way of living . . . it all takes its toll. Even when the guns are silent.'

'You weren't aware of Iona being in any kind of trouble?'

She shook her head. 'Not that I can think of. I did take the liberty of looking at her student file after your colleague called me, and there is mention of Iona making use of the student welfare and counselling service. I don't know if there was a particular issue, but she did have a few sessions with one of our counsellors. That's not an unusual occurrence though. The demand for student counselling has rocketed in recent years.'

Danny nodded. Angela Duffy had mentioned that at the Shannon Clinic. 'I'll take the details of this counselling service if you have them handy.'

'Of course, I'll jot down the number and the address.'

Ten minutes later, Danny was back out in the hot sun,

about to leave the campus, when he received a call from Jamie King.

'Stowe here, what's up?'

'Dylan Wray has died.'

CHAPTER 47

Back at her apartment, Rose closed the curtains against the blank expanse of the night. At times, the view across the harbour made her feel vulnerable, as if she were being watched, even though she knew that was ridiculous. The cost of her upbringing was a sense of wariness. Always expecting the worst and having to second guess every movement. That sense had only been heightened since returning to Northern Ireland. The need to check under a car for devices, varying routes to work, and always being watchful hadn't disappeared overnight for her colleagues as dissidents proved to be a continuing threat. Although police stations looked less like fortified military bases, there were still real challenges to working in a society used to seeing the police as the enemy.

Rose sat on the sofa, kicked off her shoes and yawned. Tiredness felt like a familiar old friend, always hanging around. Yet, despite the tiredness, her brain felt wired, as if she needed to remember something she had forgotten. The case was getting to her. When she was at university she'd had the same feeling when it came to studying, that she could never do enough to feel satisfied and confident in her ability.

Later, when she was lost to sleep, her phone rang. Instantly, she knew it was Danny. Who else would be calling her at this ridiculous hour of the morning? For a second she felt regret – or was it sadness – that life beyond work didn't exist for her. Usually, she would say that's the way she had designed it, but lately, there had been a sense of missing out. That she had limited her life by choosing work over relationships.

'What's up?'

'Did I wake you, Rose?'

'It's 5 a.m. Yes, you woke me,' she said, though she knew whatever he had woken her for would be worth it.

'I've been thinking about those dolls hanging in the tree.'

'Yeah, what about them?'

'We've been working on the assumption that they alluded to the five people in the cottage. What if they don't represent them? What if the dolls are the Mulligan children?'

Rose sat up and rubbed her eyes, her other hand pressing the phone against her ear.

'A doll for each abandoned child?'

'Exactly. It makes sense. Whoever went into the cottage armed with a knife did so in a planned manner. They knew who they were after and obviously had a reason. The graffiti and the five dolls are messages.'

Rose leaned against her pillows. 'There's something else that's been bothering me. Don't you think that it's a strange coincidence that the Mulligan case came up for review just before the murders?'

She could practically hear him thinking, turning it over in his mind.

'Who could have known?' she asked.

'I don't know.'

'Meet me in an hour?'

'Okay, I've got to feed the chickens first so it will be closer to seven.'

'Chickens?'

'I'm down home with the parents, got to do my bit.'

The roads were quiet. Not a sinner up at this hour of the morning on a Saturday. Rose had agreed to meet Danny off-site, away from the station. Sometimes you needed to take a breather, to think outside the box and being somewhere different helped.

'Right, here you go,' said Danny, handing her a sausage sandwich, brown sauce leaking out the side.

'Thanks, I think. I'm sure I'll regret eating that the minute it's down.'

'The least I could do after waking you up so early this morning.' The motorway café was starting to catch some passing trade. People stopping in to grab a coffee before they embarked on the rest of their journey.

He sat opposite her and she took a sip of her coffee, savouring the tarry taste and the mellow warmth it offered.

'Ahh.' Danny sighed, drinking his own. 'Nothing like the first coffee of the day. You can't bate it with a big stick. Pure nectar. Right, get this down us and then to business,' he said, biting into his sandwich. 'I think we need to consider where the decision to look into the Eden Mulligan case came from. The case file had been flagged up before the Dunlore murders. Who made that call to McCausland and why now?'

'Could be a coincidence, timing wise,' Rose suggested.

'It's possible, but we don't do coincidences in this job. Too convenient. McCausland said the call came from the very top. He said that pressure to look into the case had come from the first minister and deputy first minister. He implied it was to be a cursory exercise, to appease certain sections.'

Danny drained his coffee. 'The dolls and the Mulligan graffiti scrawled on the wall aren't enough on their own to make this about Eden's disappearance. There has to be another link. Something more substantial that we are missing.'

'Maybe,' she said. 'I'm thinking of McCausland's assertion that back in the day things were different, that they had bigger concerns than a runaway mother. But who decided she had run away, and why were they so quick to dismiss the case as not being worth investigating fully? They are the questions that bother me most.'

'Any luck with the priest?'

'St Aloysius' parish secretary wasn't able to help, but she did say that there was an association of retired Irish priests based in the diocese. Maybe that's where I need to go with my inquiries.'

'What next, then?'

'First, you buy me another coffee, then we go visit Iona again.'

CHAPTER 48

'I hate these places,' Danny said, turning to Rose as he showed his ID to a camera tracking their movements in the front lobby. 'They give me the creeps,' he whispered as Rose shot him a look telling him to behave himself.

The glass doors opened, permitting them to enter the coolness of the reception area, where they were met by an orderly wearing a uniform of a navy-blue polo shirt and dark trousers. He introduced himself as Adam and asked them to follow him to the day room. 'Dr Duffy is expecting you,' he said in a broad Ballymena accent. 'What's it like out there? Sun still shining?'

'Aye, it's going to be another baking hot day, for sure.' Danny said, following him down the corridor.

They were a taken to a cosy room set up with sofas and a television, wide glass doors leading out to a patio area filled with an assortment of potted plants. The scene looked like it had been set up to resemble a regular living room instead of a hospital setting, but there was no disguising the cameras in the corners and the one-way mirror built into the far wall.

Iona sat perfectly still, her back straight, looking into space with a slightly dazed expression. She wore a simple white cotton blouse and a dark blue skirt, which at once made Danny think of a nun. They weren't exactly the kind of clothes you'd expect a young woman to choose and were generic enough to suggest someone had bought them for her.

'Iona, how are you? It's us back again. We need to talk to you about what happened. Do you think that would be okay?' Rose asked.

She gave a slight nod. Rose looked to Danny, as if to tell him to let her take the lead, and they sat on the sofa opposite Iona.

'Is it okay if we record our conversation?'

She nodded.

'How about you tell us again what you know, what you think happened?' Rose said, after turning the recording device on.

'I don't really remember it all. I've told you already. Just bits and pieces. Parts of the night are coming back to me but I don't want to remember. It's too awful.' Her voice was childlike, high pitched and quivering.

'That's okay. Whatever you can tell us will be good. A small detail might seem insignificant, but could actually make all the difference.'

She nodded.

'Okay, what is the last thing you can recall before the hospital?' Rose leaned close.

'Running. Running on grass, hurting my feet, tripping over

273

a root and being so frightened. But it's strange, I'm not frightened for me. It's the others. I know they are in danger and all I can do is run. I can't save them. I don't even try.' Her breathing was ragged, her skin waxy and pale.

'It's okay, Iona, we know this is hard, but you are doing really well.' Rose spoke quietly as she leaned across and took Iona's hands, looking into her eyes. Danny willed himself to sit back and let Rose do her thing. He itched to wade in and ask the questions, but he respected Rose's authority in dealing with Iona. They still didn't know for sure if she was a victim or a suspect.

'We need you to try and remember who you were running from. Who was in the cottage?' Rose continued.

They had to tread carefully, if Iona shut down or did anything to harm herself again, they wouldn't get another chance to question her.

She stopped, her eyes wide and staring. 'I don't know. I can't stop myself. I'm hurting them with the knife. Over and over again. There's blood on my hands. It's warm.' She started to cry, shaking and twisting her hands like she was being held by someone and needed to fight them off. 'I can't do this. I can't!' Her voice was raised, and she looked panic-stricken.

Back in the car, Danny sighed and thumped the steering wheel in frustration. 'This fucking case. I can't get a break. She's in there messing with us. All this softly, softly approach is getting us nowhere.'

He sighed again, putting the keys in the ignition, but not starting the engine.

'Sorry. I'm pissed off. For a second I thought we were going to get somewhere with her this time.'

'What is it about her that has got under your skin?'

'I don't know. The mystery of it all, I suppose. It's clear she didn't do it, yet she claims she did. Why? What has driven her to feel like this, to be so desperate to take the blame?'

'It's her desire to take responsibility for the deaths that we have to look at.'

'Yeah, at this point, what I really want to know is why she believes she did it.'

'This case has really got to you, hasn't it?'

'They all do, one way or another. You know what it's like, we don't exactly get to switch off at the end of the day.'

'No, but that's not all, is it? Iona has got to you.'

He turned to Rose and shrugged.

'I suppose you're right.'

'She reminds you of Amy, doesn't she?'

'No, well . . . not exactly. They look nothing alike. I suppose it's her fragility, this place, knowing what it looks like to see someone lose themselves so completely to whatever tricks their mind is playing on them . . .' He looked down at his hands.

'You can't save all the broken girls in the world, you know.'

'That's not what this is. I just want to do my job. Get the right result.'

She nodded.

How could he explain how he felt about Amy and this case? He knew something of what Iona was going through, that sense of fractured reality where what she believed was at odds with the rest of the world. Just like Amy and her issues. His life had been wrecked by Amy's illness and the break-up. Now he had to put himself back together again and work was all that he had to hang on to.

Rose looked at him directly. 'It has to be someone she had built up a relationship with. Someone she trusted. Iona could be the link to the Mulligan case we've been looking for.'

'You think she knew the Mulligans? And that one of *them* did it?'

'Like Joel said, all the previous inquiries into Eden's disappearance messed Eamonn up. They promised him all sorts of resolution, and all the time it was just raking over the past, making him more and more desperate,' Rose said.

'I don't know if I could see him being desperate enough to murder three people though. I could see him doing something, some grand gesture, but this? I'm not so sure.'

'Hypothetically speaking, if one of them did do it, what would the motive be? Revenge? Some sort of vengeance?'

'Maybe. They're all pretty damaged.'

'I'd say so, but that doesn't necessarily make them murderers.'

CHAPTER 49

'Kaitlin can we meet? I need to talk.' Rose held the phone under her chin while she scanned the document on the screen in front of her. Searching the database for Evelyn hadn't been easy. She didn't have the necessary security clearance that Danny had, and she didn't want to alert him to her search just yet. Still, she was able to put Evelyn's name and date of birth into the computer to see what it would throw up.

Rose could hardly believe what she was reading: *Classified Information. Access denied.* Whatever Evelyn had been involved in was protected under security protocols. She knew information of this nature was sensitive and could be potentially explosive. Discovering her mother's name being protected in this way meant it was much worse than she'd imagined. She had expected to uncover something, but seeing Evelyn's name protected as classified was gut wrenching. Whatever she had done, it was murky.

She'd arranged to meet Kaitlin in a café off Dublin Road. It was dark and dingy, not at all like most of the swanky sandwich places dotted all over that part of the city.

'What's the emergency?' Kait said as she approached Rose and slid into the booth.

'No emergency, I just wanted to talk. We should order something first.'

They both studied the menu and placed their orders.

Kaitlin looked at her expectantly. 'Well, what is it?'

'Ma. I want to know what you know.'

'There's nothing to tell. You knew her as well as I did. Just because I stayed and you moved away doesn't give me some great insight into her. She was a creature of habit. Liked to keep the house just so. Didn't go out much towards the end.'

'That's not what I mean and you know it.' Her words sounded sharper than she'd intended.

'Roisin, the past is better off left alone. Why are you raking over old ashes?'

Rose shrugged. 'It's my job to rake over them. I'm working on the Mulligan case and I can't ignore the fact that we lived in the same area as Eden Mulligan. If Evelyn was involved, I need to know.'

'No, you don't. She's dead and she isn't coming back, so any idea you have of retribution and justice has gone with her.'

'The Mulligan children need answers.'

'Why would you think our mum had anything to do with *that*? Have you found something that would suggest as much?'

'No, but that's beside the point.'

Kaitlin sighed. 'Listen to yourself. It's ridiculous! Plenty of people supported the republican movement. Our mother carried the grief for our father and sure, it turned her bitter and hard, but that doesn't mean to say we need to know the ins and outs of her life.'

'I remember the calls in the night. The times she would go off on some unexplained errand. Are you telling me that's not suspicious?'

'Who knows. Maybe she was having an affair.'

The sandwiches arrived, and they began eating. 'Would Pearse know anything?'

'No, and don't go there. He's a header, in case you hadn't noticed. He doesn't approve of you working for the police. It's best you keep your distance.'

'Another hardliner in the family. That's all we need.'

Kaitlin shrugged. 'People can experience the same life and have different perceptions of what's right and wrong. You shouldn't be so quick to judge.'

Rose finished her sandwich. 'I better get back to work.'

She stood and Kaitlin did the same. 'Stop looking for problems. Let the dead lie in peace. You shouldn't go looking for trouble.'

Rose placed a twenty-pound note on the table to cover the bill, kissed her sister on the cheek and headed out into the sunlight.

Back in the office Rose sought out Danny and found him on the phone. As she was waiting for him to finish, Malachy strode across the room and indicated for him to wind up the conversation.

'What is it?' Danny said placing the receiver into the telephone base.

'I've just been down to the university following up on Iona's use of their counselling service.'

'Well?' Rose asked.

'Guess who's on their books as a part-time counsellor?'

'Who? Come on Mal, don't leave me hanging,' Danny said.

'Lizzie Mulligan.' Malachy looked suitably pleased with himself.

'Christ!' Danny said, standing up.

Everything felt as though it was on a knife edge. This was the break they needed to connect the Mulligan family to the murders.

'What do we do now? Send a squad car to pick Lizzie Mulligan up?' Malachy asked.

'I don't know if now is the right time to pull Lizzie Mulligan in. It's the break we need and it's an interesting connection to Iona, but we need more information,' Rose said.

'You're right,' Danny said. 'We do more digging.'

CHAPTER 50

'What would you say to your younger self if you had a chance?' Danny said, staring into his cold coffee. Rose could see he was morose. The pressure of the case was getting to him. She suspected he was also feeling depressed about his divorce. She'd never met Amy, so even though she knew from Danny she had her problems, Rose's sympathies lay with him. If Amy knew how miserable he was over their break-up, maybe she would have felt different; fought harder to keep their marriage together. Rose felt a flicker of sadness that she had no one to feel so strongly about her.

'Me? I'd say get a good haircut and don't let men fuck you over. What about you?'

'I'd say run and don't ever come back. Don't join the police and don't try to understand women.'

Whatever Amy's problems were, they were beyond his ability to fix, but it was clear he wasn't over her or his marriage. He needed to face the fact that it was over instead of holding on to the past.

'Come on, Danny boy. You need to put Amy behind you and get yourself out there.'

'Out where, Rosie?'

'Out on the field, or in the sea, whatever stupid name you want to call it. Out there where you can meet other women and have some fun. Sign up to Tinder or something.'

'Believe me, another woman is the last thing I need. I've sworn off you lot for life. Christ, can you imagine if someone in the station got wind of me being on Tinder? I'd never hear the end of it.'

'Catch yourself on, culchie boy. They're all on it. It's the only way to hook up these days.'

He watched her use the wooden stick to swirl around the froth on her coffee.

'So, are you on this here Tinder thing or have you got someone waiting on you back in London?'

She looked up at him and held his gaze for a second. 'No, it's just me.'

'Do you remember when we used to go to that student dive at the end of Slater Street?'

'Oh God, what was it called? Mojo's, or something.'

'Yeah, that's the one. We'd always try to get the corner table away from all the regulars. Sort of still feels like that now. Us trying to claim our own corner.'

'You're still missing Amy. Trying to recreate something from the past to make up for what you think you're missing in the present.'

'I didn't realise I was on the couch, Dr Lainey.'

She looked down. He didn't want to hear her professional opinion.

He sat back in the chair. 'Well, one thing's for sure, I don't have time for Tinder – this case is sapping my strength.

Have you any idea of the number of officers I've pulled in to work overtime? McCausland is having a hissy fit and I've sweet eff all to give him.'

'Tell you what, come and have a read through the stuff I've gathered on the Mulligan case. You might see something I've missed.'

'Rosie, I've too much of my own to wade through.'

'Suit yourself. Stop wallowing and do something proactive. Self-pity is not a good look. I know the case is dragging at this stage, but you know the score. Right when you least expect it something will fall into place and you'll get that buzz. The one that makes you feel indispensable and at the top of your game.'

'Do you promise?'

'Nope. You have to make it happen.'

She gave him a look that was meant to say: buck yourself up.

'No one said that this job was going to be easy.'

'It isn't always about the job, you know.'

She rounded on him. 'Danny, I know you've had a shitty break-up, but come on, it's over. Move on.' Knowing Danny as she did, she realised he needed her to be hard on him. Needed to make him think that he had every right to look to the future. His nature meant that he was still harking back, hoping to fix that which was broken.

'You can be a hard bitch at times, Rose Lainey.' His voice held a hint of mirth.

'Well, sometimes you just have to get over yourself. The world hasn't ended.'

'Remind me never to cry on your cold shoulder again.'

She saw that look he used to give her. The one which made her heart race and scare her. The one that made her wish there was a chance of something more between them even though she had promised herself long ago never to go there. She smiled and gave him a playful whack with the back of her hand. 'Any time, cowboy. You know where to find me for sympathy and tea.'

His phone buzzed and he took it from his pocket. He read the text.

'What is it?' Rose asked.

'The dig site has been identified and they are breaking ground tomorrow.'

CHAPTER 51

Rose walked across the field towards the dig site, thinking of how her mother's death was beginning to affect her. She had had another uneasy night, this time punctuated by dreams of visiting her mother's grave only to find it had been moved. In her dream, she had stood with wilting flowers in her hand, looking for somewhere to place them, knowing that her mother wasn't in the grave she stood at. When she woke, it was to feel weary and anxious, with a sense of hopelessness, of having no purpose. She resented Evelyn for having such a hold over her.

She had spent so much of her teen years feeling resentful towards her mother. But it went deeper than normal parental clashes. Everything Evelyn stood for rankled with Rose. They were like opposite arrows on a compass.

Now Rose was visiting the site where Eden's remains could be buried. The Commission had acquired information initially suggesting Tyrella beach, in County Down, could possibly be the place of the burial. However, a subsequent, anonymous tip-off to the Independent

Commission for the Location of Victims' Remains, had indicated that the search would be better carried out on bogland at Killymoon, in County Tyrone. It was hard to trust any of their information but what choice did they have?

Rose thought about a school project she had done on Vikings and their burial rites. They had looked at images of prehistoric bodies dug up from Ireland's peat bogs, buried along with their jewellery, gold headdresses and weapons. Here she was about to look at a scene of excavation to search for Eden.

As part of the peace process the IRA had undertaken an agreement to release information about people they had 'disappeared'. Since then, they had admitted to three further cases where people were taken and killed. It was thought that there are probably others. The ICLVR had been created by a treaty between the Irish and British governments, to gather information on the disappeared and to search for the remains of the victims. Their information was supplied by the IRA through intermediaries, often priests, and with the assistance of forensic archaeologists from the University of Bradford. Excavations across the border in the mountains of County Wicklow, the beaches of Co Louth and the bogs of Co Meath and Co Monaghan have been carried out. Rose knew that the digs could take months and involve huge areas.

The land in front of her looked like it had been scoured, cleared of anything that had previously stood in the way of the mechanical diggers sitting at the side of the plot. Mounds of earth sat like mole hills in formation. Tens of them, row after row. The smaller mechanical diggers were busy removing layers of topsoil, placing it in a mound at the side of the site that had been marked out by a temporary-looking fence made of wooden posts and thick plastic orange string.

Kevin Wright, one of the team from the university, waved when he saw Rose and she walked towards him, noticing a large map in his hands.

'You found us then?'

'Yes.' She took a moment to look across the land that surrounded them. 'This is a big undertaking.'

'Six acres, we're looking at, and that can't be done in a day. Here, this is the grid we're working on.' He held the map open for Rose to look at.

'As you can see, we've divided the site up into twenty blocks. If the information is to be believed we should find remains within the next day or so. This is Marie McPeake. She works with the families and offers support during times like these.' Marie was tall and thin with thick dark hair to her shoulders. She had an air of someone who oozed empathy.

'Hello Marie. I'm Dr Rose Lainey, consultant forensic psychologist working with the PSNI. I've been working on the Mulligan case.'

Marie reached out her hand. 'Hello. Some of the family are coming down later to see the site. God help them. It must be a form of purgatory, living with the knowledge that their mother had been taken from them and murdered. If we find her remains, then at least they can gain some sort of closure. Give her a Christian burial. In my experience of working with families like this, that is all they ask for, to be able to bury their loved ones. And give them peace.'

Rose nodded. She had enough experience to know that finding the remains wouldn't change anything much. They would still be left with questions and no sense of justice.

Kevin stepped forward, his mud-caked boots sinking into the boggy ground. 'This is Gabriel Logan. He is heading up the forensic side of the dig.'

Gabriel was tall with swarthy skin and dark curly hair. He had the beginnings of a beard and was wearing a dark-coloured short-sleeved shirt. He was ridiculously good looking, like a brooding Heathcliff, but his green Hunter wellington boots and the camera hanging from his neck made him look like a festival goer who'd made a wrong turn and ended up in the middle of the dig by mistake.

'Hello, Gabriel, I think we've spoken on the phone. I'm working on the investigation,' Rose said.

'Yes, Rose, how are you doing? Some size of excavation site, isn't it?' He had a mild Scottish accent, probably from some posh part of Edinburgh.

She nodded. 'How is it going so far?'

'Normal field archaeology takes time and patience. This type of dig is so much more complex. We aren't dealing with pieces of pottery or flint; this is human remains, someone's loved one, and we have to be mindful to not risk damaging any vital piece of evidence.'

'Not every search proves successful. There's a lot of disappointment in these types of digs,' Kevin said.

'I've counselled the family to be prepared. Sometimes finding nothing is worse than finding a body,' Marie said.

The mood was sombre and Rose could see they were all genuine in their respect. This wasn't some dig to uncover historical artefacts. Their hope was to find Eden and to put her to rest.

'Come over here and I'll talk you through what we've done so far,' said Gabriel. Rose followed him to a makeshift office in a mobile shed. On the wall, a map of the site was covered in Xs and pinpoints.

'We are working our way steadily through this section today.'

'You're attached to the university?'

'Yes, Bradford, the department of archaeological and forensic sciences. We specialise in bringing the disciplines together.'

Rose looked at the images he was showing her on an iPad.

'These are photographs of other sites we've worked on. It will give you a sense of what we are doing and what we hope to find.' Rose looked at the partially preserved body in the image. Skin, leathery and brown, coated bones.

Another image showed a site after the dig was complete. The landscape looked like something alien. 'As you can see, the terrain bears the scars of our work. It's a strange set-up. In order for the Good Friday Agreement to work, the families we are working on behalf of have to accept a lack of restitution and justice. Their lack of closure is the price asked of them.'

They turned to the sound of approaching voices. Marie appeared at the door with Lizzie Mulligan. She was dressed in a calf-length, straight, sand-coloured skirt with a white V-neck T-shirt. Her dark, glossy hair was pulled back into a low ponytail. Everything about her looked pristine, considered and smart. A direct contrast to her brothers.

Gabriel closed the iPad and turned to shake Lizzie's hand. 'Good to meet you,' he said.

Lizzie nodded. 'I felt that one of us should be here. Just in case. Eileen wanted to be here but she's working.'

Rose welcomed her into the stuffy office. 'This can't be easy for you, Lizzie.'

'Please, sit down,' Gabriel said, offering her a stool and she sat.

'I haven't been as active in pushing for the police to find out what happened to our mother – the boys took more of an interest in all that. I wanted to move on. To try to put it behind me. But the truth is, there's no escaping it. Not really.' Lizzie paused. She was dry-eyed and her voice was steady. Rose noted her composure. She was a self-assured woman.

'The day they took our mother, they took our childhood too,' Lizzie said. 'What chance had any of us? You can't thrive with no mother or father to care for you.'

Rose could only murmur in sympathy.

CHAPTER 52

Gabriel stepped forward and began explaining the process of the dig: what they were hoping to achieve by the close of the day and what she could expect. She listened patiently.

'If we find anything significant the state pathologist will come down. Her office will carry out the post-mortem and the formal identification of remains once they leave the site.' Gabriel then made his excuses and went back to work.

Rose appreciated the opportunity to speak with Eden's daughter alone. 'Lizzie, I know you and Paddy were initially taken in by the Atwoods, and that Paddy left following allegations of abuse. What happened?'

'The Atwoods weren't bad people. They did their best for us, but Paddy, well, he was a handful. He acted up. Got into trouble at school and at home. It was as if he was trying to push everyone away from him.'

Rose nodded. 'What kind of trouble?'

'He tried every trick in the book to annoy them, but they had the patience of saints. When he threw stuff, broke ornaments or destroyed books, they calmly explained why it was wrong. Eventually, he worked out the only way to hurt them was to make stuff up. That was when he began making allegations against Alan. Said Alan would strike him with a belt and would lock him in the shed overnight. All lies.' She paused for a moment. 'Paddy tried to wreck any chance I had of being part of a real family. The worst of it was, he accused Alan of watching me. He started blocking up keyholes with tissue paper to prevent Alan from allegedly spying on me. Kept insinuating that there was something in the way Alan looked at me. He wanted to destroy Alan. I told anyone who'd listen that it wasn't true. Alan and Linda weren't my parents, but what they offered us was a damn sight better than Moss Street. I had my own bedroom, pretty flowery curtains, even a dolls' house for frigsake. I thought I'd landed on my feet and I sure as hell didn't want Paddy ruining it for me. Alan never made me feel uncomfortable for a second. But after everything with Paddy he withdrew. He was cordial and kind but no more; frightened to get too close.'

She sighed and steadied her breathing. 'Eventually, Linda and Alan couldn't take any more, and Paddy was sent away. Broke my heart all over again, but I knew they didn't have a choice. Something inside Paddy was damaged beyond repair. He couldn't help it.'

Rose could hear the hurt in Lizzie's voice. Her face had drained of colour and she looked washed out in the brightness of the day.

'What about your relationship with Paddy? How did it survive?'

'I saw him on and off at prearranged visits with social workers sitting in, watching us. Things between us were never the same, but he's my kin and my twin, so I get him.

I understand. He was hurting. What they offered was so nice, so safe and lovely, that he had to destroy it. It was self-sabotage. I can see that now, looking back.'

'You work as a counsellor, I believe?' Rose couldn't help herself. It seemed too good an opportunity to not bring up Lizzie's occupation.

She nodded. 'Yes, I'm self-employed.'

Lizzie went to say something further when suddenly they heard Gabriel shout.

'Halt!'

They both froze. It could only mean one thing.

CHAPTER 53

'Stay here. I'll see what's happening,' Rose told her.

'No, I'm coming too. If they've found her, I want to be there.'

Rose and Lizzie made their way across the boggy field. The atmosphere was strangely electric, but Rose could tell the team were containing their excitement out of respect for Lizzie. Gabriel walked forward to meet them halfway.

'We've uncovered bone so this part will be slow. We have to be careful not to destroy any evidence.'

'How soon will we know if it's Eden?' asked Rose.

'It has to be her. It's where they told us to look,' Lizzie said, her voice cracking. Rose could see her body was leaning forward, as if every fibre in her being was dragging her towards where her mother might lie.

'I'm afraid that we already suspect it's not her,' Gabriel said gently. 'We're pretty certain we are looking at male remains.'

'No! Not again.' Lizzie wailed as if she had been physically struck. She buckled in on herself, her body lurching forward, and Rose put her hand out to steady her. 'Lizzie, I'm so sorry. I know this isn't what you wanted to hear.'

'No, no, no,' she said, her voice a raw gurgle of pain and tears. She walked away from them, clearly wanting to be alone.

Rose turned to Gabriel. 'What next?'

'We determine the size and condition of the grave before we disturb too much. We usually can get an idea of the gender quickly, depending on the pelvis and skull size. That's what makes me certain this isn't Eden Mulligan. Come over and have a look.'

The forensic archaeologists in Gabriel's team stepped back to allow him to bend over the opened grave. Rose peered in. It wasn't particularly deep, maybe five feet down, if that. The remains were still mostly covered by the brown clay soil but a few parts were clearly visible, where the soil had been carefully scraped and brushed away, exposing partially rotted clothing.

'What can you tell looking at it now?'

'The male pelvis has a narrower, heart-shaped pelvic inlet, see here?'

Rose looked at where he indicated.

'Women have wider pelvises in order to give birth and there's differences to be found in the shape of their skulls, too. But, mainly, we look at the pelvis.'

Rose looked at where he was pointing with a metal rod.

'It's a narrower angle where the two pelvic bones meet than what you would find on a female.'

'So, you're sure it's not Eden?'

'No. It's not her.'

CHAPTER 54

Sometimes the dead don't stay dead. They reach up through the dark clogs of earth and crawl through your sleep with a rancid, flesh-rotted grasp that tears at your neck and forces you to face realities you'd rather not.

Rose knew that dredging up the past was not always a good thing. Secrets within families stay hidden mainly because that's how they want them to be. Her own family was no exception.

Finding Sean Torrent, the IRA commander that Rose suspected her mother had links to, hadn't been too difficult. Under the terms of the Good Friday Agreement, there were plenty of his sort walking the streets as free men. He had managed to navigate his way back into Belfast society, still protected by the auspices of the state. Sean Torrent could go about his business as long as he kept his head down, whereas a couple of decades ago, he would have received a bullet in his head for talking to the police.

Smuggling illegal fuel, running brothels, and selling drugs were the current concerns of the men who had previously traded in bullets and bombs. Back in the day, Torrent was thought of as the dog's bollocks around Rose's area. Evelyn certainly held him in high esteem. So high, in fact, that Rose wondered if she had been willing to risk her life and her children's lives to do his bidding. It wasn't unreasonable to think that she was in deep enough to have caused serious injury, if not death, to those considered to be legitimate targets. There was only so much digging up of the past that Rose wanted to do though, and she realised she may never know how far Evelyn went in her devotion to the cause. Perhaps Kaitlin was right, and their mother's secrets were better off buried with her.

The pub was referred to as a social club, a backstreet dive where knock-off drink was sold at knock down prices. Rose pressed the buzzer and the man on the other side of the security camera released the lock and let her in.

She walked through the dark hallway and found herself in a dimly lit bar. There was a green, baize-covered snooker table in the middle of the room, where two young men – one with a shaved head and the other with his hair pulled back into a topknot – were in the midst of a game. The quick, sharp clack of the cue and the balls made her feel on edge. She headed towards the bar and then froze. There he was, sitting on a stool, drinking a pint of beer, looking down at his phone. She was sure it was him.

He hadn't changed too much. Tall and dark, the years hadn't diminished him. She took a seat to the side to gather herself and have an opportunity to study him. She let her eyes drink him in for a moment, registering every detail: his tall height, the slouch of his shoulders, the angle of his nose that seemed so familiar, the set of his dark grey eyes. His hair was thinning, but what was left of it had been cut short. It still held its dark colour despite the threads of grey coming through. His stature made her think of a politician, or someone used to being in charge.

He turned, as if suddenly aware of her intense scrutiny, and caught her looking.

She took her chance and walked towards him.

'Sean Torrent?'

'Who's asking?'

She could see his eyes flit to the door, as if assessing the possibility of a quick exit should he need it.

'Rose Lainey.' She flashed her ID. 'I want a word.' She hoped he wouldn't recognise her. The last time she had crossed paths with him had been when she was sixteen. He had let his eyes linger over her tight-fitting T-shirt then, before asking if her mother was at home.

The barman looked up from the sink where he was washing a jug. 'I don't want any trouble.'

'You won't get any,' said Rose. 'This is a friendly chat.'

Torrent stood up from the stool and she could see that he was uneasy from the way he shuffled his feet. A man with no secrets to hide wouldn't be so ill at ease. It abruptly reminded her of why she was here.

'I need to ask you some questions about Eden Mulligan.'

She examined his face for movement. Nothing. Almost too steady. It was a well-practised look. Sean Torrent was clearly someone who knew how to take his time when it came to responding to unwelcome questions.

'As I'm sure you are aware, Eden went missing in July 1986. I am carrying out a review of the case and your name has come up.'

The clatter of the snooker balls rang out as the topknot took the break.

'Came up in what context, exactly? I was only a teenager when she left.'

'The context isn't relevant. And what makes you say she left?'

'Everyone knew Eden. She was one of those girls. Loved herself too much. She probably ran off with someone.'

'What's that supposed to mean?'

He shrugged. 'She wasn't the type to waste her life hanging around the poky streets of Belfast. Someone like her had big ideas, big dreams. Even as a teenager I could see that.'

Rose wasn't sure why she felt uneasy.

'Did you ever speak to Eden?'

'No, didn't get that close. No such luck.' He gave a hard, bitter laugh.

'Eden got involved in something. Something that could have placed her in danger. I think you might know what that was.'

'We were all involved in something in those days. That was how you got by. Hustling. Trying to keep alive. You can't pin it on me.'

'Not everyone worked that way, making sure to keep themselves safe at the expense of other lives. I'm pinning nothing on you. Just asking a few questions. If you don't want to have a friendly chat here, I can get a car to come and take you to the station.'

Rose thought of her mother and how her family life had been caught up in the type of rhetoric he pushed. Freedom and revolution packaged up with bombs and bullets. She caught her breath. There was something so visceral in how she felt about him, how she felt connected to the past he represented. It was as if her childhood was woven through with everything he stood for. She could easily imagine taking a gun and putting it to his head, to right the wrongs he had committed. She wouldn't lose any sleep over it, that much she was sure of.

'For fuck's sake. Can I not enjoy a quiet pint without being harassed?'

'You would have been aware of the Mulligan family. Probably went to school with them.'

'So what?'

'So, what can you tell me about them?'

'They were the same as the rest of us. Skinny wee runts roaming the streets.'

'At what point did you become involved with the paramilitaries?'

He jerked his head to the side. 'I don't know what you're on about. I don't need to tell you anything.' He said the words dismissively, as if he could brush her off like a piece of inconsequential dust.

'I think you'll find that you do. You see, I know more about you than you think.' She allowed herself a beat of pleasure at having the upper hand in this strange dynamic.

'It was easy for you to use the people around you, the friends you grew up with, and trample their lives to save your own skin. Do you sleep easy at night? Or do their ghosts haunt your dreams?'

He sneered, his mouth twisting in contempt. 'Catch yourself on. I don't know what the fuck you're going on about, love.'

'Don't call me *love*. I want you to understand that I know more about you than you think. More than you could ever guess at.' She narrowed her eyes and spoke quietly. Somewhere in the back of her mind she had yearned for this meeting. He represented everything she hated about her mother. Sean Torrent was the quiet knock at the door that signified her mother disappearing into the night, to clean up God knows what atrocity.

'You don't remember me, do you?' she asked.

'Should I?'

'I'm Evelyn Lavery's daughter.'

His expression switched; his eyebrows knitting together in puzzlement.

'What do you want?'

'I want to know why my mother answered to you and I intend to find out.'

Rose turned and walked out the door, glad to leave the stench of the dive bar behind. Her eyes took a second to adjust to the brightness of the day. Sean Torrent was never going to tell her what she wanted to know but she needed to make him aware of her presence. She wanted to be the bane of his life, the way he had been the bane of hers.

Her phone rang and she saw Danny's name flash up.

'What's up,' she said as she answered.

'They've found another body at the dig site. It could be Eden.'

'I'll be at the station in half an hour. Wait for me.'

Within an hour, they were on their way to the site.

Danny parked their car beside a Land Rover and they got out. The ground was rough and muddy. Rose cursed herself for not having a spare pair of boots at hand. As they walked closer to the site, they could see all activity had halted, waiting for their arrival.

'That's Gabriel. He's in charge,' Rose said, indicating to Danny the tall fella standing by the mobile hut with a group of others.

'Christ, he looks like Poldark.'

Rose laughed. 'I'd noticed.'

They approached the group and Rose introduced Danny to them.

'Well, we've another body, then?' Danny said.

'Yes, buried alongside the first one.'

Rose stepped forward. 'Do we know yet?'

'Yes,' he said before she could get the rest of the words out. 'It's female. The Mulligan family have been notified of the finding.'

CHAPTER 55

Danny woke up the next morning with a saying of his father's in his head: if something says it's a duck, and it walks like a duck, the chances are, it is probably a duck. The words bothered him all the way to the station. Why, if Iona Gardener was claiming to be responsible for the murders, was he so determined to disbelieve her? In order to get his head around it, he went back to the beginning.

Iona arrived, on foot, at the station at Larchfield. She said the others were dead and she did it.

He pulled up the CCTV footage of Iona arriving at the station that night. Frame by frame, he studied it. There she was, dishevelled and covered in blood that turned out to be mainly her own, but also some of Dylan's. He froze the frame and zoomed in. Her eyes were wide. Her whole demeanour said she was scared. She was shaking so violently that one of the officers ran out from behind the reception hatch to assist her, but she fell before he could reach her, hitting the floor and blacking out.

Danny picked up his phone and called Rose. 'Are you free? I want to run some stuff past you.'

They met in a small meeting room away from the bustle of the incident room and the dank hole of the basement office. It was functional, sparse, and cool, thanks to air conditioning. Malachy joined them, keen to be kept in the loop. Danny knew he was guilty of turning to Rose to discuss every aspect of the case and had to watch his step there. It didn't do to freeze out a lead partner and Malachy deserved to be treated with the same respect. The trouble was, Danny liked how Rose worked. Their shared history and friendship meant that he knew how she operated. He could rely on her. She was firmly based in the real world but was attracted to the lofty theories and paradigms of academia. Given half a chance, Danny would bet she'd eventually hide away in some university department. For whatever reasons she didn't care to share with him, he knew she was hiding something or running from something. She had always been that way, giving little of herself away. Any time they talked about home and family when they were students, she deftly deflected the questions.

'So, what do we need to do?' Malachy asked.

'I'm trying to get my head around a few things. I suppose I want to know what kind of person maniacally attacks five people and then arranges three of them in a bed. And then there's the Iona Gardener angle – how did she escape and why does she claim to be responsible?'

Rose sat on a chair at the table while Danny stood against the wall.

'I keep coming back to Iona. Did she fight her corner? Had she fled before the attacker had finished off?'

Rose leaned forward. 'In other words, what was so special about Iona to save her? What cracks has she hidden from us?'

'Yes.' Danny pointed to Rose. 'That's it exactly. Her connection to Lizzie Mulligan, what can we make of that?'

'On one hand it could be nothing. But, if Lizzie and Iona had grown close, had some sort of personal connection, then maybe that is why the murderer sought out the friends in the cottage.'

'And we don't know that she escaped. Maybe she was spared,' Malachy added.

'But why spare her?' Danny asked.

'A week ago I'd have said finding a link between Iona and killer might help to answer that question, but now with Lizzie being the link between the cottage five and the Mulligans I'm all out of fresh ideas.'

'So, based on what we've gathered so far, what kind of murderer do you think we're looking for?' Danny asked.

Rose frowned. 'As I've mentioned before, there is some evidence that stabbings like this are connected and related to sexual deviation. We are talking about someone with severely disturbed emotional relationships. The assailant could be expressing something – a pain or anger – that has remained buried for a long time that has only just been triggered.'

'So, a nutter with a deep-rooted jealousy?' Malachy asked.

'Not necessarily jealousy. Maybe something more complex than that.'

'Can't you come up with anything better than that?' Danny knew he was being unfair but his frustration was getting the better of him.

'You can't expect her to be able to draw you up an

instant diagram of who did what and why. Catch yourself on, Stowe,' Malachy chastised.

'Right, Mal. I know, but I'm under pressure, here.'

'Aren't we all?'

A silence fell between them.

Rose leaned forward in her chair. 'Look at the weapon. A knife used in the way it was speaks of rage. Something barely contained was unleashed in that cottage. To stab someone is hard. You see them up close. You feel the knife sink into flesh, hear the sucking of sinew and muscle tear away, and see the blood. It's provocative and visceral. And yet, the scene at the cottage showed us a killer who was merciless despite the intimate nature of the crime. It makes me think it's possible that we are dealing with a dissociative episode. Someone who has figuratively stepped out of their body while they created a scene of bloodied hell.'

Danny scratched his head. 'We're back to the beginning and no further forward.'

The next day, Danny and Rose travelled to the pathology lab to meet with Gabriel Logan. The second body had been found buried in a former cut-away peat bog, meaning that the site had to be drained before the excavation could begin. This time it had been female remains unearthed from the bog cased in clay and dirt. They both knew what the news could mean to the Mulligan family. The secrets that had put her there would be resurrected soon enough.

The lab was set up with the skeletal remains from the dig site displayed on two steel tables.

'I think it's always better to talk through findings with the remains in front of us. It will all be in the report, but I thought you'd want to hear this from me direct,' Logan said.

'Yes, thanks,' Danny said. 'We appreciate that.'

'The exhumation team is made up of the lead anthropologist, a photographer, the surveyor, and a field assistant in charge of the systematic collection of physical evidence. Once a body has been recovered, we do everything to ensure that vital evidence is not damaged. It's like doing your job, only throwing tons of soil and decades on top,' Logan said.

Danny nodded. 'I can see it's a complex mission.'

An almost complete skeleton was laid out with two bones tied together with discoloured cord. Most of the bones in the partially completed jigsaw puzzle were a dirty yellow colour, others an earth-darkened brown. Danny noted there were obviously pieces missing. Next to the pieces of bone, there was a stainless-steel washing table, complete with deep sinks and sieves probably used to clean the debris.

'We appreciate you moving fast on this one,' Danny said. 'You know how difficult it is for the family. They are desperate to know if it's their mother.'

'Northern Ireland isn't the only place dealing with disappeared people. I've worked on similar forensic excavations in Argentina and Colombia. The not knowing what has happened and where their missing family members' remains might be becomes a huge psychological issue. There's something barbaric in not affording someone a proper burial. So, yes, I appreciate the sensitivities.' He led them closer to the table.

'As you can see, we don't always obtain a complete skeleton,' Logan said. 'The bones can't always be separated from other matter at the exhumation site because of time or the level of risk of damaging what we are trying to extract. The sieves help filter small items, such as wrist and foot bones, to avoid them being lost. Depending on the type of sample, we clean it with a soft-bristled brush like this.' He held up a short stubby brush. Danny watched Rose lean in closer to have a better look.

'Then the remains are placed on the metal table in correct anatomical positions so that we can work systematically, examining every bone, to provide an inventory of our findings. Each bone is marked with a serial number and recorded.

'I've kept you waiting long enough though. You want to know what we've found.'

'Yes. Can you confirm that the second body found was Eden Mulligan?' Rose asked.

'It's her. We were able to run the dental records through the system.' He could scarcely hide the excitement in his voice. The find was a professional win for him and his team.

'And there's something else.'

'What?' Danny asked.

'She was pregnant.'

CHAPTER 56

The next day, Rose went to see Eamonn Mulligan. He had requested the meeting, asking Rose to be at Joel Ellis's office for ten o'clock. She parked on a side street and walked the short distance.

She walked down Deramore Avenue thinking that Belfast was showing its true colours in the sunlight. The red, white and blue of the past few weeks had died away. Previously pristine Union flags now fell dissolute against lampposts, already fading in the harsh sunlight. Everyone looked weary and ready for the heat to break. The promised rain still hadn't come. She passed a group of teenage girls, squawking and laughing at something one of them had shown the others on her phone. Only a few decades ago their lives would have been so different, dictated by intimidation and the threat of violence. Eden Mulligan's Belfast would have been worse again. Opportunities for work were limited, with working class girls depending on factories or shops for jobs. Life coloured by the constant sense of being the 'other'. Now, Belfast was a vibrant city full of creatives, young professionals, and a steady trade of tourists coming to view the peace walls and the *Game of Thrones*' film locations. Times had most definitely changed.

She reached Joel's office and found Eamonn already there. Joel told them to make themselves at home, he would give them space and time to talk and return in an hour. Rose thanked him and poured herself a glass of water.

'Well, Eamonn, what's on your mind?'

'I need to tell you something. Now that the dig has unearthed our mother, I feel it's time.'

Rose nodded. 'Okay, what do you need to say?'

'I've never told a soul this, not even Joel. He knows I've struggled with the past, yes, and he's been good to me. I know he blames himself for the beating I got, but they'd have come after me anyway at some point.'

Rose reached for the jug of water on the table and poured another glass of water, before passing it to him. 'Go on.'

'There are people among us who knew all along what had happened to my mother. Do you know how hard that is to live with? To know they were walking the streets unaffected. Breathing the same clean air and enjoying the beauty of a summer's day?

'You said something the other week, at the Europa: that we might all know something of significance without realising it. Well, for years there was something that I kept buried. I didn't think it had any bearing and I didn't want to dwell on it.'

Rose sat forward.

'You have to remember, I was a child. I didn't even understand what I was seeing until years later. It was late and I was sleepy.'

'Okay Eamonn, take your time.'

He took a deep breath.

'Something had woken me. At first, I thought it was Cormac snoring or one of the girls gurning over something, but then I heard it again. A low rumble of voices and something else I couldn't distinguish. It was definitely coming from down the stairs. I climbed out of bed. I can remember noticing the moonlight and how it illuminated the whole room, making it look like I was viewing it through a blue lens. Funny how little details like that stay with you.

'I crept down the stairs as quietly as I could and went towards the room at the back of the house. But then something made me hesitate. I don't know what it was but somehow, I knew I shouldn't make myself known. I pushed gently on the door, opening it just an inch. It was then that I saw them.'

'Who, Eamonn, who did you see?'

'My mother. With him – Father Ryan.'

He stopped and refilled his glass. 'There he was with her. She was sitting on his lap, her head thrown back as if she was possessed by the devil himself. Her nightdress, the cotton one she always wore – white with little sprigs of blue flowers – was open and her breast was exposed. He was worrying at it with his face. His hand was between her legs. She was my mother but not my mother. The strangeness of it unnerved me. My world skidded to a halt. Everything felt wrong and rotted. I felt sick and quietly backed away from the door before either of them saw me.'

Rose could see a flush of heat scorch his face. She couldn't tell if it was shame, embarrassment, or anger. Dancing flecks of dust were illuminated by the morning light, but the room felt strangely still.

'I was only about five or six. Too young to make sense

of what I was seeing – like I said – but I knew what they were doing was wrong. I thought of my daddy, away working and how he would be so angry that this priest was in our house at night time. I crept back to bed, shaking, and spent the rest of the night tormented by the image. But then, the next morning, all was normal. The girls were fighting over socks, Cormac was giving me dead arm punches and Ma was bustling about the kitchen making us porridge. I figured, how could she be so ordinary if the night before had happened? In my mind, that scene had changed everything, but everyone was acting like it was a typical day. I couldn't make it right in my head, you know?'

'You were very young, Eamonn.'

'In the end, it was easier to try to pretend I had dreamed it. I tried to block it out. Now though, the image keeps coming back to me. It's like a spool of thread unravelling. Things I didn't know I knew are swirling round my brain. I can't get any peace.'

He looked totally dejected and lost. 'I can't help thinking, what if I'd told someone then. Would anything be different now?'

CHAPTER 57

Edmund Ryan. He was a like a bad smell that hung over the case notes. From Katy Carberry's recollections, to the testimony, there was something not right about how this man presented himself to the world. Why did he suddenly move away after Eden's disappearance and why was the testimony available to Rose suggesting he was dead when she knew for a fact he was alive?

Rose picked up the phone and dialled Marni in Boston. It would be late afternoon there, so she hoped that the parish secretary would still be around.

'Hello, is that Marni?'

After some pleasantries, Rose enquired about Father Ryan. She wanted to be certain that Marni had been exhaustive in her search.

'Yes, he is most definitely alive. We received a Christmas card from him last year, and I've just found out our Monsignor and he occasionally share letters.' Rose could hear the glee in her voice. Marni appeared to have enjoyed

313

Sharon Dempsey

her digging around. She was probably one of those real-life crime fanatics that like to think they could piece together a murder investigation from the safety of their living room sofa.

'In fact, I've been able to get the address for you of the retirement home.' She practically sang it. Rose took down the details and hung up. Marni would be congratulating herself for being a useful citizen.

Belfast to Bray. It couldn't be that far, could it? She looked it up. It was on the far side of Dublin. Two and a half hours of driving.

She found Danny at his desk.

'Fancy a road trip?'

'Will it take long?'

'Mmm, it might do.'

'Where to?'

'Bray,' she said, certain he would tell her to piss off.

He shook his head. 'Rosie, you are a frigging distraction. Please tell me this has something to do with the case and that it might be worth my time.'

'It has something to do with the case and it will be worth your time. I hope.'

She told him about Eamonn's story of finding the priest with his mother when they were on the road.

'If Eden had been having an affair with him, then that puts him in the frame,' she said, looking out the window. Danny was driving. The sun was setting over the hills and the sky was streaked amber and indigo, with a suggestion of a storm coming.

'Possibly. It's definitely worth checking out, but priests

314

get moved from parish to parish all the time. His time at St Malachy's could just have been up.'

'But he vanished out of Northern Ireland. Wound up in Boston. That suggests to me that he – or the church – was putting distance between himself and Belfast. I want to know why. It isn't a leap of imagination to think the church was protecting him. There's been plenty of examples of paedophile priests being sheltered. Send them to confession and park them in some other parish until their crimes have been forgotten. Ryan could have been sent away for a reason connected to Eden.'

'True. Rose, find something worth listening to on that radio. If I have to hear shite music all the way to Bray, I'll be a grumpy bastard by bedtime.' She turned through the radio channels until she picked up Hozier.

'Ah Christ, that's as bad as Ed Sheeran.'

'Fine.' She kept searching and only stopped when she'd found Melody's Echo Chamber, knowing he'd stop complaining.

'Look, we're passing over the infamous English border.'

'Don't you mean the Irish border?'

'Nope, Tonto. Common misconception. The English imposed the border on the Irish, remember.'

He started talking in a send-up of Ian Paisley. 'Even I, as a fully paid up member of the Ulster Protestant community, can accept that reality.'

'And look at all the hassle it's caused with Brexit.'

'Serves them right. Soft border or hard border, it's all about protecting territory and political gain.'

Rain began to fall, heavy rods drilling down onto the car, as the sky darkened with menace.

'The sunshine wasn't going to last forever. At least my Da will be happy that the farm's getting a soaking,' Danny said.

At some point, Rose drifted off to sleep. She woke when they had reached Dublin. Even though it had gone seven o'clock, the traffic was still heavy.

'Shouldn't be too long now. Do you fancy stopping for a bite to eat before we track down yer clergyman?'

'Yes, definitely.'

They pulled into a restaurant and headed inside.

After the waiter had taken their orders, Rose decided to try to be the type of friend she felt Danny needed. She knew his marriage breakdown still played on his mind. It went against her personality to pry, but she figured that in order to help him through it, she was expected to ask difficult questions.

'So, Danny. What's going on with you and the divorce?'

He shrugged. 'Same old shite. Paying solicitors for f-all. Trying to keep Amy from blaming me for everything from a broken fingernail to the state of the world.'

'That bad?'

'Yep.'

'You know you can talk to me, don't you?'

'Aye, but talking shite and crying on your shoulder over a glass of whiskey isn't a classy look.'

'Danny, come on. We've been friends for a long time.' She reached out and took his hand.

'Don't be giving me sympathy, woman, or I'll start gurning. No one wants to see that when they're tucking into their greasy burger.'

'All right, no sympathy,' she said taking her hand away.

'But if you need me to listen, even if you are talking shite, I'm always available.'

She hesitated and wondered if she should clarify. 'Available' sounded like a come on, but then she figured she was being over sensitive. They were firmly in the good friend and work colleague zone. She'd made sure of it.

CHAPTER 58

The retirement home for priests was nothing like Rose imagined. At the back of her mind she'd pictured a *Father Ted* set-up, full of cantankerous old men and subservient women pouring endless cups of tea. The reality was more clinical and business-like. It was a cross between a small hospital and a hotel. The Saint Columbanus Retirement Home sat off a busy main road into Bray, sheltered by trees and shrubs. The automatic doors led into a reception lobby, where Rose asked a small Eastern European woman if she could speak to Edmund Ryan.

'Father Ryan is in the chapel for evening prayers. You are welcome to wait until he is finished, but you'll need to sign the visitors' book. Please wait here until he returns,' she said, looking up from the computer screen.

Rose and Danny sat on a pale blue fabric sofa in the lobby to wait. A statue of a saint – probably Saint Columbanus, Rose assumed – stood looking down on them with a book carved into his stone hands. There was a hushed reverence about the place and the steady tick of a grandfather clock was the only sound. Danny looked at her, eyebrows raised. They waited for a bit until the receptionist cleared her throat and said, 'Evening prayers have ended, so if you want to make your way through to the great room, it is down the corridor, the third door on the left.'

Ryan was waiting for them, as if he'd had some fore-warning that he had visitors. The great room was a large living room dominated by a huge bay window that looked out across a pebbly coastline. Ryan was seated with a book on his lap and a serene expression on his lined face that made Rose think of the statue. He looked frail and wizened, as if life had been sucked out of him, leaving him desiccated. His sparsely covered scalp looked raw and exposed in the fading light. Rose noted he wasn't wearing a collar, but then, she didn't know if priests were obliged to always wear them.

'I hear you have come to see me,' he said with a feeble voice, muffled by mucus. He coughed to dislodge something and spat into a cotton handkerchief that he then secreted behind his back.

'We're from the PSNI. We need to ask you some questions about your time at St Malachy's parish in the eighties,' Rose said.

He laughed, a dismissive wheeze of a chuckle that sounded like an asthmatic donkey braying. 'I'm afraid you're too late if you've come to chase me about my involvement with the republican movement. We won the war and then our comrades sold us out for power and a pay cheque, signed by the Queen of England herself.'

Rose wasn't going to waste time. 'We are interested in Eden Mulligan. How did you know her?'

He startled, as if he hadn't expected to hear Eden's name.

'Oh, so soon? I thought we'd have a warm-up first. Eden was a parishioner. I administered to her spiritual needs.'

'Is that all you administered to her?' Danny asked with a sneer in his voice.

'I don't know what you mean by that.'

'We have reason to believe you were in a relationship with Eden Mulligan. Within weeks of her being taken from her home in July 1986, you fled Belfast. Can you account for your sudden departure?' Rose asked.

'I was moved to America by my bishop. It was a great opportunity.'

'A great opportunity to raise funds for the IRA and oversee gun-running from a safe distance.' Danny didn't hide his disdain.

'So what? You can hardly prosecute me now for my involvement with the republican movement. We've moved on, or haven't you police noticed? You really think it's in anyone's interest to harass a retired priest on the basis of murky hearsay?'

'No, but if you were involved with Eden Mulligan's disappearance, I will make damn sure you're charged and held to account,' Rose said.

'Now, now, haven't you heard of the arrangement? Any information leading to the unearthing of remains is exempt from being used in court proceedings. We were at the table putting these provisos in place while you two were probably still in nappies.'

Danny leaned forward. 'Who were you working for?'

'I don't work for anyone but the Lord our Father. I'd advise you to drop your line of enquiry.'

'Is that a threat?'

'Don't go hearing imaginary conversations.' He coughed

again and wheezed. 'I don't have long to live. Lung cancer. Convenient, you might think, but I've had my life. My work here is done, as they say, but as a parting gift, I did inform the Commission for the Disappeared as to where they might find Eden. You have no case against me. To tell you more would be a goodwill gesture. Perhaps it could even be cleansing.'

Rose balked at his nerve. To suggest that he was doing something good by revealing his secrets was sickening. Dusk fell over the room, casting shadows. A rumble of voices from the hallway died away and then the grandfather clock from the reception area began to chime.

'So, you admit that you were responsible?'

'No, dear,' he said patronisingly. 'That is not what I am saying. I was a priest. I was privy to certain sensitive information. That does not make me her executioner.'

'You're sick. You were involved in denying five children a normal childhood and you sit there talking about goodwill,' Rose said.

'If it's justice you're after then you need to go back to partition.'

'Why did you give Father Dominic permission to share your confession? The testimony was incomplete.'

'Well, settle yourself down and I shall finish what I started.'

Rose looked at Danny. He was entranced, waiting to hear what they had come for.

CHAPTER 59

Ryan leaned back in his chair. 'I was the messenger, nothing more. We went into the priesthood together, much to the delight of our mothers. Edmund and I were thick as thieves back then.'

'Wait, you're not Edmund Ryan?' Rose asked, incredulous.

'No, I needed to get out of the country and Edmund unwittingly assisted me. My name then was Peter. It's not difficult to swap identities. Neither of us had family to worry about us, or question where we were. Our mothers were both dead. No one thinks to look at a man of God too closely. Even when Edmund disappeared, covering it up wasn't too hard. We said he had been removed from the parish. Moved on to better things.

'I went to Boston. They treat their priests with great respect and love over there. I settled into the parish under his name and managed to keep any minor indiscretions under wraps. Before the peace process there were priests like me who had to step up, do what was necessary to keep the republican movement in line. I may have over-

322

stepped the mark a few times. You really shouldn't underestimate the respect afforded to priests. It paves our way.' He smirked.

'Edmund, well, he liked the ladies. Eden wasn't his first and he did care for her. Cared for her so much that he was willing to risk everything for her. We couldn't allow that.

'He was a charming bastard. He had the whole place eating out of his hand. They thought he was one of them. A man of the people. You've got to understand that priests in those days were removed, set apart like glorified martyrs in waiting – living saints among the people. But Edmund, he was different. He acted like he *was* one of the people. I suppose when it came down to it, he was. Just another selfish man, out to take what he could. In this case, Eden.

'She was his woman. Not that it was common knowledge. God knows it was all clandestine, *Thorn Birds* style. I'm sure Eden didn't know what had hit her when he turned on the charm. A lonely woman that looked like her needed a man. Someone to tell her she was beautiful, to hold her and make her feel desired. He wooed her. Cried on her shoulder about his conflicted conscience, no doubt. Hard to resist that which is forbidden.

'Anyway, the two of them managed to keep their love affair secret for long enough. Well over a year, I believe. Until it all changed. She was like a brood mare. Got pregnant at the drop of a hat. When she told Edmund she was carrying his child, he panicked. Came to me looking for a solution.'

'What was your part in it?' Rose asked, her voice steady and calm but Danny could sense she was seething.

'Edmund talked of running away. Leaving the priesthood

and bringing up Eden's five children as his own. He even talked of setting up a community of priests who had found themselves in a similar predicament. Men of the cloth who couldn't or wouldn't keep their vow of celibacy. It was clear to me that he would be better off if I dealt with the problem for him. I thought in time he would have grown tired of her anyway. That he would set his sights on another, more promising woman. Men like him rarely stay faithful. So why risk everything he had built on one woman?' He paused, staring out at the darkening view.

'Edmund had set her up a bank account. Promised her that they would find a way to make it all work out, but I didn't know that until much later. Not that it would have made any difference. I wasn't about to let him destroy what we had built. We had worked together all our lives. Played as boys, pretending to carry the host, practising saying the creed. We were made for service. Service of both church and country.

'Edmund was instructed to tell Eden to meet him at the parish house. The plan was to get him on side and to take Eden away for a period of time. Long enough for the pregnancy to be hidden and the baby to be handed over to the convent sisters to pass on for adoption to a rightfully needing couple. Except Edmund wouldn't go along with it. He was still full of ridiculous plans to bring the child up and to take care of the Mulligan brats. In the end, he left us no choice.'

'Eden was killed?'

'She was told that Edmund wanted to discuss their future. A car was sent for her in the middle of the night. These things don't intentionally happen. Not always. She fought like a banshee when we took her to the safe house across the border. Tempers were flared.

'When Edmund realised what had happened, he begged to be executed and buried with her. If we refused, he said he would go to the police.'

CHAPTER 60

Rose woke at dawn and found herself lying on Danny's bed with his arm draped around her. They had talked until after 2 a.m. and then decided to sleep. It seemed silly to go to her own room and they had been relaxed enough to put their heads down where they were. At one point in the night she felt herself easing into the crux of his body and he'd responded, wrapping himself around her. She didn't want to think beyond the here and now. There was no point second guessing how they felt about each other.

Danny groaned and rolled over. 'Christ the night. My mouth feels like something's died in it.'

'Well, don't breathe near me then. First point of business is to buy a couple of toothbrushes.'

'Aye, boss. I'll put them on expenses.'

'Danny, there's something I need to tell you.'

He exhaled. 'Go on.'

'I came back to Belfast for my mum's funeral.'

'Christ, Rosie, why didn't you say?'

She put up her hand. 'No, listen. We weren't close. In

fact, I hadn't spoken to her in years with good reason. I've never told you this because, well, I was ashamed.'

'Of what?'

'Of my family, of where I come from, all of it.'

'Why? What are you on about?'

'My mother was a republican and I've reason to believe she was an active member of the IRA.'

'Shit, Rose.'

'Exactly. I knew you'd feel like that. If you want me off the case, then fine. I understand.'

'Would you let me process this before jumping the gun? There's no reason for you to come off the case . . . unless you've uncovered a connection. Have you?'

'No, nothing, but I have run her name through the system and it's coming up as classified. That's as far as I got.'

'Right. There must be a good reason for that. I'll do some digging of my own, if you like. So, that's why you kept me at arm's length all these years? Never saying too much about home.'

She shrugged. How could she explain the shame she felt?

They were on the road to Belfast by eight thirty, sustained by coffee and croissants. Rose was driving and was determined to get back before they lost any more time.

'So, Rose, our wee road trip was worthwhile. What did you make of the priest's story?' Danny said.

'I think it's the confirmation we needed that Eden was murdered, and a cloak of paramilitary provided the perfect cover. We can also be fairly certain now that the second body uncovered is Ryan's.'

'But where does that leave us with the Dunlore murders?'

'What if they were carried out to draw attention to Eden's disappearance? To make us re-open the case?'

'You're thinking that someone close to Eden, someone invested in finding out the truth about her, did it?'

Rose thought how strange it was that death in Northern Ireland appeared to be sanctioned if it was for political gain. There was an almost unwritten and unspoken rule that people who had been involved in the paramilitaries got what they deserved. She thought of Eden and her children, trying to get by in life. She had found herself caught up in something she had no power and control over and had paid the ultimate price.

Danny turned to Rose. 'We need to talk to her children again.'

CHAPTER 61

Back up north, the rain had finally come. The sky was a shifting mass of low cloud. For a second, the cloud cleared, and it seemed as if the sun was returning with a vengeance, but then there was a muffled rumble of thunder in the distance.

Danny was silent. Rose could tell he was thinking. She watched him, saw the quiet intensity and wondered about the thought processes going on in his head. The case was at a critical juncture. They couldn't afford to get this wrong.

'We need to question each of the Mulligans. Starting with Cormac,' Danny had said.

Following a few phone calls, they had discovered that Cormac Mulligan was working on a building site near the foot of Cave Hill. A new development of houses had sprung up and Cormac was getting labouring work by the day. They parked the car and approached the site. The sky had turned a deep violet, like a livid bruise. The air crackled with electricity, the long-promised thunderstorm imminent.

Danny spotted him first. 'He's over there, look.'

Cormac Mulligan was dressed for the building site, wearing a reflective vest and a hard hat. He was talking to someone and had a pickaxe in his hand.

'Let's go have a word.'

Cormac was none too impressed to have his working day disrupted.

'For Christ's sake, it's hard enough for me to get work without me bringing coppers onto the site.'

'We need to talk to you, Cormac. There's a few issues we need to tie up. We'd appreciate it if you came down to the station.'

He put the pickaxe down and turned. 'You have got to be effing joking. I said all along you lot would never help us. You put us through hell. *Again*. There's only so much of this that any one family can take.'

'Cormac, we are asking nicely, but if you force us, my colleague here will bring you in the hard way,' Rose said.

He looked defeated and shouted over to his foreman that he had to go sort something out.

'If he docks my pay, I expect to be reimbursed.'

'What's this about?' Cormac asked, taking a seat in the interview room.

'We need to know where you were on the night of twenty-eighth June.'

'How the hell am I expected to know what I was doing weeks ago? I was probably working or watching television back in my flat. Take your pick. What day of the week was that?'

'It was a Saturday.'

'Well that's easy then – I was at Rosario football club. I coach the under sixteens.'

'It shouldn't be too hard to confirm your alibi then,' Danny said.

Rose leaned forward. 'Cormac, your family must feel desperate to have the mystery surrounding your mother's disappearance solved. How far would you all go to see the case resolved?'

'What kind of question is that? We've done everything in our power to find out what happened. You promised all sorts that you can't deliver. Told us that you were on our side and then you come to my worksite and bring me in for questioning? The problem lies with the RUC and then the PSNI in not doing more. Don't try to lay it at our feet.'

Rose resented his tone but couldn't work up enough anger to fire back at him. She wasn't the RUC; she hadn't messed up the first investigation and she was doing everything to solve the case now. She had no right to feel stung by his accusation of police indifference to his mother. Every time she looked at the case file she, herself, was struck by the lack of due care and attention. She couldn't help feeling that it was because Eden was a mother from a Catholic community.

'I'm just doing my job,' she said. More than anything, she wanted to be done with Cormac and his family. And to be done with the nagging worries she had about her own mother.

Later that day, Rose returned to her case notes on the Mulligan family. Cormac's alibi had checked out. He had been coaching a night-time football match and had several witnesses to vouch for his whereabouts. Paddy's checked out as well. He had been propping up Bittles bar until closing and had been sleeping it off in a doorway until the

Home Safe bus, a Christian charity looking after the home-less, scooped him up and took him to a shelter for the night.

Rose knew that without the psychological or physical protection they need, children who experienced the loss of a parent often go on to internalise fear and anxiety. Their abandonment giving rise to shame and that, in turn, making them believe that they aren't worthy of love. This was the crux of the pain from which they needed to heal to have full and meaningful lives.

It was to be expected that, having endured emotional and physical abandonment, the Mulligan children would experience persistent psychiatric disorders such as anxiety, post-traumatic stress, aggression, impulsiveness, delin-quency, hyperactivity and substance abuse. What a legacy, she thought. While the daughters Eileen and Lizzie appeared to have fared better than the brothers, she knew that women were better than men at masking problems – they could maintain the semblance of a normal life while battling private demons. And that left Eamonn. The baby of the family. Or was she looking at the wrong son entirely? There was that feeling again. A deep sense of unease. Something bothered Rose about Paddy and she needed to know why.

CHAPTER 62

Danny had a lot to consider as he headed back to the station. He drove past the security camera and waited the five seconds until the fortified gates slowly swung open for him. When he reached his desk, he checked his messages, and then told Tania to gather the team for an update at noon. Magee sat over on the far side of the room, talking into his phone, while Jack Fitzgerald and Jamie King were bent over a computer.

Danny needed Rose to talk through their findings to date. She was the first person he looked for the minute he came through the station gates. He could no longer deny that she was under his skin. All the shit he had been through with Amy made him extra wary. He wasn't in a fit state to embark on a new relationship, let alone one which he knew would mean so much to him. Rose was pretty much perfect. Too bloody perfect for him. If he'd any sense he'd play the field for a while. Get all this angst out of his system. Settling down hadn't done him any favours in the past.

* * *

When he finally tracked Rose down, she was raring to go.

'Paddy Mulligan, we have to bring him in,' she said, barely stopping for a breath as they walked down the stairs to the basement office. They could be sure of peace down there.

'I've been thinking along the same lines. We do need to bring him in, but first, hear me out. I'm sure there was more than one intruder in the cottage that night. If it was Paddy Mulligan, he was only part of the story. Someone else knew what Paddy planned to do. They may not have been involved in the killings, but they interrupted him, and set about clearing the scene of evidence. It would explain why Iona was able to escape.'

'But the blood and mess, it was everywhere. The scene was hardly clean,' Rose said.

'Yes, but no prints worth filing were found, no weapon. Someone was methodical enough to do a sweep. Someone who had more presence of mind than the killer. The bodies were placed in that bed. Whoever was there that night helped Paddy do that.'

'Are you thinking that Lizzie was there? It would explain the two contrasting aspects of the crime scene – a bloodbath and yet, a tidy exit. And the motive was definitely to draw attention to the Mulligan case, to make us reopen the investigation,' Rose said.

'And Eden Mulligan? What about her case?' Danny was pacing around the room, the pieces beginning to slot together.

'She was the price paid to cover up Ryan's indiscretions.'

'So how did Paddy Mulligan know about the five in the cottage?' Rose asked.

'Lizzie knew Iona in a professional capacity. Perhaps Lizzie set Iona up, sent Paddy to the cottage?'

'Yes, and it goes towards explaining why Iona felt responsible.'

'He wanted to replicate the family set-up. The five children left behind. Their childhoods were virtually killed the night their mother was taken. That's what he said to me,' Rose said.

'Exactly. Could the cottage murders have been interrupted by one of the other Mulligans, who knew what Paddy planned to do?'

'I don't know. It's possible.'

CHAPTER 63

By the time they arrived at Paddy's flat, he was gone. There was only one place he could be. Rose was sure of it. They drove down Ormeau Road weaving in and out of traffic, past the old Victorian gas works that was now an office complex, the red brick wall running the length of the road. She turned left onto Hyde Street, and pulled up at number thirteen. The house was derelict, condemned by the council as dangerous. A faded council notice had been stuck onto the metal door, stating 'STAY OUT: Unsafe'. The windows were blocked up with bricks and the front door was fixed shut with an outer metal barrier.

The street was quiet. Kids were playing with a frisbee farther down the road but this section of blocked-up houses was ghost-like. Shells of another life long gone.

'Danny, you cover the front, I'll go around the back,' Rose said, running off before he could say otherwise.

'You can't go after him. You're not police. Stay in the car, Rose!'

'No, you need me to talk to him. He'll respond to me.'

'No! Rose, stay put. I'll radio for back-up.'

But she didn't listen. Rose was sure that once Paddy knew the game was up, he'd realise the only way out would be to kill himself. She needed to be the one to reason with him. To tell him that she understood his justifications. To make him feel heard. She ran up the entryway, dragged an old, partially burnt out metal bin close to the wall and heaved herself over. Her ankle rolled as she hit the ground, making her cry out in pain. The backyard was a tangle of broken bottles and weeds creeping through the cracks in the concrete, but she could see the back door had been forced. She cast around, looking for something to prise it open with and found a discarded brush, its bristles rotting. With a final push, she managed to force it wide enough to gain entry.

Inside, it was dark. A smell of something putrid hit her nostrils, making her recoil. It was an animal-like musk, undercut with decaying flesh. A cat, or a rat perhaps, had become trapped and had died. The heat of summer had produced an overpowering stench. She felt her way through the hallway and climbed the stairs, hoping they wouldn't give way beneath her weight.

As she approached the landing, she heard him.

'You worked it out, then.'

She followed the voice into the bedroom at the back of the house, where she found him sat crouched against the far wall. A knife in his hand glinted in the meagre light. Suddenly, she wished she had listened to Danny. She had no gun for protection and her psychological insights meant nothing in the face of a dangerous man cornered. Light spilled in through the roof where the tiles had come dislodged and the ceiling had rotted away. It was enough to illuminate the darkened room. His pallor was blue, as if the blood had been sucked out of him.

'I thought that other cop would have been the one to bring me in. It's his case after all.'

His voice wavered. Fear.

Rose walked slowly into the room, wishing she had a gun trained on him.

'DI Stowe and I are working together. He knows I'm here.'

'Worried I'm going to knife you too?'

'Reach for anything, one false move, and they won't hesitate to pump you full of lead. Paddy, it's over. You can't run.'

'I'm running nowhere. None of you understand. Time and time again we told you all. Tried to make you see what it is like for us, living like this. When I have trouble sleeping, I come here. It's not as bad as it looks. It's still the same wallpaper.' Rose looked at the wall where he indicated with a flick of the knife, seeing the faded grey and green geometric pattern that screamed eighties.

'It's the same roof over my head. It might be falling down now, but it's still my home. The last place I had her. This is where it all started. Where it's all going to end.'

In the distance, a helicopter circled overhead, a steady rattle. A dog barked in the street and someone told it to shut the fuck up.

'You planned all of this didn't you, Paddy?'

'You didn't leave me with any choice. The five in the cottage were a necessary sacrifice. If the police had done their job in the first place, none of this would have happened.'

He was deluded and justifying his dark actions to himself.

Rose felt adrenaline pump through her veins and willed herself to keep him calm and talking.

For a brief second, Rose thought of her office in London with its safe, predictable rhythm.

She stared at Paddy, watching the tendons bulge in his arm like cords beneath the skin as his grip tightened on the knife.

'Your mother wouldn't want this.'

'She was special, you know. She wasn't like anyone else I have ever met.'

'That's the way it is with mothers,' Rose said. 'We love them beyond all else.' She thought of her own mother. The days Evelyn had spent in the hospital before she'd died. How, even if Kaitlin had told her, she wouldn't have gone to see her. And how, now, part of her regretted that she hadn't had the chance to make amends.

'Paddy, you can't get away with this.'

'I never intended to get away with it. Don't you see? I only wanted to make you take us seriously. To dig a little deeper. The others. They would never have understood. Only Lizzie knew I had it in me to do it.' His jaw was set tight, as if he was actively containing his anger. He rocked back and forth slightly, making Rose think of a child wanting to be soothed by its mother.

'The other police, they had no respect. Blamed her for everything. Said she'd another man on the side. That she'd run off and left us. We knew she'd never do that. If only you could have seen her, dancing in the kitchen, the radio playing the top ten, her face all lit up with love for us.'

He fell quiet as he remembered her, this woman who had meant everything to him.

'It was Lizzie's idea, originally. She said once what we

needed was someone important to die and to be able to link the two cases, to make the police have to open our mother's file and examine it properly. We all had some difficult conversations over the years but that one stuck in my head. It wouldn't let go of me.'

'Did Cormac help you?'

'No. What's any of that matter? I did it. Me, only me.' His lip twitched, a tell that his brother was possibly involved.

'Really, the only thing that separates me and Cormac is conviction. I had the balls to do it.' He slumped forward, the fire gone out of him. He was like an exhausted animal, spent by the chase and ready to give in.

'The planning gave me a focus. I knew what I had to do and finding the five of them was like a gift from the gods. Iona, she thought she could fix me. Make the pain go away. So bloody naive. Full of all her education. Trying to save the world. Just like Joel before that.'

'How did you meet Iona?'

'She came to me. Lizzie had met her through her counselling work and put her in touch with me. She was looking for information to help with her dissertation. Some fancy title about the disappeared and transgenerational trauma. She said so many young people today are committing suicide because of the difficulties their parents and grandparents faced during the Troubles. She wanted to know what it was like for me, being brought up without parents, living through all of that. What could Iona ever know about what it was like for us?' A shadow fell across his face. He looked utterly dejected, his head hanging down to his chest, almost as lifeless and grotesque as the dolls he'd fashioned and hung from the tree at the cottage.

To the side of him sat a wooden dolls' house. By the

looks of it, it was handcrafted and was a reconstruction of the house they were standing in. Paddy noticed Rose looking at it. 'I made every part of this. It had to be perfect. I worked hard to make it so. The tiny hallway leading to the narrow, steep staircase took forever to get right. See them stairs and the bannister? That kept me at it for months.'

She peered into it now, seeing that, through the dolls' house, he could visualise and recreate the life he'd had back then.

He placed his finger and thumb into the door and pulled it to open the front of the house. The front wall swung back in one fluid movement, allowing her to see the whole tableau he had created. The downstairs was set with the replica 1980s sofa. He had made a television that sat in the corner, its spindly aerial fashioned out of copper wiring. The fireplace had been constructed out of miniature, mosaic tiles. He had built out the tiny hearth and had even thought to place a poker by the side.

'Upstairs, the beds lay exactly in the places they should be. My mother's and the girls' facing the narrow window at the front of the house, and the boys' bed in the backroom overlooking the yard.

'The hard part was placing the dolls. I worked so hard on the house, considering every detail and thought about where each of them should be positioned.'

Suddenly, the stairs creaked. Rose held her breath, thinking it was Danny, but suddenly the door banged open and there stood Cormac.

'I knew you'd be here, hiding among the memories. I've come for answers, Paddy. Why? Why did you do this?' He took little notice of Rose as he strode across the dust-covered floor and Rose watched as he squared up to his brother.

'For you, Cormac. For all of us. Don't you see that? It was the only way to make them listen. To make them see what we had lost. Deep down you know I'm right. It was the only way. No one cared about our Ma, no one but us.'

Cormac looked away, as if it was too painful to look directly at Paddy. He leaned against the wall with his hands on his head.

'Why them?' Rose asked, breaking the silence. 'Why the young people in the cottage?'

Where was Danny? Surely, he should have been here by now. Adrenaline was pumping through her veins and she could feel her heart thump in her chest.

'There were five of them. The perfect little unit. Tight they were, just like us. I'd helped Iona with her research and every now and then I'd spot them around the university. There was something about them, the way they stuck together, always hanging around each other like there was no one else they'd rather be with.'

Rose could see Cormac out of the corner of her eye. He was bent over holding his head in his hands.

'It was Iona showing an interest in Ma's case – well that's how I knew that they were the right ones. I realised that I could do something to make a difference. It was a sacrifice of sorts. That's what it was. A sacrifice so that we could get to the truth.

'Iona pretended that she cared. That she was interested in what had happened to us and wanted us to be able to find closure, but we were no more than fodder for her essays. That was all. A means to getting her degree. She knew what our mother meant to us, she knew that we had nothing when she was taken from us.'

Rose let out a weary sigh. He was so damaged that in his mind this was all perfectly logical.

'Fuck, Paddy. What have you done?' Cormac wailed. Rose put her hand up to silence him.

'You followed them to the cottage?' she asked.

'I knew that was where they would be. She liked talking to me. I thought she was trying to understand what it was like back then. How it was for us growing up without a mother or father.' His eyes had a haunted look about them, as if he was held hostage to the past. Rose could hear Cormac crying softly. He was watching the final disintegration of his family.

'How long were you watching them for?' Rose asked. She could hear sirens close by.

'About a week. I had to be sure. To know that their lives were worth the sacrifice.'

'Who helped you, Paddy? There was someone else in that cottage with you. Someone helped you carry the bodies and place them on the bed.'

He shook his head and continued talking as if he hadn't heard Rose's question.

'In some ways, knowing something about them made it easier, not harder. I felt a connection with them.' He talked without looking at her. 'They died to save my mother. I'm not crazy, I didn't think she'd be found alive. But I knew, one way or another, their deaths would help unearth the secrets that had gone with our Ma. If we can find out what happened on that night in July, then maybe I can rest, you know?

'I'm tired. So tired. We all are. We deserved answers after

all this time. Their deaths aren't on my head. Not really. If the police had investigated properly in the first place it would never have come to this.' He rubbed at his neck.

'This stops here, Paddy. It's gone too far,' Rose said, her voice sounding calmer and more authoritative than she felt.

He looked directly at her and she saw despair in his eyes.

'It's already over. We can bring my mother home now. I didn't expect to get away with it,' he said, and pressed the knife to his throat.

'No!' Cormac shouted. 'No! Paddy please don't hurt yourself.'

'Get down on the floor! Put your hands behind your head. I am arresting you in connection to the murders in Dunlore cottage.'

Rose turned to see Danny standing at the door with his gun trained on Paddy. Suddenly, there was a roar of footsteps on the wooden floorboards and the room was full of police officers.

There was a scuffle of bodies. Rose turned to see Paddy was on the ground, being handcuffed.

'You took your time,' she said to Danny.

'Just letting you do your thing, Dr Lainey. I'd the sight on him from above. Next time, wait in the car and don't go running off acting like a cop.' She looked up and saw a gap in the boards of the ceiling. Danny must have climbed up from the back of the house and watched them while waiting on back-up.

'Do you really think there'll be a next time?' Rose asked, glad the stand-off was over, that they had Paddy and that the case was almost solved.

'I would bet on it,' he said, smiling.

CHAPTER 64

The next morning Rose was in the basement office when Danny arrived at the door carrying two coffees.

'Thought you could do with this,' he said, handing her one of the mugs. 'You did well, Rosie. You kept him talking and got the confession.'

'Well nothing's on tape but we'll have enough to move forward.'

It seemed obvious now that the repressed anger, the heightened anxiety, and the shame of the Mulligan children's abandonment, would eventually spill out into something ugly and evil.

'We've cleared the Moss Street house. Paddy had been sleeping there on and off. He'd set it up like his lair, with a sleeping bag, a small gas stove, some canned food and his carpentry tools. He'd made that dolls' house there too and created the creepy dolls from ones belonging to Eileen and Lizzie. Each one made for him and his siblings. Five children. Five dolls.'

'There's still one more part of the puzzle missing though,' Rose said.

'Yeah' Danny said. 'Lizzie.'

The rain had eased and the heat from the previous weeks had dissipated, leaving the air fresh and clean. Danny and Rose were sat in the pool car, waiting for Lizzie Mulligan to arrive at her home; a semi-detached house off the Antrim Road.

'There she is,' said Rose.

To look at Lizzie Mulligan, you'd think she was a well pulled together middle-aged woman, looking after her family, going to work, counting down the days to the next bottle of prosecco to be shared with friends. Nothing about Lizzie suggested anything sinister. She was too smart for that.

It wasn't just how she looked – the high cheekbones, the haughtiness in her demeanour, the set of her full mouth pulled tight over her sharp white teeth – but also in the way she carried herself, like she was worth something. Rose knew a woman like that in the right environment would succeed in anything she'd put her mind to. People respond to beauty.

Eden had been tarnished because of her beauty. If she'd been born in Edinburgh, Manchester or London, she could have had a different life. One of privilege bestowed on her simply because she looked a certain way. As it was, she'd found herself in Belfast amidst the Troubles, a ridiculous name for a bloody war of intimidation and brutality.

Lizzie Mulligan's outlook and potential had been limited by poverty and a broken, motherless family. Rose had seen it before. Families can get by without a father, but an absent mother leaves a void that can't be filled. Lizzie, like the rest of her siblings, had been emotionally wounded. She hid it well beneath the good haircut and the stylish Karen Millen jacket, but take away the trappings and Lizzie was as broken and sad as Paddy, Cormac, Eileen or Eamonn. Maybe more so.

Overnight, Rose had tried to fathom the workings of Lizzie's mind. In some ways, Lizzie had distanced herself so completely that she didn't hold herself to account. Absolved herself from all guilt simply by trading one harm off against another. Her brother was expendable, beyond salvage, his life deemed worthless. The secret bond of twins, forged in the shared space of the womb, had been broken, savagely so.

Danny got out of the car as Lizzie approached. 'Lizzie Mulligan, we need to have a word. We'd like you to accompany us to the station.'

'I want my solicitor,' she said. Her hand, glinting with a diamond ring, flew to her hair in a nervous gesture.

CHAPTER 65

The interview started out with Lizzie refusing to answer their questions and her solicitor sitting stony faced and impassive. Rose explained her analysis: Lizzie had decided way back, as far as that first adoption placement, that her brother was of no use to her. So she spun lies about the adoptive father, made Paddy feel that he had to defend her. Damaged any chance he had of a normal life. Why had she done it? Probably because she'd decided that her life could be better without him. Placed in a new family, she could reinvent herself and take the chance to have a normal life, one maybe even better than the one she'd left behind in Moss Street.

'Lizzie, we know what happened. I understand your process. How you worked your brother Paddy, manipulated him and made him do your dirty work.'

She smirked. 'I can't be held to account for what he did.'

The solicitor put a hand up, indicating to Lizzie to stop responding.

'What changed, Lizzie?' Rose could see a shift in her features, a softening. Something breaking.

'Starting my own family, it caught up with me, made me start thinking about our Ma and what we'd missed. Over the years I'd no interest in the crusade Paddy and Eamonn were on. I'd no trust in the authorities to do what was right, and to be honest, I knew that they couldn't bring her back.'

Somehow the idea of finding out what had happened to Eden had ossified into something dark and putrid, Rose thought.

'My client does not have to answer any questions.'

Lizzie turned to her solicitor. 'Forget it, Marcus, I need to talk. It's over.'

She turned back to Rose. 'I couldn't bring her back but thought maybe we could avenge her death. Not like track down those who'd done it and bring them to justice – more a sense of restoring the balance. It was clear in my head that someone had to pay, and it wasn't for our Ma's life as much as for ours – the kids that were left behind, left to rot.'

'How did you get your brother on board?' Rose asked.

'He was easy to work. That's the thing about damaged people, they are always looking for someone or something to save them, make it all better. He thought I could do that. He only had to do as I said and all would be okay. He'd take his last dying breath knowing he'd made the ultimate sacrifice to make right what had happened to our mother. Twisted, fucked-up logic. God, men are so easy to play.'

'How did you do it, Lizzie? How did you make Paddy believe in you? To commit the murders?'

'The oldest trick in the book: guilt. My own brother, entranced by the thought of the bond between us. The years apart had allowed for the intensity of brother and sister to fade but when we met up there was a pull, strong and indisputable.

'All it took was a faraway look, my hand resting on his a second too long. We all have that strong desire to belong, to have a bond. His weak mind couldn't compute that he was being played. Deep down, he felt connected to me and I played on that until it felt like he'd do anything for me and our family. It was always there, that echo of us as kids, me and him. Two peas in a pod, our Ma would say. In the days after she vanished, we would lie in my bedroom in Moss Street, telling each other stories about our Ma and hoping that one day she would show up,' Lizzie said.

'He leaned on me to protect him. I was the closest thing he had to our mother. That meant something to him. And even though there were times when I thought he didn't have it in him, he was brilliant. He did get the job done. What I hadn't counted on was him bringing Eamonn into it. At some point, he'd left Eamonn a long, rambling voicemail telling him that he'd be going away for a long time, but that he was okay with that because he was not right in the head and that he had only done what he had, to help clear our mother's name. As if the reason overrode the action. The rumours of our mother abandoning us or being a tout had eaten him up. He wanted it known that our Mum would not have left us.

'Then he asked Eamonn to look after me. Eamonn rang me in a mad panic. "*What's he on about, Lizzie? What's he planning to do?"* I knew then that he had fucked it up. He wasn't meant to bring anyone else in on it.'

Danny stood up. 'Lizzie Mulligan, I am charging you with conspiring to murder. You do not have to say anything . . .'

CHAPTER 66

Later, Rose and Danny updated ACC McCausland and accepted his congratulations on solving not one, but two cases. Eamonn Mulligan had been arrested along with his brother, Paddy, and sister, Lizzie, leaving Cormac and Eileen bewildered and sad. It would take some time for them to accept the turn of events.

'I've got to hand it you, Stowe, I didn't think the Eden Mulligan case merited our time and energy. I thought it was going to be one of those cold cases that never gets solved. Well done,' McCausland said, looking pleased. For once he was giving them his full attention.

'Thanks, Sir. I've been lucky to have Dr Lainey's insights. I don't think I would have cracked this without her.'

Rose appreciated Danny's recognition, but it was the combination of psychological input, diligence and investigation that had got the job done.

'Of course, Lainey, you've to be congratulated too.'

'Thank you. We're heading out to see Iona Gardener

now to fill her in on what has happened. Her doctor thinks she needs to hear it from us,' Rose said.

'Well, get it wrapped up and enjoy your weekend. You both deserve a few days break.'

Iona was with her parents in their Shandon Road home, having been discharged from the hospital. Her memory was still sketchy, but she had a better understanding of the events and was recovering from the trauma. There was still a look of anxiety about Iona, as if panic was just beneath the surface ready to bubble up at any given provocation. The superficial injuries had healed, though one had left a faint scar on her left cheekbone.

'Thanks for agreeing to see us, Iona,' Rose said, as she sat on a dark green velvet sofa in the Gardeners' living room. 'How are you?'

'The doctor says I'm doing better. Some days I agree. Others . . . well, I'm not so sure.'

'You've been through a lot. It's not going to be easy, but with the right help you'll get there,' Danny said.

'It's just not fair. My friends didn't deserve this. I feel so guilty for bringing it to our door. If I hadn't become involved with Paddy Mulligan, this would never have happened to us. My stupid dissertation seemed so important at the time. That's laughable now. My friends are all gone. I keep thinking of everything they will miss out on – marriage, kids – all the big milestones of life.'

'You couldn't possibly have known how dangerous Paddy Mulligan was,' Rose said gently.

'We moved into the Dunlore cottage thinking our lives were just beginning.' She breathed out in a sigh. 'Now life looks totally different. I can't imagine ever enjoying a good conversation or laughing. Can't see how I'll ever feel happy again.'

'I'm sure it all seems insurmountable now,' Danny said, 'but give it time.'

'The guilt eats me up. I feel responsible. If I had never met Paddy Mulligan . . . '

Rose reached over and took Iona's hand. 'You shouldn't blame yourself. The Mulligans, Lizzie and Paddy especially, were damaged people and they used you.'

Iona looked exhausted.

'We'll go now and leave you in peace. Take care and if you need us, to talk about the case or anything, well, just call me,' Rose said, standing up.

It was all she could offer Iona.

EPILOGUE

It was as if after everything that had happened – her mother's death and returning to Belfast – Rose had been forced to a place she couldn't come back from. Not without changing everything about herself first. Standing in her rented apartment, she looked out the window, across the expanse of dark water, and felt a contentment that she thought had been lost to her. Her life had taken an unexpected turn, delivering her back to Belfast, and here among the embers she had felt some sort of renewal.

There was a contentment in reconnecting with her family. And, of course, having Danny in her life again was worth returning for. Tomorrow she would see if she could extend her contract with the PSNI. It was time to stop running, to unearth the shards of the splintered bones of her childhood and to heal the hurts.

Danny had kept his promise to look into Evelyn's past and what he turned up was shocking to both of them. Evelyn Lavery had been an informer. She had worked for the state passing on covert information that had helped to secure the arrest of three members of her own community. Rose had shaken her head, not sure how to take it in.

'She wasn't in the IRA?'

'Technically, she worked for them as part of a clean-up squad who would be called upon to clear evidence. She also occasionally moved weapons and transported people.'

'But all that time she was working undercover?'

'Yeah, Rosie.'

It would take a while for Rose to process this new image of Evelyn. She had questions still unanswered, but at least she felt she was closer to knowing the truth. It was time to make amends, to get to know her brothers and sister all over again as adults.

She slid back the glass door and stepped out onto the narrow balcony, breathing in the muggy air and letting it rest deep in her lungs before exhaling. There was no sense of danger in the atmosphere. Belfast was different, but so was Rose.

ACKNOWLEDGEMENTS

Thanks to the following people who make my life im-measurably richer:

Liam, Kate, Owen, and Sarah, my loves. Special mention to Daisy, our cat, for putting up with me taking photographs for Twitter and Instagram.

My Mum, Jeannie for being amazing, especially during the difficult years of which we've had more than a few.

To Katie Loughnane, Sabah Khan and the entire Avon and HarperCollins team, thank you for welcoming me into the fold and for transforming my story into a real-life book! I have enjoyed every minute of the process.

Lina Langlee, agent extraordinaire. Thank you for your support, your calm, measured approach and for taking a chance with me.

Neil Ranasinghe for answering my annoying questions and reading an early draft.

Amy H. Deeken, M.D. for answering my pathology questions.

Damian Smyth, Head of Literature, Arts Council NI for the ongoing support.

The Northern Irish crime fiction community – too many to name individually.

Thanks to Joan, Katie, Tracey, Andrea, Roma, Deborah, Zoe and Donna for the friendship and laughs.

And to you my reader, thank you for buying my book.

AUTHOR'S NOTE

Who Took Eden Mulligan? is based in fictional and real places in and around Belfast.